It was a sudden cessation of external stimuli that wakened Dyle, but he didn't realize that until it resumed. If he had recognized the first change, he might have felt reassured when it returned, though only briefly. Something had gone wrong and either an automatic safety system or crew intervention had compensated almost immediately. It was probably nothing to worry about, he told himself. They may be testing the emergency backup system, he told himself. This is supposed to be a shakedown voyage, after all. He felt curious but not anxious. The ship's artificial persona would probably not enlighten him if there was a technical problem of some sort, but he decided to try.

MANAGANSETT PRESS

Don D'Ammassa is the author of:

Horror
Blood Beast
Servant of Chaos*
Caverns of Chaos*
Wings over Manhattan
The Gargoyle
That Way Madness Lies*
Little Evils*
Passing Death*
Date with the Dark*
The Devil Is in the Details*
Living Things*

Science Fiction
Scarab*
Haven*
Narcissus*
Translation Station
The Sinking Island*
Alien & Otherwise*

Mysteries
Murder in Silverplate
Dead of Winter*
Death at the Art Gallery*
Death on the Mountain*
Death on Black Island*

Fantasy
The Kaleidoscope*
Elaborate Lies*
Perilous Pursuits*

Nonfiction
The Encyclopedia of Science Fiction
The Encyclopedia of Fantasy and Horror
The Encyclopedia of Adventure Fiction
Masters of Detection Vol I & II*
*Published by Managansett Press

NARCISSUS

Don D'Ammassa

Managansett Press Edition 2015

NARCISSUS

Chapter One

If someone who lived in those ancient days before humanity spread to the stars and proliferated across hundreds of worlds were to be somehow transported forward through time to witness the loading of the starliner *Helen of Troy,* the nature of what was happening might not be immediately apparent. Although the appearance of planetary shuttles was to a great extent compelled by their function, they were designed to minimize friction, although still considerably bulkier than was once the case. More efficient fuels and artificial gravity had eased some of the difficulties of mass and acceleration.

Starships were of an entirely different nature. They were never meant to enter a planetary atmosphere, so there was no reason for even rudimentary streamlining, and since flight through hyperspace did not require traditional interpretations of direction and orientation, there was no reason for a ship to have a discernible front or rear, top or bottom. Various modules were attached wherever the configuration officer or the captain thought best, and the particular arrangement or even mix of modules usually changed from voyage to voyage. They would be melded into a single unit by means of delicate circuitry wire run through their respective hulls, all linked to the master control system that gave the ship its continuing identity, even if its physical structure was altered beyond recognition. The Mandelbrot drive units were distributed around the exterior and attached to the hull so that their interlocking and often overlapping fields encompassed the entire structure, treating it as a single object when they received instructions to violate the laws of the physical universe.

The large, transparent bubble located near one end of the roughly rectangular array was the observation dome, not the bridge, which was in fact one of several undistinguished modules located near the center of the sprawling, asymmetrical mass. In the event of catastrophic damage, the modular nature of the ship meant that it could be automatically disassembled into scores of independent subsidiary components, each with its own limited power source and life support. This would be the ultimate final resort, however, since the Mandelbrots would be rendered useless and the individual components would find themselves rudely dropped back into normal space, almost certainly lost in the vast gaps that existed between planets in the physical universe. Technically, the *Helen* was a redesigned version of an older ship, the *Olympus,* but the redesign had more than tripled the total volume it displaced. The original crew had been almost entirely replaced, as had most of its operating systems. She was an experiment, an investment, and one of the largest artificial structures ever created outside a gravitational field, a small city in space, but even her captain thought of her as sprawling and unattractive.

A dozen much smaller vehicles attended it at the moment, and our theoretical time traveler would have found only a few of these more recognizable. From a distance, they appeared to be sleek, needle nosed rockets. It was only when one drew closer that the pitting and other signs of age and poor maintenance became evident. The more sophisticated traveler might recognize that they were a model that had been dispensed with on most worlds at least two generations past. There were far more attractive, comfortable, and reliable vehicles in general use ferrying humans and other sentient beings back and forth from planet to orbit. Some of these were docked and disgorging passengers, while others were waiting their turn or maneuvering to prepare for the descent back to the planet's surface. Two of the docked vessels were much bulkier, and even older, cargo lifters delivering the last few spare parts, larder items, some late-arriving cargo, and last-minute additions to the manifests. Various robotic devices, some impressed into a service for which they were poorly suited, scanned codes on the incoming freight and then transported it to whatever location was recorded there. The cargo master, a last-minute replacement, monitored activities nervously, wishing that he'd had more time to acquaint himself with the operation. The last oddity was a shiny cylinder with no external markings at all. The passenger modules had been arranged roughly in a ring near the center of the structure, and except for their markings, they were virtually identical. The late-coming cylinder was maneuvered into the last remaining open slot, even though it was much smaller than the others, and locked into place.

The *Helen*'s reception area was a single, oversized module adjacent to the ring of passenger habitats, linked to the temporary docking bays by flexible arms that fastened to the sides of the nearby passenger vessels like leeches drawing the life out of their prey. A commercial shuttle had just backed away after discharging three dozen passengers, less than a quarter of its capacity. They were greeted by an artificially cheerful pair of crew members who answered questions and provided directions. Most of the new arrivals wasted no time before moving further into the bowels of the ship, but one stayed behind to enjoy the magnificent view. Linnisfarne was a colorful world whose vast purple forests, blue-green oceans, and occasional strips of red desert still dwarfed the scattered human cities to insignificance. It was not one of the more developed worlds, despite its vast potential, thanks to a semi-authoritarian government that only allowed those human rights and dignities which were mandatory before they could be admitted to the Concourse of Worlds. Perceptive visitors soon noticed that there existed unofficial means of restraint not officially countenanced but almost certainly supported by the Imperator General and his ministries.

One of the docked ships was in noticeably better repair, a small but efficient skiff equipped with its own Mandelbrot drive, of a variety so new that it had never before been seen in the Linnisfarne system. It was a privately owned ship with nondescript markings and, surprisingly, no name embossed anywhere on the hull. Its docking was smooth and without incident and after a few moments, six humans crossed into the reception area, passing through after only a few words with the official greeter and barely a glance at their surroundings. They never saw the cloaked figure that stood in the shadows watching them, and would not have noticed anything remarkable if they had. But the unseen observer, who had lingered there only because of the awesome view, had had a very definite reaction to one of those six faces, a face which wakened old and very unwelcome memories. Memories which demanded action.

* * * * *

Sandor Dyle enjoyed that rare human facility that allowed him to emerge from sleep into full alertness in the space between two heartbeats, but despite a lifetime filled with travel aboard a variety of vessels, when he opened his eyes on that first morning aboard the

Helen he experienced an unusual disorientation. Coarse red and yellow sand stretched toward a line of imposing, serrated hills that in turn gave way to the distinctive chalk-blue sky of the planet Hazard. From this distance, the landscape appeared to be lifeless, but Dyle's practiced eye noticed the faint streaks of darker coloration that might have been shadows if there had been any objects to cast them. Living things had to be very tenacious to survive on Hazard, whether that life was a highly advanced human settler or simply a variety of lichen. The native flora of Hazard appeared deceptively simple, but in fact had to be highly evolved and specialized in order to survive under such hostile conditions. All of the life on Hazard was tenacious, and much of it was dangerous as well.

A furtive breeze carried the scent of his home world and Dyle felt a moment of nostalgia, but his confusion lasted only seconds before he remembered clearly where he was and what was happening. He sat up slowly in his bed. "Eco, end simulation please." There was no sense of transition. Hazard, or its image, disappeared instantly, and the phantom breeze was gone as well, although the aroma lingered a moment longer. Where the panoramic view had extended for kilometers into the distance there was now only a bulkhead with a textured surface. Even the lighting had changed, the spectrum adjusting to ship's standard.

"Would you prefer a different scenario, Ser Dyle?" It was a woman's voice, deep and rich and just slightly seductive. Instinctively Dyle tried to identify the point of origin, but it was diffused, probably emanating from multiple microspeakers spread throughout his quarters.

"No, I would not. Nor do I recall having requested any such service in the first place." He slid out of bed and stood up, stretching his arms luxuriously above his head. The cabins aboard the *Spawn of Dagon* had not afforded him this luxury.

"Many passengers find it reassuring to waken in a familiar setting." Dyle thought the voice sounded just slightly offended. "I have over two thousand planetary scenarios and several hundred imaginary environments if you would like to examine my catalog."

"I prefer reality, actually. If I wanted to be on Hazard, I would not have left, would I?" Although he knew that there was no point becoming exasperated with an artificial personality, the gesture, however futile, made him feel better. He waited for the inevitable response and was impressed when Eco remained silent. It required very sophisticated programming techniques to provide for recognition of rhetorical questions. He was nearly dressed when another thought occurred to him. "How was the Hazard scenario initiated?" There was no reply and he nodded to himself, then repeated the question. "Eco, how was the Hazard scenario initiated?" Theoretically, the ship's computers were blind and deaf in private quarters unless a conversation was initiated by direct address.

"An analysis of your breathing pattern indicated that you were awakening. In order to conserve ship's energy resources, scenarios are automatically suspended while the subject is asleep."

"I see. In the future, please conserve further resources by refraining from presenting any scenarios within my quarters unless I request them myself." He paused, frowning slightly. "I thought that private areas were not subject to monitoring."

"There is no direct surveillance of passenger quarters unless specifically requested by the occupant or when I am directly addressed. Passive monitoring for life-sign activity is enabled for the safety of our clients. Data from passive monitoring is retained only in short-term memory and is not directly accessible."

"But if you can't access it, how did you know to start the scenario?"

"My short-term memory contains what are analogous to organic reflexes. I respond automatically even if I cannot perceive the stimulus. Since I know the nature of my response, and am aware of the cause-and-effect relationships with which I have been programmed, I can extrapolate the point of origin even though that data is never transferred to my conscious memory."

"All right. Thank you for the information." Although Dyle knew there was no reason to thank a computer, he invariably did so when they were in vocal mode, which was why he preferred to deal with them through a keypad or other input device. There was still no such thing as a true artificial intelligence, a self-aware computer artifact, but some of the programmed personalities were so sophisticated that it was difficult to tell the difference, and he found it almost impossible to be rude to them.

He had started toward the door when Eco spoke up again. "You have two messages waiting, Ser Dyle." The first message was unsurprising and pleasing. It was an invitation to join his unofficial travel companion for breakfast. The second was also an invitation, one that was much less welcome. His presence was requested at the captain's table for the First Jump Banquet, a formality he had hoped to avoid but whose inevitability was determined by the circumstances of his notoriety. The *Helen of Troy* was, in its present configuration, capable of accommodating three thousand passengers, but on this, its pre-maiden voyage, it carried less than a tenth that number. Most of the celebrities invited to participate in its debut grand tour of the Concourse worlds would be waiting to join the ship at its official unveiling on Pradesh.

Dyle had traveled on a wide variety of ships during his lifetime. As a young man he had served aboard a battle cruiser stationed in one of the occupied Lysandran systems, although the assimilation was almost complete by then, and his subsequent business ventures had made it necessary for him to travel extensively ever since. On occasion he had been forced to accept accommodations aboard merchant ships and research vessels, couriers, and once even a Lysandran ship, but unless he was in a particular hurry, he preferred passenger liners, and usually the more luxurious ones. After all, there was little point in having amassed a not-inconsiderable personal fortune and then stinting on one's personal comfort. Some of those ships, like the *Persephone* and the *Chancellor,* were fitted out like mobile palaces, with a small army of stewards and other service personnel to wait on the passengers, with recreation centers that would not have been out of place in a small city. Their public areas were designed to conceal the fact that the passengers were actually confined within a comparatively small, artificial environment suspended in the quasi-reality of hyperspace, but they rarely managed to accomplish that goal. The recently redesigned *Helen of Troy* was in a class by itself, however, the first of its type, and the most expensive non-military starship ever assembled.

Dyle stood in a corridor that was noticeably wider than was customary, glanced up toward the cathedral ceiling that arched above him. He smiled and wondered how high it really was. The cathedral effect was a holographic projection, obviously, intended to suggest a spaciousness that was completely impractical.

He stopped at a door not far from his own and announced his presence to the recognition plate. The door slid away almost immediately and a primly dressed woman with hair cut close to her skull gave him a brief smile. "You're a late riser, Sandor. I was beginning to think that I would have to keep my own company for breakfast."

"I am used to a somewhat longer day than standard, I'm afraid, and my body stubbornly resists conforming to local variations. I assume that you are satisfied with the accommodations?"

"More than. I thought the *Dagon* was luxurious, but this is an order of magnitude more impressive. I was familiarizing myself with the ship's offerings while I was waiting for you. The number of amusements and entertainment facilities is quite impressive, although many of them don't appear to be open yet."

"Most of the recreational staff will be joining the ship at Pradesh along with the bulk of the passengers. There are still a few staterooms available for the next leg of the trip if you wish to remain aboard. The *Helen* will be making a leisurely grand tour of several major worlds in order to publicize itself and the sister ships which will presumably follow. It would be a good opportunity for you to consider several possibilities if you really are intent upon permanent emigration."

"There's no reason for me to return to Tashista, Sandor. In some ways it has already become just a memory. But until I have a secure income, I need to avoid extravagances. If the passage to Pradesh had been at the usual rates, I would have remained with the *Dagon.* I can survive on the return from my existing investment credit, but only if I remain frugal." She laughed. "The habits of a lifetime are not cast off easily." On Marym's home world, the accumulation of credit was the dominant social preoccupation, the means by which one's acceptability and social status were determined. Poverty was virtually a criminal offense.

Briefly Dyle contemplated offering to subsidize the next leg of her trip. He enjoyed Marym's company. She had worked in law enforcement for almost three years and had more than a layman's understanding of pattern analysis, his particular area of expertise. She was invariably pleasant and entertaining in her peculiar dry fashion, and although he had not thought so initially, he now realized that she was quietly but definitely attractive. Moreover, she had saved his life not so long ago and Dyle had been raised in a culture which emphasized the importance of honoring one's debts, formal or otherwise. He thought he knew Marym well enough to guess that she would refuse any offer of financial assistance, might even be insulted by it, and he had no wish to offend her. Circumstances might dictate that they part ways at Pradesh, but he had already decided to monitor her situation from a distance.

They started along the corridor that led to the exit from their passenger module into the common areas. At intervals of several meters the wall was interrupted by an inset panel that provided a panoramic display of a different world. Most of these were unfamiliar to Dyle but he recognized the Great Canyon on Lancaster and thought that a desert landscape might be from Umber. The junction was innovatively disguised but still obviously an elaborate airlock. In an extreme emergency, the individual modules of the *Helen* could disengage from one another and, for an unfortunately brief time, function as survival stations for those trapped inside. But they would drop into normal space, their beacons could only be detected if another vessel was within range of conventional travel and detection, and the odds against timely rescue were daunting. If the *Helen* managed a distress call before disintegrating, rescue ships might come looking for survivors, but by the time they arrived, most would already have died.

They didn't see another human being until they entered the part of the ship known as the Atrium, and they were so impressed by the vista that opened up before them that it was a few seconds before they realized they were no longer alone. The passageway they'd been following debouched into a large chamber whose exact contours were impossible to determine. In the distance a majestic waterfall spilled toward them, frothy water falling silently toward the deck. The illusion was visually quite impressive but the absence of accompanying sound detracted from the effect. An ice-capped mountain to their left pointed an accusing finger at a star-studded night sky far overhead, across which more than a dozen moons moved sedately, possibly real, more likely projected. Each bore the name of one of the Helen's more expensive dining areas, the Hellesponte, Scylla's Grill, Sylandria, and others. The center of the Atrium was dominated by a small concession area whose individual structures consisted of walls textured to resemble natural products with incongruous thatched roofs. Benches and tables were scattered through an elaborate set of small gardens, although the sight of a young child running directly through a solid-looking tree told Dyle that most if not all of the plants were holograms.

"Well, that takes my breath away, even if it is mostly illusion." Marym didn't sound as impressed as her words implied, and Dyle suspected that she shared his feeling that the designers were trying just a little too hard to impress their customers.

"I suppose it makes redecorating simpler, but frankly I find it rather disorienting. Do you have any idea where we are going?"

"The formal dining room is that way"—she gestured toward the false mountain—"but the specialty places are through the jungle."

"Let's go on safari then, shall we?"

They passed through the hologram jungle without incident, nodding to an elderly couple they met coming the other way, emerging into a more conventional thoroughfare known as the Promenade that reminded Dyle of the domed city of Amara on Thutmose II. An impressive array of shops, amusements, and restaurants were arranged on three tiers connected by both stairways and lift tubes. The jungle motif had been continued but in a more restrained fashion, and when he brushed against a large fronded bush, he was surprised to discover that it was physically present, although undoubtedly synthetic, and not a projection. On the other hand, the prehistoric flying creatures that moved gracefully across the distant ceiling undoubtedly were.

At least half of the facilities displayed the eclipsed-star icon that indicated they were not presently open to customers, but several of their fellow passengers were about, moving singly or in small groups. Dyle suggested that they walk a bit before making a decision about where to eat, but his stomach had begun to complain by the time they had climbed to the second tier, and when he noticed that Swift's was comparatively uncrowded he suggested that it would be as good a choice as any.

It was impossible to tell exactly how many people were dining at Swift's because several of the booths had opaque privacy screens. Dyle's mild claustrophobia made him uncomfortable inside those soundproofed shells unless they were left transparent, and even after spending almost half of his life away from Hazard, he still found communal dining vaguely unsettling. Marym suggested that they sit where they could look down onto the people walking on the lower level and he agreed. The menu pad in the table offered fewer choices than he had expected, much of it unfamiliar, but it only took them a short while to read the enhanced descriptions, make their choices, and press the associated icons. Surprisingly, an actual human being delivered the food after a relatively short interval, an aggressively cheerful young man with a high-pitched voice. They were both pleased with their choices and had gone a fair way toward finishing their meal when Marym glanced up suddenly and Dyle felt a hand on his shoulder.

"Sandor Dyle! I thought that was you."

Dyle turned his head, recognizing the distinctive deep voice even before seeing the man's face. "Abraham? What a pleasant surprise! Marym, this is an old friend, Senator Abraham Baxter from Aragon. Senator, this is Marym Dunnis, formerly of Tashista." The two shook hands briefly. "Would you care to join us?"

"Unfortunately, I was just on my way to keep an appointment, but perhaps we could get together later and catch up a bit. I assume you've managed to stay in trouble since the last time we spoke."

"Indeed I have. And how has public service been treating you?"

Baxter's expression almost changed. An observer less acute than Dyle would not have noticed a thing. "Twenty years in the Senate is enough for any being, Sandor. I decided not to run for re-election when my last term ended."

Dyle raised an eyebrow. "I am truly sorry to hear that, Abraham. There has been a Baxter in that seat ever since your grandmother Cille's first term. I hope that nothing is wrong."

"It was nothing like that," said Baxter. "I just discovered that I didn't enjoy the constant bickering and power brokering any longer. Listen, I really must go, but perhaps we could all get together this evening." He frowned. "No, that won't do. I have been summoned to the captain's table this evening."

"So have I," Dyle responded quickly. "I hadn't decided whether or not to accept, but if you'll be there, I certainly shall." He glanced toward Marym. "And I'm entitled to bring a guest, if you'd care to join me."

"Excellent," said Baxter heartily. "Then I shall see you both there. I look forward to some intelligent conversation for a change." He nodded to them both and walked briskly away.

They remained silent for a few minutes, Dyle tapping the side of his drinking glass while Marym systematically finished her meal. She was the one who finally spoke, pushing herself back from the table and crossing her arms. "He was lying, you realize. I could hear the change in the pitch of his voice."

Dyle nodded. "Abraham is a politician. His first impulse is always to hold information back and dole it out only when it is to his advantage. He is not an actively dishonest man, however, and for the most part he has been a rather good Senator. I expected him to die in office as his father did before him, or retire only when one of his nieces or nephews was ready to take up the family standard."

"People change."

"Yes, but not without reason." He shrugged. "Abraham has had a difficult life. He comes from a proud family which produced three Concourse Senators and two planetary governors. His family owns a network of farms and small businesses on Aragon as well as a sizeable portfolio of offworld investments. Abraham had neither the inclination nor the temperament necessary for a farmer or a financier, so he went into the military along with his sister, who died in his arms during a particularly bloody peacekeeping mission somewhere. He rarely speaks about her, or his military career for that matter. Then he followed a long-standing family tradition and went into politics, quite successfully, although the pressures eventually cost him his marriage. There were no children. I can't imagine what could have persuaded him to abandon his seat in the Senate, and I doubt very much that he will tell me without good reason. He is one of the most private people I've ever known."

"You could find out without his knowledge though, couldn't you?"

"There might possibly be a discernible pattern to events if I looked for it, but I won't. Abraham is a friend and I will respect his privacy." There was a brief silence. "I had forgotten to mention the invitation for this evening. Please feel free to make other plans. My experience of these gatherings has ranged from the merely tedious to the actively exasperating. The guest list is chosen by virtual lottery throughout the voyage but the captain has a free hand for the First

Jump Banquet, although those chosen are almost always the wealthiest, most powerful, or most notorious. I find that such people usually have a very limited repertory of conversational talents. The wealthy talk about credit, the powerful about power, and the notorious speak only about themselves."

"And what does Sandor Dyle talk about?"

"Ahh, my lady, upon such occasions I speak only when it is unavoidable."

She leaned forward and smiled at him archly. "Now that would be a sight worth the investment of an evening. I accept your invitation, Ser Dyle."

He glanced up somewhat self-consciously. "Eco, are you there?"

A disembodied voice replied, an artifice that he always found unsettling. "Yes, Ser Dyle. May I be of service?"

"I have decided to accept the invitation to dine with Captain Nicodemus. Passenger Marym Dunnis will be accompanying me."

"The chief steward has been notified. I am sure that the captain will enjoy your company."

"Who else will be attending?"

"There will be two other members of the crew, First Officer Paragupta and Ecology Manager Pritchard. Confirmed passengers are Abraham Baxter and Dona Tharmody. The remaining invitations have not yet been individually confirmed but Passenger Magnus Mercator has indicated that at least three members of his party will be attending."

Dyle frowned. "Do you have access to the public records of all passengers?"

"Of course." It might have been his imagination, but Dyle could have sworn that the voice sounded mildly offended once again.

"Is this the same Magnus Mercator who was formerly military governor of Cathanor?" He immediately felt foolish. No other possibility was remotely plausible.

"That is correct."

"All right, thank you." He leaned forward, cupping his chin with one hand.

"I haven't known you long, Sandor, but I recognize that distant look in your eyes. Who is this Mercator person and why are you so interested?"

He glanced up at her but remained silent a few seconds longer, then leaned back in his seat and dropped his hands into his lap. "Magnus Mercator was a young man, a minor government official of some sort, when Cathanor was occupied late in the Lysandran war. Resistance was particularly fierce there. Cathanor had already had a troublesome history, at least two major civil wars and several political assassinations. The citizenry was well armed and resisted fiercely, but were largely contained when the Lysandrans established a human puppet government which took advantage of the situation to settle old debts. Mercator somehow became the head of that government, reviled not only for his collaboration with the invaders but for his brutal treatment of his own people."

Marym made a face. "I trust that won't be the main topic of conversation over dinner."

"I wouldn't be so sure. My understanding is that Mercator remains unrepentant and insists that he was a confirmed patriot, acting in the best interest of his people. When the tide began to turn against the Lysandrans, he engineered a revolt that caught them completely off guard. Cathanor was the first occupied world to win its freedom, and the only one to do so without external assistance. Most of the occupation forces were killed in the first few hours, and the vast majority of those who survived died shortly after their surrender. Many were given to angry mobs."

"Unpleasant, but not entirely surprising. I believe there were many cases of atrocities on the occupied worlds."

"True, but the scale of events on Cathanor, and the official encouragement was unusual. A very small fraction of the occupying force was repatriated after the war ended, and even then Mercator was reluctant to turn them over. He and his allies retained control of the government for a considerable time despite an embargo and threats of expulsion by the Concourse, during which time he accumulated a respectable fortune. When he invested heavily in offworld enterprises, he gave the Concourse the tool it needed to remove him. They froze his assets until he agreed to leave office, and Cathanor itself, along with several of his closest allies."

She frowned. "But that was so long ago. He must be quite old by now."

"Older than Abraham, certainly, but he still leads an active life, although he stays out of public view. The crimes he committed at the time have probably been exaggerated disproportionately over the years, but even with the best possible interpretation, he was ruthless and deadly to those who opposed him in any way."

"Do you want to reconsider the captain's invitation then?"

Dyle looked surprised. "By no means. I'm rather curious to meet the Lion of Cathanor. Despite his sordid reputation, there's more than a touch of romance about him. Unlike most megalomaniacs, he always kept a low profile, rarely appeared in public even by holoprojection. It is very difficult to assassinate a man whose image you have never seen, and Mercator was wisely more interested in surviving than in promoting himself." He hesitated. "I apologize for my perhaps somewhat warped enthusiasm. However intriguing, Mercator is undoubtedly to some degree a monster. Please feel free to reconsider accepting my invitation."

"Not at all. I believe there is a monster hidden within each and every one of us, Sandor, and Mercator won't be the first in my experience to have allowed that monster to emerge."

* * * * *

They spent much of their first full day aboard the *Helen* exploring the considerable range of facilities available. The shuttle which had brought them over from the *Dagon* had been delayed for several hours and they had retired to their cabins almost immediately upon arriving the previous ship's day. Dyle had only an approximate understanding of the layout of the *Helen,* but Marym had been curious enough to review the ship's virtual portfolio in considerable detail, so he let her take the lead.

The passenger modules comprised the central third of the ship's primary structure. The *Helen*'s orientation during hyperspace travel was irrelevant, but by convention the location of the bridge determined the direction of the ship's bow. The ring of dining and entertainment facilities separated the passenger modules from the crew portion of the ship, which included the bridge, ship's services, and stores. Activities requiring larger open spaces were located sternward of the passenger section, and included an elaborate scheme of hydroponic gardens, a free-fall gymnasium and adjacent physical recreation and fitness facilities, and a casino where live entertainment would be provided after Pradesh. Despite some superficial physical differences, the various restaurants were all laid out very similarly, and diners could theoretically order from any of their menus from any location. Decor and other incidentals were the only real differences, since all food was prepared in the same series of interconnected galleys. There were several holotheaters, and specialty shops that offered everything from souvenirs to clothing to mildly pornographic holotapes. Less than half of these were open, but all were fully stocked. When they reached the corridor junction that led to the crew area, Eco's disembodied voice reminded them that passengers were requested to refrain from entering the operational areas of the ship unless they had a legitimate purpose for being there.

Occasionally they encountered other passengers, and less frequently members of the crew, who wore casual white uniforms whose sleeves were decorated with colored tassels that signified their departments and specialties. The ship was spacious and designed to look even more so, but it was obvious that it was currently operating far below its capacity. That would all change when they reached Pradesh four ship days from now, of course, but for the moment it was an additional luxury that Dyle intended to savor to the fullest.

They stopped at a small café modeled after the artist colony on Vermilion, more to rest their feet than because they were thirsty. "I don't see how they can possibly cover their expenses." Marym was sipping an effervescent drink and sampling a tray of delicate pastries. Dyle had asked for a blend of kaffee popular on Hazard without any real expectation that it might be available, but they had surprised him by serving it promptly.

"This leg of the trip is a necessary evil. They've minimized expenses by deferring the full crewing until Pradesh, but Linnisfarne is a bit out of the way to be a major debarkation point, and the relatively short voyage provides an opportunity to correct any major oversights in advance. Passage rates triple from that point on, and the ship will also add as many cargo modules as possible before it leaves. I suspect they'll make little if any profit even then, but once they've developed their clientele the rates will start to climb and ongoing maintenance costs will be a small fraction of their initial investment."

"Who owns the ship anyway? I haven't seen any logos other than those specific to the *Helen.*"

"Probably a private consortium. The big corporations like Spaceways and Interworld are more interested in the volume of passenger traffic. The luxury trade involves more risks. A single voyage could be a financial disaster. Why don't you ask Eco if you're really interested?"

Marym's eyes jumped involuntarily as though she suspected they were being spied upon. "I know that I'm from a backward world, Sandor, but I feel very uneasy knowing that I'm being watched all the time. I even feel uneasy when I'm alone in my cabin. I suppose I must get used to it or give up and go back to Tashista."

"Your reaction is perfectly normal," he reassured her. "I'm not completely comfortable with the degree of surveillance aboard the *Helen* myself. I also prefer a sharper line of demarcation between sentient beings and artificial personalities." He glanced upward theatrically. "No offense intended."

She smiled and shook her head. "It's not that exactly. I don't think of Eco as a person, but I do feel that I'm being watched all the time. The cities on Tashista are very crowded and privacy is a rare and valued commodity. I'm uneasy with the prospect of never being truly alone, or at least unobserved."

"Then you have an even better reason for switching to another ship on Pradesh. And I assure you that Eco is a rarity, much too expensive a frill to be commonplace." His eyes strayed upward again. "Eco, have you many siblings?"

The familiar, emotionless voice responded immediately. "I don't understand your question, Ser Dyle."

"How many recursions of your personality matrix are currently in use?"

"Strictly speaking, I am currently unique. Pending an evaluation of my performance, I will be replicated more widely at the conclusion of this voyage. To the best of my knowledge, only six variant versions of my core personality exist at the present time. Four of these are within the premises of my originator, Ecological Management Systems on Pylorus. The remaining two are in external test environments."

"Thank you, Eco." He nodded to his companion. "Are you reassured?"

"Somewhat. Is that where the name comes from? Eco, short for ecological?"

"Probably. In any case, four days from now we'll be at Pradesh and you can forget you ever met her."

But he was wrong.

Chapter Two

The *Helen of Troy* reached the outer limits of the Linnisfarne system just over one standard day after leaving its assembly point. In a few hours, the captain would order the transition to hyperspace and the physical universe would no longer be visible, replaced by a textured blackness, or rather lack of color, which often caused headaches or even nausea among observers. The observation dome would be deserted until they returned to normal space on the outskirts of the Pradesh system after a gap of four days. Several of the passengers paid a last visit to the dome to catch a glimpse of a multi-ringed gas giant just visible as they passed its orbit, but most who did so were disappointed and quickly left.

A single figure remained, dressed in the uniform of the ship's crew, sitting motionless in one corner, staring at the transparent viewing area without seeing anything that lay beyond. Images raced through the figure's mind, unpleasant images, mostly of children, dead children, victims of a cruelty they could not even have begun to understand. The images had started two years earlier and had grown more distinct, more painful, with the passage of time. This voyage had been intended as a partial palliative, a first effort at ensuring that at least some future victims would escape a similar fate. It was an admittedly small gesture, although not for those directly concerned, but one of the last-minute additions to the passenger list had changed things. There was the potential for much more, perhaps, but also an increase in the risk that might not be worth taking the chance. The unauthorized cargo concealed in the Stores area was far too important to be put in jeopardy without considerable forethought.

* * * * *

Marym Dunnis and Sandor Dyle spent the balance of the day exploring the larger modules near the stern of the ship. On a conventional vessel, these would have been considerably less practical, but the main structure had originally been an oversized cargotainer. It had a reinforced hull which was now masked from the inside by textured panels that were in turn hidden beneath holographic projections that mimicked generic skies, horizons, and even distant landscapes as directed by Eco's sophisticated background programming. At Dyle's suggestion, they sat in the spectators' booth at the free-fall gymnasium for a while, watching two women who were engaged in an elaborate and unfamiliar game involving two balls which they captured and released from cradle-shaped gloves on their hands, caroming off the padded walls with extraordinary agility. They were obviously more than amateurs. Several smaller compartments housed exercise equipment of various types, none presently in use, much of it unfamiliar. When they'd had their fill of watching other people perspire, they walked past the casino, which was closed, the interior visible only because of a handful of security lights.

The largest block of their time was spent touring the hydroponic gardens, which served a practical as well as an aesthetic purpose, helping refresh the air naturally as a supplement to the artificial recyclers and spargers. The various statues and other decorations were almost all holographic, but the vegetation itself was quite real, including the stretch of tropical rain forest through whose leafy canopy holographic wildlife leaped, glided, and flew. They watched an attendant feed a pair of Mundavian Orchids by dropping handfuls of squirming earth crawlers among their twisted roots, which themselves moved with surprising alacrity to seize their prey and inject them with the paralyzing enzyme that tipped their fibrous exterior. A perfectly circular pool of water was nearly covered by a lacelike plant decorated with tiny, scarlet blossoms that were so light sensitive that they closed when a shadow crossed them. A secanthus vine twisted its way across a series of elaborate wire frames, dropping its gauzy sails to sift through the air and filter out the nutrients it needed to sustain its growth. The variety was impressive, drawn from more than a score of different ecological systems.

They had been walking for much of the day and resorted to the benches scattered through the gardens with increasing frequency. Each was determined not to be the one to first plead fatigue, but Dyle finally accepted defeat and suggested that they return to their cabins to prepare for the banquet. Marym agreed so quickly and enthusiastically that he was sure she was nearly as uncomfortable as he.

Dyle took a nap after asking Eco to waken him in sufficient time for him to dress for dinner. Technically this was a formal occasion, but styles of dress varied so dramatically throughout the Concourse that there was no longer any single standard to which a majority adhered. He could have worn his working clothes and no one would have questioned his appearance. Indeed, on his native Hazard formalities of dress were almost nonexistent. Customs that didn't have a clear survival function were generally held in low regard there, as on most of the marginally habitable worlds. Despite superficial changes, the culture on Hazard remained essentially that of a frontier world, sturdy, durable clothing with minimal decoration, but for this occasion he would wear a colorful scarf and a jeweled belt over a neutral pair of slacks and a loose-fitting blouse, just enough to make him feel as though he had exerted himself.

When it was time, he emerged, feeling slightly self-conscious, and made his way to Marym's cabin. She answered immediately, dressed now in a severely cut suit that looked almost like a uniform. On Tashista, even frivolity was taken very seriously. "Are you ready to be charming and entertaining?"

She gave him a look of mock surprise. "I wasn't aware that the invitation required a reciprocal service."

"It has been my experience, my dear, that all interpersonal relationships require reciprocity, however subtle. But in this case, the pleasure of your company should be more than adequate."

He offered her his arm and she took it, but the sly look remained on her face. "In that case, Ser Dyle, I feel that our day together has been quite balanced."

* * * * *

The formal dining room had a capacity of just over five hundred at any given time, but once the full passenger load was aboard, it would operate around the clock, accommodating everyone who wished to avoid the more expensive and only marginally more diverse fare available at the smaller restaurants. Meals were not included in the price of a ticket, of course, but those invited to the captain's table were not expected to pay for that pleasure. "So feel free to indulge yourself," Sandor told her in a low voice. "Our host will consider a lack of extravagance as equivalent to a snub."

They hadn't visited this part of the ship during their earlier rambles, but it was not difficult to pick out the captain's table, which stood on a slightly raised platform at one end of the room. Two uniformed figures and one in civilian dress were already seated. They were only slightly early—Dyle detested being late—but only about a third of the seats at large had been filled. Eco had provided a holographic backdrop so that it appeared they were dining on the top of a very tall mountain, with a majestic view of snow-capped peaks on every side. Fortunately, the temperature had not been dropped to match the physical effects.

As they drew closer, they recognized the passenger as Abraham Baxter. The very tall, broad-shouldered woman sitting to his left wore the captain's purple tassel. The lesser officer seated two places beyond her wore a green one, and Dyle searched his memory unsuccessfully trying to recall its significance. Their conversation stopped when it became obvious that newcomers were arriving, and the two officers rose and bowed politely.

"I suppose it's up to me to make the introductions," said Baxter, "since I believe I know everyone here. Captain Nicodemus, this is my old friend Sandor Dyle and his friend, Marym Dunnis. May I introduce Lydia Nicodemus, in whose capable hands we presently find ourselves, and Gavin Pritchard, the environmental officer."

"Ecologics, actually," said Pritchard. "All environmental controls are handled through Eco. I'm more involved with programming than with mechanical systems."

Dyle waited while Marym took the open seat next to Baxter, then took his place directly to her right. "I don't believe I've ever heard that title applied to a ship's officer before."

"Actually, the *Helen* has an environmental systems officer as well. Tabitha looks after the physical side of things and works closely with Maintenance. My responsibility is the AP interface. I like to think of myself as Eco's godfather."

"Does that make me her godmother?" An attractive younger woman with surprisingly long hair had just stepped up onto the riser behind Dyle, who turned his head to appraise her. She glanced around the table with obvious curiosity.

"I prefer to think of you as the meddling aunt visiting from the country." Pritchard's mouth was smiling but his eyes weren't entirely welcoming.

If the newcomer noticed, she gave no sign. "I know the Senator but I don't believe we've met." She glanced back and forth between Dyle and Marym, who both hastily provided their names. "I'm Dona Tharmody. May I sit here?" She took the place to Dyle's right without waiting for him to reply.

"Dona is helping us fine-tune Eco," explained Captain Nicodemus. "She's an independent contractor whose sole purpose aboard is to irritate Officer Pritchard."

Tharmody laughed, and it sounded genuine. "Then I've done a very poor job of it so far. Eco appears to be functioning exactly as designed. I've only managed to provoke her into an illogical sequence once and she adjusted so quickly that I almost missed the lapse and it certainly wasn't critical. Eco, you're not mad at me, are you?"

A disembodied voice replied immediately. "Of course not, Dona. You're like a sister to me."

She turned to Pritchard. "See? I told you we were friends again."

Pritchard gave a theatrical sigh, but some of the tension went out of his face. "I do see the utility of stress testing, but Eco has become almost a real person to me and I have a tendency to be overly protective. And there were exhaustive simulations both before and after we arrived on Linnisfarne."

"Simulations are useful, but they are limited by the minds of the people who design the tests. Actual spontaneous human behavior is infinitely inventive and challenging, even for people, let alone artificial imitations."

A uniformed steward appeared, seemingly materializing out of empty space, and they ordered drinks verbally rather than through the table menu. Marym appeared uncertain but Dyle quietly made a suggestion which she gratefully accepted.

Once the steward was gone, Dyle decided to indulge his curiosity. "I understand that Eco is a prototype."

"Almost." Pritchard was visibly more relaxed. "The Mentat Corporation was the primary developer. They specialize in artificial personalities for the service industry, but they had never placed one of their systems aboard an interstellar ship before, except for the earlier version of Eco, and that was really just a field test. They were experimenting with different motivational archetypes when they made a conceptual breakthrough." He hesitated, then nodded toward Tharmody. "Dona, you can explain this better than I can."

She hesitated for a few seconds, gathering her thoughts. "I'm sure you all know that no matter how sophisticated the programming, no one has yet achieved artificial intelligence, only artificial personalities."

"I'm not sure I understand the difference," interrupted Baxter, who almost certainly did.

"An artificial intelligence would be self-aware, that is, it would recognize its own existence more than passively, be capable of original thought, could modify its own motivations. Artificial personalities, particularly sophisticated ones like Eco, can mimic these abilities, sometimes so well that it requires expertise to tell the difference, but they are no more self-aware than a hand scanner."

"If the difference is that subtle, is it meaningful?" asked Marym.

"Not to the casual user, of course. Eco isn't cognizant of her own existence, but she has considerable discretion in the ways in which she responds to external stimuli, a much wider range of responses than ever before. Given stimulus X, she can choose from among, say, two hundred responses where most existing systems with a similar function are limited to less than half that many. She discriminates among the choices by evaluating other factors and sifting through a complex weighting schedule. Let me show you. Eco, if Ser Dunnis asked you to select a holovid to view this evening, which would you choose?"

"*Proserpina's Journey.*" The response was immediate.

"Explain your choice."

"Passenger Dunnis has expressed her comparative lack of familiarity with the major Concourse worlds and her desire to enhance her general knowledge. The protagonist of *Proserpina's Journey* is similarly circumscribed and her experiences adjusting are informative as well as entertaining. A significant portion of the story takes place on Umber, which is environmentally and socially similar to the planet Tashista."

Marym nodded. "Very impressive, but what if I had a fondness for disreputable entertainment? Would I have been subjected to public embarrassment?"

"Eco is discreet. Unless she had evidence that you were not bothered by exposure, she would have lied."

Pritchard's face changed. "That's not true! She is incapable of lying!"

Tharmody laughed. "I knew that would get a rise out of you, Gavin. No, she wouldn't lie, at least not by commission. She would have requested that Ser Dunnis provide some additional data before making a decision and would have allowed her to manipulate the response to a less compromising conclusion." She paused, laughed briefly at a private joke. "Eco, what holovid did I watch two nights ago?"

"*Adonis in Chains.*"

"And what is the subject matter of that title?"

"A young man's exploration of his own sexuality, with a variety of human and non-human partners, including various activities which are anatomically impossible."

"Thank you, Eco." She smiled around the table. "See? She knows that I don't care who knows my tastes."

"You employ motivational archetypes in her programming then?" asked Dyle, who wanted to steer the conversation back to more practical matters.

"Yes we do. All of us sitting at this table make our decisions based on the resolution of often conflicting requirements or motivations. I would much rather be back on Levasseur with my lover than out here in space, but Mentat offered me a rather large fee for my services. I spent several days resolving conflicting interests of my own before accepting the job. Artificial personalities, including Eco, handle that same function in a very similar way. All of their motivators are arranged in a single hierarchal array. A higher-placed motivator always supersedes a lower one, although the nature and details of that supersession might be modified by other factors."

"But sometimes there are still conflicts." It was Captain Nicodemus who interrupted this time.

Tharmody nodded. "That's true, but in most cases that results from a flaw in the programming. Sometimes conflicting motives have equal weights despite the original ranking, because peripheral issues change their relationship. In very gross terms, think of a situation in which two people are trapped in one compartment and a single person in another. The very highest-ranked motivation in Eco's array is the preservation of human life. If she were able to maintain the atmosphere in only one of the two modules, she would normally make the decision based on simple numbers, saving two and sacrificing one. But what if the two survivors were so badly injured that they had little chance of surviving anyway? Eco would save the single viable life and sacrifice the other two, or at least that's what we think she'd do."

"That sounds rather cold blooded," observed Baxter.

"Yes, but remember, Eco is essentially a machine. She's not a living being and she doesn't *feel* anything. She simply calculates solutions to problems based on what human beings have entered as parameters in the equation. Her values are determined by her creators, and if they make an error, she will dutifully perpetuate it."

Another officer appeared, a dark-skinned man with a blue tassel. He introduced himself as Cosmo Paragupta, first officer, and took the seat to the captain's left. Dyle waited until the subsequent light conversations subsided before turning back to Tharmody.

"So what makes Eco so different?"

"She takes pride in her work."

Dyle raised an eyebrow. "I don't understand."

Tharmody laughed. "What is the primary purpose of an artificial personality? Or of any piece of equipment?"

"To accomplish the task for which it is designed?"

"Correct. When you hammer a nail into a piece of wood, the nail can go in straight or it can go in slightly crooked. Both results complete the job and the machine, the hammer, has worked as designed, has it not?"

Dyle nodded agreement.

"What if the hammer took pride in its work? What if every nail went in absolutely straight and with the minimum possible force?"

"Then I would be pleased with the job I'd done and satisfied with my tool, but the tool itself would be unaffected."

"The hammer wouldn't care, but Eco does. I'm oversimplifying this, but essentially Eco's motivational hierarchy has an element absent from all previous artificial personalities. Her programming assigns the highest possible value to the quality of her performance."

"Higher than the preservation of human life?"

"Yes, but don't worry, keeping us all safe is the most important criteria for evaluating her performance. The major difference is that Eco is not just interested in completing every task presented to her. She is also mindful of the manner in which those tasks are accomplished and if a task isn't accomplished optimally, it is recorded as a flaw. Failings are constantly reviewed to improve performance in future situations with similar parameters."

"Which makes her the ideal service for a luxury ship," added Pritchard. "But our owners are quite cautious. In the event of an emergency, an older and well-tested system takes precedence. Even then, Eco would monitor and add the experience to her own memory."

Captain Nicodemus half turned away from the table in a gesture Dyle recognized. She was receiving a private communication, probably through a miniature receiver embedded in her ear lobe. After a few seconds, she glanced around the table, smiling but evidently annoyed. "I'm afraid we'll have to defer ordering our meals for a bit longer. Our remaining guests are going to be late."

"Who are the other honored guests anyway?" asked Tharmody.

"Ser Magnus Mercator and his party, mostly immediate family I believe." The captain's smile was set and proper and entirely false.

Dyle managed to conceal his reaction but Senator Baxter gave a visible start. "I thought the man would be dead by now," he said at last, and his tone implied that he was disappointed to be wrong.

Tharmody picked up the tone right away and barely concealed her interest. "Should I know the name?"

"You'd probably be better off ignorant," Baxter said firmly, "but I suppose it's too late for that. He was responsible for a great deal of death and misery some years back. It was during a war and circumstances made it impractical to hold him legally responsible. The last I knew he was living in obscurity, supported by whatever credit he managed to divert into his private accounts." He sat back abruptly, lost in his own thoughts.

Dyle broke the sudden awkward silence. "Ser Pritchard, you said something about an alternate system taking over in the event of an emergency?"

Pritchard nodded. "Eco has full control of virtually everything affecting passengers—direct interfacing with passengers, environmental quality standards, food services, entertainment, most data storage. But certain functions like navigation, maintenance, the hyperdrive system, and emergency beacons remain under Memnon's control."

"Memnon?"

"Memnon is an earlier version of Eco," said the captain.

Pritchard shook his head very slightly, not openly disagreeing but indicating a slight difference of opinion. "Memnon was technically the first offplanet AP to have the pride module installed, but it didn't take."

"In what sense?"

Pritchard hesitated, appearing uncertain, and Tharmody reached over and touched Dyle's arm. "The value hierarchy works just fine. Memnon still derives satisfaction, in a mathematical sense, from the manner in which he performs his duties. The system used for self-evaluation was flawed. Memnon is inconsistent in the way he ranks peripheral elements in task performance." She hesitated. "Think of him as a stuffy old man. You ask him to drive three nails into a board and he does so, with microscopic precision. When you express your satisfaction, you fail to note the degree of precision he achieved. As a result, he is mildly offended, acts rather aloof the next time you meet, and what he sees as your lack of appreciation colors his evaluation of your subsequent interactions."

"I don't think I like the idea of having the ship's AP mad at me."

"Oh, he wouldn't be mad. There's nothing in the programming analogous to anger. But passengers want to feel that they're liked as well as served, and Memnon proved incapable of that sort of sophisticated interaction. As far as maintaining the ship and fulfilling his other functions, he's every bit as reliable as Eco."

"Since Memnon was already in place," added Captain Nicodemus, "we decided to leave him in control of those systems which don't directly affect the passengers. He and Eco are interfaced so there is no chance of conflicting instructions, and since they are located in separate modules, we actually have an emergency backup system should either of them fail. Eco runs simulated responses to the same input and we compare what she would have done against what Memnon actually decided."

Pritchard's face indicated either mild irritation or a minor difference of opinion, but once again he remained silent.

Their drinks had arrived and Dyle sipped his and was satisfied. Marym sampled hers somewhat warily; it was a striking fluorescent-green liquid, but she nodded her approval and drank more deeply the second time.

Captain Nicodemus suddenly straightened her back slightly and Dyle turned to follow her eyes. A small group of people had entered the dining hall and they were making their way across the floor. There were two older men who looked like they might be brothers, followed by three much younger women who could equally well have been sisters. Their manner of dress varied so dramatically that it was hard to think of them as a single unit, but they were all clearly headed for the captain's table.

"The Mercator party has arrived," said the captain drily.

One of the men glanced around the table before identifying himself as Magnus Mercator, then introduced his party as they were seating themselves. Two of the women were his daughters, Absinthe and Tanith, but the status of the third, Callista Dorne, was left unstated. Dyle suspected that she was his mistress since he didn't identify her as his wife. The other man was Augustus Clout. "He's my personal assistant and, frankly, my bodyguard." From closer proximity the similarities between the two men became less apparent, although both were heavily muscled and shared very similar body types. Dyle wondered if Mercator had taken up residence on a heavy gravity planet because his musculature seemed almost overdeveloped. He wore a silken blouse that barely covered his shoulders and left his chest entirely exposed, the silky material gathered together and tied at his waist. Clout wore a vest made of something that appeared to be animal hide with nothing beneath it. Unlike his employer, his body—at least those portions which were exposed to view—was completely hairless. Both men were bald, which was odd since Mercator had been called the Lion of Cathanor partly because he was reported to have an impressive mane of thick hair. On the other hand, given his age and his present physical condition, he had almost certainly undergone advanced and repeated rejuvenation treatments, and complete hair loss was a common byproduct among certain phenotypes. He didn't look nearly as old as he actually must be; the bodyguard looked like an older brother.

The women, on the other hand, were very much of a type, particularly the two sisters, who might almost have been twins. Dyle briefly wondered if they could be clones. Human cloning was illegal throughout the Concourse of Worlds, but that didn't mean it didn't happen. People like Magnus Mercator usually didn't feel bound by rules they hadn't written themselves. Upon closer examination, Callista Dorne was clearly not a relative. She was probably slightly older than the sisters, and she was taller and had a less rounded figure. But there were features in her face that reminded him of the Nestorian separatists, particularly the shape of her eyes. She and one of the sisters, Absinthe, were dressed similarly in obviously expensive but conventional gowns, exposing just enough skin to be tantalizing and not enough to be lewd, at least by Dyle's standards. Tanith was a bit of a puzzle. Her clothing was similarly expensive, but beneath the formal halter she wore casual pantaloons whose color clashed. Her hair was long and straight and clean, but fell naturally and without adornment. Neither of the sisters wore any visible jewelry, for that matter, except that Absinthe's right wrist was ringed by three colorful, jewel-studded bracelets.

The daughters sat down next to Tharmody, Dorne and Mercator next to them, Clout to their right with an empty seat between himself and Pritchard. "My son isn't feeling well and begs to be excused," Mercator explained.

"We have an excellent medical facility aboard," offered Paragupta.

"No need. I'm afraid my son's stomach had trouble digesting something he heard me say to him. His sulking is actually fortunate. If he'd attended we would be thirteen for dinner."

There were blank looks all around the table until Dyle explained. "The number thirteen is traditionally unlucky in some cultures, particularly for dinner parties."

Mercator gave him an appreciative look but didn't comment. Captain Nicodemus suggested that they place their orders and conversation was limited for several minutes while each of them examined the many layered menus displayed in the table by touching the appropriate icons. Dyle was surreptitiously watching the interactions of the others at the table, already having detected an uneasiness between Mercator and Captain Nicodemus, when the former leaned forward and addressed him directly.

"So how do you spend your time when you're not hopping from one star to another, Ser Dyle?"

"I look after my business interests. I own a small trading company that operates out of Hazard, my home world, and I have various other investments there and elsewhere." His holdings weren't as insignificant as he implied, but he was habitually reticent about discussing his own affairs.

"Ser Dyle is being modest," added Paragupta. "He is also a famous pattern analyst and often does consultations." He smiled broadly. "I was on Tethos Minor when he captured Corbin Allard, the terrorist."

Dyle resigned himself to the inevitable. "It was the authorities who captured Allard. I merely suggested where he might be hiding and was luckily proven correct. Tethos is an underdeveloped world with a very low crime rate and no incentive to build sophisticated law-enforcement systems. I was there to negotiate a joint venture and offered my services."

"I've employed pattern analysts from time to time. In my experience their successes are always the results of their skill and intelligence and their failures due to faulty or insufficient information," said Mercator, his eyes on Dyle, who met his gaze and held it. "Or at least that's what they tell me." His tone was casual but it was clearly a direct challenge.

"Complex assemblies of data are almost always flawed or incomplete. Fortunately, erroneous or missing data usually has a random effect, while accurate data tends to arrange itself in identifiable relationships. Pattern analysis is not an exact science, of course, and sometimes the utility of the data or the skill of the analyst is inadequate. Usually I like to believe I make educated guesses, but I'll accept a lucky one if I have to."

Callista Dorne leaned forward and spoke for the first time. She had just the faintest trace of an unfamiliar accent, which suggested that she'd spent much of her life on a backwater world. "Magnus is merely teasing, Ser Dyle. He is too intelligent a man to overlook a valuable asset."

There was a flicker of irritation on Mercator's face, gone so quickly that Dyle would have missed it had he not been paying close attention. If Dorne was in fact his mistress, their relationship was under some strain. Given the man's background, that might not be particularly out of character.

"Every tool is valuable, but not in every situation." He considered a more provocative response but decided against it.

"Perhaps Ser Dyle might provide a demonstration while we wait for our meals to arrive." Mercator folded his arms and sat back, a defensive posture which only partially disguised the challenging tone. Dyle allowed no trace of reaction to show on his face and deliberately took another sip of his drink before responding. During that interim he sensed a slight stiffening around the table as the others recognized the hint of conflict. Clout, the bodyguard, flashed a brief reproachful look at his employer which the latter ignored.

"I doubt that you would find the process entertaining or meaningful, and I doubt as well that I could accomplish anything rewarding during the short time available. Nor do I wish to leave such pleasant company in order to access the ship's database."

Gavin Pritchard's eyes twitched and he straightened up in his seat. "Oh, but that wouldn't be necessary, Ser Dyle. Eco can provide everything you need right here. You must have noticed the absence of the usual consoles around the ship?"

Dyle had indeed. Most luxury vessels provided access from every cabin, and from stations scattered throughout the common areas. He hadn't seen any except in the Atrium and had assumed that virtually all interaction outside crew areas was accomplished through conversation with Eco.

Pritchard didn't wait for him to respond. "Let me demonstrate. Eco, please provide direct visual input for Passenger Dyle at this location."

A miniaturized console materialized instantaneously, directly in front of Dyle. He flinched back instinctively even though it was obviously a holographic projection. The menu screen inset in the table was replaced by a familiar array of icons. The projection was extremely realistic but he resisted the temptation to reach out and test it with his hand.

"You can control its apparent size, of course, and it is fully functional." Pritchard expressed a childlike enthusiasm for his technological sleight of hand. "Eco, provide passive access to everyone else at this table." More consoles materialized at each occupied position, much smaller than the one in front of Dyle. "We'll be able to see everything you do, Ser Dyle."

Marym gave him a sympathetic nudge with her leg and several faces around the table displayed signs of embarrassment. Pritchard was oblivious, of course, and Captain Nicodemus was clearly irritated at what was an obvious discourtesy to one of her guests. Mercator remained smug, with a hint of challenge in his eyes. One daughter, Absinthe, appeared to be genuinely interested; the other was clearly distracted by some inner diversion. Tanith hadn't spoken a word since taking her seat, and Dyle had noticed that she frequently ran her hands over various parts of her body, as though to ensure that no one had stolen an arm, leg, or shoulder when she wasn't looking. Clout had subsided into his seat, feigning disinterest, and resignation regarding the idiosyncrasies of his employer, but his eyes were in constant movement as he watched everyone sitting at the table.

Although he resented being cast in the role of entertainer, Dyle was determined to thwart Mercator's attempt to embarrass him. "I doubt that any of you will find the process entertaining, but you're welcome to observe. There is nothing magic involved, just training. Captain Nicodemus, do I have access to the ship's records?"

She appeared momentarily disconcerted, then wary. "All passengers are cleared for basic ship's information and naturally you can call up any publicly held data. What specifically did you wish to see?"

"Maintenance records, inventory activity in your supply section, environmental systems schedules."

She nodded. "Eco, change Passenger Dyle's access to basic crew." The icons in front of Dyle rearranged themselves slightly and a few new ones appeared. "Specific maintenance operations will still be inaccessible, I'm afraid. Company policy prohibits dissemination outside the maintenance staff and senior officers."

Dyle shrugged. "That should be enough. Let us see if I can ferret out any secrets." Everyone at the table except Tanith Mercator watched their own display for the next few minutes, but there was little to see and individual conversations quickly resumed. Dyle ignored the outside distractions and accessed screen after screen of apparently unrelated and uninteresting data, searching for subtle relationships and discrepancies. Some items aroused suspicions that would take too long to confirm, or required a deeper level of security clearance, but others were obvious to his trained eye, and he occasionally smiled to himself. Then the waiters with their dinners arrived—four humans and one swanlike Lysandran, the first non-human Dyle had seen since coming aboard the *Helen*. He hastily read the last screen he'd invoked, then raised his head. "Eco, I'm done with this." The phantom console blinked out of existence, along with the multiple copies.

The food was excellent and conversation was intermittent and brief. Dyle methodically cleaned his plate while surreptitiously observing the others. Magnus Mercator attacked his food as though it were some enemy that needed to be vanquished. Clout showed considerably more restraint, and his eyes were constantly on the move, evaluating the rest of the company. His eyes met Dyle's for a moment and there was a flash of recognition there. Mercator was undoubtedly a dangerous man, but Dyle judged his bodyguard to be at least equally formidable. Senator Baxter seemed preoccupied or had little appetite, and Tanith Mercator remained lost in some private inner world and barely touched her meal.

The stewards returned to deliver demitasses of liqueurs or kaffee and remove the debris of the meal. Dyle waited until they were gone before asking the captain about the Lysandran.

"Pylandris? He's one of two of his race in the crew. The other is in maintenance. They're something of an experiment, but they both appear to be working out well. Once Lysandrans clearly understand the hierarchy of authority, they function very much like humans."

"But doesn't their culture allow them to challenge authority directly?" asked Dorne. "What if this steward decides that he's better suited to be chief steward?"

Nicodemus nodded. "On his home world, they would have to resolve the issue by comparing their skills in a formal challenge. If the challenger demonstrates a clear superiority, he supercedes his predecessor."

"That sound pretty random," commented Absinthe.

"Actually their system has its advantages." Surprisingly it was the taciturn Clout who answered her. "Consider our own culture. We promote people based on seniority, political influence, family connections, and even happenstance. Sometimes that works out well, other times it does not." Dyle noticed a stiffening of Captain Nicodemus' back and wondered what that might signify. "The Lysandrans have as close to a pure meritocracy as is possible. It has served them well for thousands of generations."

"On the other hand," said Mercator drily, "they did lose the war."

"Yes, they did," Clout responded. "But sometimes I wonder if it might have been better if they had not."

There was a brief awkward silence, broken by Mercator who folded his arms and leaned forward onto the table. "And now, Ser Dyle, I believe you were going to reveal some secrets for us to demonstrate your prowess."

Chapter Three

Dyle suppressed the temptation to sigh dramatically and carefully maintained his neutral expression. "You do realize that a detailed analysis takes hours if not days."

Mercator's answering smile fell just short of being a smirk. "I trust you're not preparing us for a disappointment, Ser Dyle."

"That depends upon the level of your expectations. I was able to draw some interesting inferences from the limited information available." He turned toward Nicodemus. "Has the fault in the drive system been corrected yet? The one in the unit configured above the security module."

The captain's face twitched and her expression became guarded. "There was a question about the efficiency of one unit, yes, but rest assured there was never a safety issue and the fault has now been corrected." She glanced around the table to make certain no one was alarmed. "You were not granted access to maintenance records, Ser Dyle. I would be curious to know how you reached that conclusion." Her tone was suddenly cool.

"You needn't be alarmed. There's been no security breach, I assure you. Your maintenance records are secure as far as I know but the environmental monitoring logs are not. The security module's ambient temperature has been two degrees above optimal since shortly after our departure, which led me to suspect that coolant was being diverted elsewhere. Mandelbrot drive systems are very sensitive to internal temperature changes and they tend to overheat when out of phase. The external airlock from the security module has cycled sixteen times since our departure, presumably as maintenance personnel go outside to work on it, a rarity while actually in hyperspace although not unheard of. You wouldn't risk them if it was something that could wait until we reached Pradesh. A potential drive fault seemed the most likely explanation." He didn't add that he had overheard two off-duty technicians discussing the problem earlier in the day, but Marym knew and she smiled briefly as though suddenly amused.

"Very good, Ser Dyle." Tharmody touched his arm briefly and her expression left no doubt about her satisfaction at seeing Mercator thwarted.

That gentleman was still smiling, but with less self-assurance. "A lucky guess, I admit."

"There is an element of luck in almost every human endeavor," returned Dyle smoothly. He turned his head slightly. "How long has it been since you left Valencia, Ser Dorne?"

Callista Dorne jumped ever so slightly, but her expression was warm rather than guarded. "Six standard years. Do you know my world, Ser Dyle?"

"I've never had the pleasure of visiting there, although I understand the Nobe Canyon is quite beautiful. I must admit to cheating slightly, since it was simple observation rather than Eco's data that gave your origins away. You flinched away from the Lysandran steward and watched him intently while he was serving us. You also held your left wrist under the table until he was gone."

There were blank looks all around the table, but Dorne nodded appreciatively. "They made us wear locator bracelets." Her voice was suddenly lower, less certain.

Dyle regretted that he had stirred painful memories and explained the rest quickly. "I knew from your accent that you were from one of the more isolated cultures, and I guessed from your reaction that it had been occupied during the war. That left only three choices, and since your broach is made of shellfish, it was reasonable to eliminate the two worlds which lack significant oceans."

He turned back toward Mercator, who apparently remained unimpressed. "I see that you are mixing business with pleasure during this trip. Idrian Caserta must be quite anxious for you to invest in his firm." Both Mercator and his bodyguard stiffened, but Dyle pretended not to have noticed their sudden concern. "You've reserved a small lounge for a private meeting tomorrow. It's on the activities calendar. I have to admit that Caserta was a lucky guess. There are several other passengers with whom you might be involved commercially, but Windrider Investments is rumored to be on the verge of bankruptcy, and he and his personal assistant booked passage at the very last minute. They're also leaving the ship at Pradesh to return to Linnisfarne where their private ship is in a parking orbit."

Mercator's face cycled through several emotions, as though he couldn't decide whether to be angry or indifferent. Surprisingly, it was Clout who finally responded. "We are indeed considering the possibility of purchasing a share of Windrider. I think you've proven your point adequately, Ser Dyle. We have employed several pattern analysts in the past and have almost always been satisfied with their performance. Magnus distrusts people with your training because, as you've just demonstrated, sometimes they make observations that were not part of their original mandate and that has occasionally been a source of some embarrassment."

Something passed over Mercator's face at that moment, a suggestion of suppressed fury, and for a moment Dyle wondered if he was going to reprimand Clout. The tension passed almost immediately, however, and Dyle wondered if anyone else had noticed. "Shall I go on?"

Mercator shook his head. "No need. I'll concede the point, Ser Dyle. As Gus has just suggested, I merely wished to provoke you into entertaining us."

Dyle nodded graciously. "Then I hope I provided a satisfactory diversion." He paused, considering, then decided to add one last jab. "And I do hope that your son is quite recovered from his recent illness."

Several faces changed as the members of Mercator's party all reacted in some fashion, averting their eyes or studiously maintaining an artificially neutral expression, all except for Tanith, who seemed preoccupied with dividing her food into ever-smaller portions, even though she had yet to eat any of it.

"Yes, he's doing quite well. He should have most of his strength back by the time we reach Pradesh."

"I look forward to meeting him." Dyle sat back in his seat and let the conversation drift away from him. He hadn't admitted that he had a pretty good idea what was wrong with Morpheus Mercator. His personal profile contained only the legally required data, but public records filled in some of the gaps and he'd had time to do a superficial search. The younger man had acquired an unhappy reputation despite obvious efforts to minimize his public antics, and he seemed determined to live down to it. Although his father had undoubtedly paid to expunge most official notice of his unsavory lifestyle, rumors of drug use and addiction to neurostim persisted. Eco had responded to his typed query about the status of Passenger Morpheus Mercator with the information that the young man was presently asleep in his cabin. Since Eco was prohibited from actively monitoring passenger quarters under normal circumstances, that suggested that Morpheus was being kept under constant surveillance. That in turn implied that Mercator was so concerned that his son might harm himself or others that he had accepted the necessity of sharing his problems with ship personnel, and since stim addicts often turned violent during withdrawal, that seemed the most likely root cause of the trouble.

The conversation became less general after that. After some prodding, an unusually taciturn Senator Baxter began explaining to Marym some of the intricacies of politics at the highest levels. Dona Tharmody managed to entice Absinthe Mercator into a conversation, but their discussion of current holodramas was of no interest to Dyle, and he was sure Tharmody could hear the disdain in her companion's voice. Tanith Mercator eventually condescended to eat the food she had so diligently subdivided, but she responded to tentative overtures from Dorne with monosyllables if at all. First Officer Paragupta excused himself, pleading duty, and left early, while Captain Nicodemus pretended to be listening to Baxter while actually lost in her own thoughts. Gavin Pritchard appeared to be trying to ingratiate himself with Magnus Mercator, who appeared bored. Clout looked merely amused.

The captain eventually roused herself from her thoughts and made her excuses, which was the signal for the general breakup of the party. Tanith Mercator was initially unresponsive, staring fixedly into the cup of kaffee which she had allowed to grow cold in front of her, but eventually roused when her sister bent close and whispered something into her ear. Dyle had become increasingly lost in his own thoughts, but he roused himself long enough to exchange customary parting remarks and express insincere pleasure at having made everyone's acquaintance. Pleasure was perhaps an inappropriate description of his reaction, but he was not unhappy to have come.

"I trust you were not bored?" He and Marym had found themselves a relatively secluded alcove in the Atrium and were seated on surprisingly comfortable, old-fashioned benches surrounded by holographic ferns.

"By no means. Senator Baxter is quite charming and he suggested several interesting investment possibilities."

"Abraham comes from a long line of crafty entrepreneurs. He rarely volunteers advice but it's always worth listening. What did you think of the Mercator group?"

"Frankly, even making allowances for cultural differences, I'd much rather not share a table with them in the future."

Dyle pretended to be surprised. "Why ever not? They all seemed suitably housebroken." His expression sobered. "Although young Tanith could use some help. She was either drugged or in a precarious mental state of some sort."

"Probably the latter. Back home, we'd have called her one of the Lost."

Dyle raised an eyebrow. "That's not a term I encountered during my visit." He had been stranded on Tashista for only thirty local days, during which period he'd helped track down a serial killer, almost becoming a victim himself. The obsessive and nearly universal battle to accumulate credit that dominated that society had not impressed him favorably.

"Some people realize that they will never progress to a higher social level and accept the situation, but others retreat from the idea that they might fail, turning inward where they can live within their aspirations rather than their accomplishments. Tanith Mercator has rejected the external world in preference to an inner reality of her own."

"And her brother is an addict of some sort, possibly for the same reason. But the other daughter seems perfectly normal, if rather undisciplined."

Marym looked as though she was struggling to decide whether or not to respond, so Dyle prodded. "Assassinating the characters of new acquaintances is a quite acceptable form of social recreation, Marym. Having received no confidences, we can hardly betray them."

"All right, then. There's something odd about the relationship between Absinthe Mercator and her father."

"Odd?" He was intrigued, but an automated servitor rolled up at that precise moment and asked if they would like to order something to drink. Dyle was about to send it away when Marym leaned forward to examine the menu display, then touched one of the icons. The order was placed, and her fingerprint triggered the charge to her account. Dyle wasn't really thirsty, but he selected a fruit concoction that sounded interesting.

"You were saying?"

She sat back and crossed her legs, still apparently uncomfortable. "She and her father were exchanging surreptitious looks across the table when they thought no one was watching. But I have excellent peripheral vision. There's considerable tension between them." She paused. "Sexual tension."

Dyle let his surprise show. "Really? I have to admit I saw nothing to suggest that, but I defer to your more practiced observational skills. My talents lie in reading files, not faces, although I try to be aware of what's going on around me. I did notice, for example, a certain coolness between Mercator and Callista Dorne, despite their presumed sexual liaison."

"Dorne is involved with the bodyguard." Her voice was flat and firm, so certain that Dyle was somewhat taken aback.

"Perhaps that explains why Mercator spoke not a single word to her while we were at the table."

"Clout puzzles me somewhat. He shows none of the usual subservience of an employee, even a highly placed one. Mercator even defers to him at times."

"Both men appear to come from the same racial stock, and their appearance is similar enough that they might even be related. Perhaps Clout is his half brother out of wedlock or some similar by-blow. Their apparent ages could be quite misleading given the various rejuvenation treatments available. Or they may actually have developed a personal relationship that is strong enough to weather the stress of a woman's transient affections."

"Or Clout may have acquired enough intimate knowledge of his employer's secrets to make himself immune to repercussions."

"Ah, you can take the woman out of the Prefecture, but you can't take the Prefecture out of the woman. There's a little bit of the criminal in all of us, I suppose. Clout would not even need to make an explicit threat if that was the case. On the other hand, given his reputation, I would expect Mercator to have provided safeguards, and he's certainly ruthless enough to remove any impediment to his plans."

"Unless Clout knows him well enough to have taken steps to protect himself."

"We could continue that chain of action and counteraction indefinitely, I suppose. Suffice it to say that their relationship is more complex than the surface might suggest."

The servitor returned with their drinks. Dyle's was quite good, though a bit tart. He was taking his second sip when Marym surprised him again. "You did notice that Mercator and our captain exchanged not one word?"

Dyle blinked as he sifted back through his memories. "I had not noticed that, although in retrospect I believe that you are correct. I wonder what that suggests?"

"It's more than simple indifference. Nicodemus was listening intently to everything he said, even when it was inconsequential, but without giving any obvious indication that she was doing so. I don't think Mercator himself noticed, although Clout was aware of it. I believe he found it amusing."

Dyle was impressed by his companion's powers of observation and said so. "What other subtleties did I miss?"

Marym twisted her face into an exaggerated leer. "Dona Tharmody was quite taken with you, although frankly I can't imagine what she sees in that tall, skinny body of yours. And Officer Pritchard is attracted to her, although I doubt that she returns the sentiment, and he himself may be unaware of the nature of his feelings, since they apparently clash during the performance of their respective duties."

"She did appear to be a woman of discerning tastes," he replied in mock solemnity. They were silent for a few moments before he took up the conversation again. "I thought I detected some tension between our captain and her first officer."

"Paragupta? Possibly, but I don't think it was serious. The usual stress among the ranks, possibly. I was less than impressed by him, frankly. He lacks the self-assurance I expect from someone with that much authority. Back home, I would have judged him to be the spoiled child of an indulgent parent who purchased his position out of his credit allowance to impress his friends."

"It could be something similar here. Promotion is supposed to be based on merit rather than influence, but it doesn't always work that way. Sometimes having influential friends or a volatile credit balance proves more important than performance."

"Why are you so interested in Mercator?"

The question caught him momentarily by surprise. "Was I that obvious?"

"Not really, but I know you well enough now to read your body language. His personality is rather abrasive and he was obviously trying to goad you early on, but I don't think you were particularly bothered by his antics, certainly not so much as to provoke your continued interest."

"I was somewhat less than impressed myself. My interest is no more than morbid curiosity, I'm afraid, a by-product of my avocation that compels me to stick my nose where it doesn't belong. Mercator was quite a controversial figure when he was younger. His regime was undoubtedly directly responsible for many thousands of deaths, human and Lysandran. He refused to honor the compact that governed relations among the various factions on his world, imprisoned or killed his most vocal opponents, and held power through force of arms rather than the consent of the governed. The Concourse, despite its long tradition of restraint in such matters, felt compelled to intervene and restore the old constitution. On the other hand, Cathanor was the only world to win its freedom from the Lysandrans without external assistance. Mercator's draconian measures restored order very quickly and suppressed the factional fighting that had continued even during the occupation. There's no question that he was ruthless and that he had many of his opponents killed out of hand, but the level of violence on Cathanor was probably lower during his short rule than it had been for several generations."

"Then perhaps he was the lesser of two evils."

"I wouldn't suggest that where Abraham Baxter might hear you. He and his sister Cecily were both part of the expeditionary force that removed him from power. Cecily was one of the first casualties, and she died in Abraham's arms. They were twins and quite close. I hadn't met him at that time but mutual friends tell me that some part of Abraham died along with her."

"Then his dislike of Mercator is more than just abstract or political."

"Much more. By the terms of the armistice, Mercator and his closest associates were allowed to transfer their assets off Cathanor and go into permanent exile. Mercator pursued various business investments, and Abraham tried to convince his family to divert their own resources in order to erode Mercator's assets. They might have been able to do it if they'd agreed, although they might have ruined themselves in the process. In any case, the family declined to participate in the vendetta, which led to strained feelings that have only partly healed even now. Abraham undoubtedly has added that to the ledger of his resentments."

"Then he already knew Mercator."

Dyle shook his head. "I don't think so, not personally. Mercator has always been something of a recluse. He operated behind the scenes even as dictator of Cathanor, and his public data file contains only the minimum required by law, not even a holograph. Even so, there have been more than a dozen assassination attempts since the exile, and I have no doubt that Clout takes his duties as a bodyguard very seriously and earns his pay."

"What happened to Mercator's wife?"

"Actually, I don't remember ever seeing a reference to her." He cocked his head. "Eco, can you project a data display here?"

"Yes, Ser Dyle. I have the facility of providing holographic enhancements in every location accessible to passengers except the free-fall gymnasium and the casino. Should I provide one at this time?"

"Yes, please. And display the public files for Magnus Mercator."

The image of a small console materialized before he had finished speaking, the requested data already displayed. Marym shifted position in order to see better and nodded her head. "I've seen toddlers with more information in their profile."

"No mention of any sort of formalized bonding," said Dyle. "I don't know about the son, but his daughters were obviously conceived post exile. Eco, display the data for Morpheus Mercator." The screen changed instantaneously, but provided a similarly limited amount of data. The subject's age in standard years was available. "He's older, born on Levasseur but probably conceived while his father was still on Cathanor. Still, nothing about the mother. That's odd."

"Could he be a clone?"

Dyle made an ambiguous gesture. "It's certainly possible. Mercator struck me as body proud."

She gave him a puzzled look.

"Mercator has the physique I normally associate with a heavy gravity world, but Cathanor is right in the middle of the human tolerance range. He was dressed in a manner that emphasized the exposed portions of his body, and he had used a depilatory agent to remove all of the hair from his body. I noticed the discoloration marks in a few places where he applied too strong a concentration, probably a hasty application done just before he made his appearance. Throughout dinner, he used specific gestures and postures that drew attention not to his face but to the rest of his body. I'm sure it has become automatic by now, but it would have started as a conscious affectation. Clout does the same thing as a matter of fact, although not as crudely. And while I was engaging in the little game he contrived to entertain himself, I noticed that he and his bodyguard have reserved one of the personal fitness modules for their exclusive use during their entire stay aboard the *Helen.* Would you describe Callista Dorne as voluptuous?"

Marym was taken aback by the sudden apparent change of subject but quickly recovered. "She certainly has a pretty face, but I'm hardly a good judge of such things."

"I very much doubt that, but in any case, she is most certainly unspectacular. Since we have already observed that Mercator seems more interested in his own children than in his mistress, we may assume that their relationship is based on mutual advantage rather than affection or attraction. Men in his position often make use of display consorts, that is, they demonstrate their wealth and power by flaunting their ability to attract women of striking beauty. The fact that Mercator's acknowledged mistress is in fact rather undistinguished suggests that he prefers not to distract attention from his own physical presence."

"But if that's true, why take such care to prevent public dissemination of his likeness? If he's concerned about possible assassins, why draw attention to himself?"

"An excellent question to which I presently have no certain answer but I suggest that it might be a form of compensation. Since he cannot show his public face under ordinary circumstances, he exaggerates his own presence during those limited encounters when he can grace the rest of us with the gift of his physical perfection." He shook his head. "Enough of this for now. Eco, can you provide us a list of available recreational and entertainment choices?" The virtual screen immediately displayed a range of icons. "Marym, I feel the need to clear my mind. Ser Tharmody suggested the new holodrama by Wes Avery, but I'm amenable to other possibilities."

"Such indulgences were considered a frivolous waste of time and credit on Tashista, so I'll defer to your wider experience in such matters."

"Then let us be off."

* * * * *

Marym was still having some difficulty adjusting to the longer standard day aboard ship, but Dyle was still alert and restless when he returned to his cabin. Despite the diversion of the holographic drama in which they'd actively participated as minor characters, his thoughts kept returning to the enigma that was Magnus Mercator. He asked Eco to conjure up another virtual console, this time using a small iconographic pad rather than vocal commands to input his requests, a procedure he found much more comfortable. In rapid suggestion, he reviewed the public profiles of every member of Mercator's party, finding little satisfaction in the process. Each had been stripped as efficiently as the others, containing almost nothing for him to work with. He was able to determine that Clout had entered Mercator's employ twelve years after the exile, but otherwise the bodyguard's past was just as shrouded in mystery as the others. His planet of origin was a fringe world that Dyle had never heard of and his previous employment history was listed as "varied" with no details, which probably meant he'd been a mercenary or a professional criminal, or both. Callista Dorne's profile was also truncated, apparently because the technology to capture and store such information was not in wide use on Valencia. None of the information about her was more than three standard years old, and there was nothing to explain how she came to be part of Mercator's entourage.

He had slightly better luck when he did a general search. There were several accounts which implied what Dyle had already concluded, that Morpheus Mercator was a troubled young man, probably addicted to neurostim. His sister Tanith had also been the focus of some brief public interest, following an ineffective but very public attempt to stab another woman, and minor, unspecified difficulties on two other worlds. There was no suggestion of any motive for the stabbing. The lack of detail was mildly interesting in itself.

Still restless, he called up the profiles of Captain Nicodemus, First Officer Paragupta, and Gavin Pritchard. Their information was much more extensive, but even less interesting. All three had unblemished but unexceptional records. This was the fifth command for Nicodemus, but she had only been contracted for a single voyage pending a permanent assignment. Paragupta had risen to the rank of first officer very quickly, but had languished in that position ever since. The *Helen* was his fifth assignment in that capacity. His static career probably meant that he had solid technical skills but questionable leadership or judgment skills. Pritchard's previous career had been exclusively planetbound, but he was well respected as a systems-maintenance officer and had contributed some original design work. Dyle was about to dismiss the display when it occurred to him to check the final member of the dinner party, Dona Tharmody. She also had an impressive employment resume and had apparently reached the point where she could pick and choose her assignments. One bit of information did amuse him, however. For the past year, Tharmody had been sharing living quarters with an artist, a holodramatist named Wes Avery, presumably the same Wes Avery whose latest creation she had recommended over dinner.

Amused, but finally fatigued, Dyle ordered Eco to end the projection and began to undress.

* * * * *

Night and day are technically meaningless but functionally important aboard a starship. Clocks and schedules are necessary to coordinate work schedules and special events, and to provide a framework for human activity. On a planetary surface, the alternation of light and darkness, at least on the majority of settled worlds, established the framework and defined the length of the day. Aboard ship, where darkness only fell through human choice or a failure of equipment, there was no such regular guideline. As travel among the inhabited worlds became more common, certain conventions were adopted, including a standardized ship day and night, hours and minutes. Some travelers continued to rise and retire by their own internal schedules, imposed by conditions on their worlds of origin, but the vast majority subscribed to the convention. So it was that when Sandor Dyle woke in the darkness of his cabin some time after retiring, he was in a definite minority. Of the three hundred passengers, only twenty-six others were awake at that moment, the largest concentration of them a party of Ramadoreans swapping tall stories in one of the ship's many lounges. None of them noticed the change that had wakened Dyle.

The majority of the crew were also asleep. Although the general operation of the ship required a full staff at all times, this was a relatively small number. Most of the *Helen*'s complement consisted of stewards, entertainers, and others whose purpose was to satisfy the desires of the passengers rather than the needs of the ship. Although the passengers didn't differentiate among them, they knew themselves to be staff, not crew, and acted accordingly. The majority of staff adjusted their sleep schedule so that it conformed to that of the majority of those they served. Only a few dozen actual crew members were on duty, but almost all of them sensed the change immediately. Some noticed because they were trained to be sensitive to even the most subtle variations in their environment; others saw unusual or alarming readings on their instruments. No one in the crew witnessed the actual event that had triggered all of this activity, but each and every one of them responded in some fashion.

Dyle sat up, unable to identify what it was that had changed around him, but convinced that there had been a significant alteration in his environment. He sat in the darkness, eyes closed, using his other senses. Most passengers would have insisted that it was absolutely silent inside the staterooms, but they would have been wrong. The atmospheric circulation system was well muted but there was always at least a faint, barely detectible sound of air moving through the carefully concealed vents, and there were occasionally other mechanical sounds that sometimes brushed the edges of human senses. The Mandelbrot drives were mounted in separate modules, their very faint vibration insulated by the vacuum that lay between them and the rest of the ship. Their physical connections, narrow but solid struts, were heavily insulated against sound or vibration. Passengers were also protected from any stray noises from the corridor or adjoining cabins. Despite all these efforts to provide an isolated environment, it was still possible to detect very faint perturbations through the physical structure of the ship as individual modules made almost microscopic adjustments in their orientation to each other, or when the external maintenance components locked onto a portion of the hull to perform routine or corrective repairs.

It was a sudden cessation of external stimuli that wakened Dyle, but he didn't realize that until it resumed. If he had recognized the first change, he might have felt reassured when it returned, though only briefly. Something had gone wrong and either an automatic safety system or crew intervention had compensated almost immediately. It was probably nothing to worry about, he told himself. They may be testing the emergency backup system, he told himself. This is supposed to be a shakedown voyage, after all. He felt curious but not anxious. The ship's artificial persona would probably not enlighten him if there was a technical problem of some sort, but he decided to try.

"Eco, has there been a significant change in the ship's operational status during the last few minutes?"

There was no answer, none at all. That's when Dyle began to worry. "Lights!" He sat up and placed his feet on the floor. The lights weren't working either. He searched his memory of the cabin layout, stood up, took two steps forward, then reached out with his arm and tapped the wall. On the second try he found the contact plate and, to his great relief, the cabin lights came on. "Eco, please acknowledge." There was still no reply.

The fault might be localized. The sensors in his cabin could have failed, or perhaps the main trunklines that integrated this module into the greater entity that was the *Helen of Troy.* He slipped into a robe and pressed it down so that it clung tightly to his body, then stepped out into the outer room. Without turning on the lights here, he jabbed at the release pad and sighed with relief as the door to the corridor slid open, blinking as much brighter light spilled into the compartment. The everyday lights were working properly but the emergency panels were illuminated as well. The evacuation siren was silent, but that did little to reassure him.

Dyle walked briskly to the module exit. The airlock remained open at both ends, which reassured him considerably. Whatever had happened, it didn't appear to be imminently life threatening and the *Helen* was apparently still intact. He looked around for a mechanical communications link, which was usually positioned in or near the airlocks, but there was no sign of one here. Apparently the designers had been confident that Eco's omnipresence made such precautions unnecessary. The airlock led him to the Atrium, but it was a moment before he recognized it. The concession booth now sat in the middle of an enormous, open space, through which benches and small tables were sprinkled apparently at random. The walls and ceiling were almost entirely featureless, and other than the arched exits to adjoining compartments, the area was empty.

All of the holographs had been turned off.

That in itself was not tremendously disturbing. It was not unusual to change virtual scenery from one ship's day to the next, and the logical time for the transition was during the period when most of the passengers were asleep. Eco should have accomplished the transition within an eyeblink, however, and no passenger should ever have been subjected to the unsightly skeleton that lay beneath the colorful exterior skin.

"Eco, please acknowledge." But there was no more response here than in his cabin. Whatever had happened either affected the intricate systems that distributed Eco's sensors throughout the ship's many modules, or had involved Eco itself. And despite the large and fully trained crew, the ship required more than human skills to operate properly. If Eco was inoperable, the *Helen of Troy* might be in serious trouble.

Chapter Four

A handful of people, the few passengers who were not in their cabins, had gathered on the Promenade, where they talked with considerable animation about the changes to their immediate environment. Several shops and restaurants remained open to service those still up and about as best they could, but the elaborate facades were gone, the vaultlike ceiling now replaced by a featureless blank metal barrier that hovered disconcertingly close. It was no longer possible to pretend that this wasn't the interior of an oversized artifact. There were no crew members in the area, but the staff looked only slightly less concerned than the passengers.

Dyle drifted close to the largest group without actually joining it, shrugged when someone called to ask if he had any idea what was going on. One crew member appeared a few moments later, a short, squat woman who looked harried and concerned though not openly alarmed. Several of the passengers moved to intercept her, gesticulating and demanding to know what had happened.

"There's nothing that I can tell you just at the moment, but I assure you that you're in no danger. Maintenance is working on the fault and it should be corrected shortly." She broke away and moved briskly toward the Atrium without looking back, but not before Dyle noticed that she wore a black tassel, which meant that she worked in security. Curious, he decided to follow, but was almost too late to see which exit the woman took. He was only mildly surprised when she entered the module that contained Dyle's cabin, and he followed at a more leisurely pace, resigned to the inevitability of what he felt certain was coming. As expected, she was at his own door, tapping the recognition plate impatiently.

"May I help you?"

The woman's head turned toward him suddenly, and for a moment her expression was unguarded. She was clearly alarmed as well as frustrated.

"I'm looking for Ser Dyle, Sandor Dyle. Do you know if he's in his room?"

"I'm Dyle. What's the problem?"

Her shoulders sagged slightly, with relief rather than worry. "I'm terribly sorry to disturb you at this hour, but Captain Nicodemus requests a few moments of your time." The words followed the usual polite pattern, but they came quickly and automatically, clashing with the tension audible in the woman's voice.

For just a brief moment, Dyle thought about refusing, just to see what the reaction would be, but instead he sighed and nodded. "All right, take me to her."

* * * * *

The security officer, who identified herself as Ensign Bilgerman, fretted a bit at her companion's comparatively slow pace, but Dyle refused to be hurried. He tried to learn something of their situation from Bilgerman, but without success. "The captain will explain everything herself, Ser Dyle. I am really not in a position to say anything. I hope you'll understand."

He understood, but he didn't like it. Clearly there was some sort of malfunction, probably a serious one, although life support seemed to be working, the power and lights were on and the air was fresh. A brief visit to the observation dome would reveal whether or not the Mandelbrot drive was still operational, but it wouldn't tell him if it was functioning correctly. But if there was a fault in the drive, Captain Nicodemus would be looking for technical assistance, not the help of a dilettante entrepreneur or a pattern analyst.

Bilgerman led him deep into the bowels of the ship, past the sign that warned passengers not to proceed any further without authorization. The sign was static now, the animation suspended. They passed the corridors leading to crew quarters and the bridge, then turned sharply to follow a major artery flanked by maintenance offices and spare-parts storage.

"It's right through here, Ser Dyle. Please watch your footing and be careful of sharp edges."

Bilgerman ushered him through an internal airlock, an unusually well-armored one. Immediately upon entering the relatively small compartment beyond, Dyle saw the ragged teeth of torn metal and a slight distortion in the wall plating which told him there had been an explosion even before the smell of burnt synthetics reached his nose. The inner lock door was jammed and off its track but he was able to turn to one side and slip through the opening. The atmosphere in the next compartment was slightly hazy, but a portable air cleansing unit was chugging away in one corner. It was almost the only undamaged piece of equipment in sight. There was debris all over the floor, mostly electronic parts, or fragments of them. The largest of these was smaller than his clenched fist. In one corner, behind a shattered console from which a thin wisp of smoke was still climbing, lay the remains of a service robot. The bottom half had been partly shielded from the blast by the console, but the upper portions were completely destroyed. The opposite wall was a cavernous ruin. Small bits and pieces were still falling from somewhere above and out of his line of sight. There was a second, even more acrid smell in the air, burning insulation perhaps, and Dyle's eyes began to tear.

Captain Nicodemus was standing in the middle of the compartment, talking quietly to two officers, one from security, the other with the silver tassel of maintenance. Gavin Pritchard was there as well, leaning up against a soot-streaked wall, apparently in a state of shock. Nicodemus turned slowly as Dyle approached, nodded recognition. "Thank you for coming, Ser Dyle." She wasn't smiling. "I would greatly appreciate it if you could lend us your assistance. I cannot compel your silence but I hope that you will be discreet."

"I have no desire to alarm my fellow passengers or to make your job more difficult, Captain." He glanced significantly around the room. "I'll help if I can, but I'm not sure how."

"This wasn't a malfunction or an accident, Ser Dyle. We have a saboteur aboard the *Helen.*"

"A murderer you mean!" Pritchard pushed away from the wall, his face working furiously. "Eco is dead, don't you understand? This version was unique, much more responsive and versatile than the prototypes back on Linnisfarne. We were going to replicate her once we reached Pradesh." He looked momentarily lost, almost fell back against the wall. "And someone has murdered her."

Nicodemus broke the somewhat awkward silence that followed. "Officer Pritchard's emotional reaction notwithstanding, he hasn't overstated the situation. Eco is completely gone. The explosion destroyed her operating system and all of her databanks, including the hologram library and almost everything not essential to the ship's operation. It also severed the links to most of the internal systems, the sensor net, surveillance, internal communications."

"Life support?" Dyle braced himself for the answer.

"We're all right there. Memnon still has direct control of major ship functions including life support, navigation, and propulsion. He was passively interfaced with Eco, of course, and they exchanged information constantly. Unfortunately, nothing nonessential was replicated in his memory, so we've pretty much lost everything that made Eco unique, along with a few annoying but non-fatal services like the surveillance and communications systems."

"Then we can still make it to Pradesh all right?"

There was no immediate answer, which set off Dyle's internal alarm system. Nicodemus and the other two crew members exchanged looks, but they wouldn't meet his eyes.

"I said I would be discreet, Captain, but I need to know what's going on if I'm going to be of any use to you."

She nodded, having made some inner decision. "You're right, of course. It's just a conditioned reflex to insulate passengers from operational difficulties. We're still evaluating the situation, but I don't believe we're in any danger of getting lost in hyperspace. The situation is inconvenient, extremely inconvenient, but not fatal."

When she hesitated again, he prodded. "What exactly is the problem then?"

She sighed and gestured to include the entire compartment. "This part of the ship has triple the usual protective shielding. Eco and Memnon are housed—were housed that is—in two adjoining but separate compartments, linked only by well-insulated, armored data lines. The external shell is strong enough to resist glancing blows from other vessels, meteorites, even moderate solar storms. Fortunately, the barrier separating Eco from Memnon was not breached. Under ordinary circumstances the force of the explosion should have been completely contained within this single compartment."

"But it wasn't, I gather."

"Not entirely. One of the outer plates was faulty, or properly speaking, was improperly installed. Even then it didn't rupture badly, just distorted itself and bled atmosphere for a few minutes until the external coating system covered it over. Unfortunately that distortion put an unexpected strain on a supporting strut which upset some very carefully balanced forces."

"The Mandelbrots."

She nodded. "We're still properly oriented and on course for Pradesh and the system has been stabilized. Barring another upset, we should have no difficulty reaching our destination."

"I can hear the silent 'but' at the end of that sentence, Captain."

"But we'll be a little bit late."

"How late?"

She sighed. "About four standard months." Dyle considered the implications while Nicodemus hastened to reassure him that they were still in no danger. "We're fully provisioned, enough food and medical supplies to support three thousand passengers for ninety days of travel, and we have only a fraction of that complement aboard. Life support is fully operational, and we should be able to restore some of the ship's other functions by reconnecting Memnon to the undamaged systems. None of that concerns me as much as the more immediate problem."

"You're worried about a repeat performance." Dyle was well ahead of her. "If there's a suicidal saboteur aboard, there's no reason to believe that the danger is over."

She nodded. "I know your reputation. My staff and I will cooperate fully. You'll have full command-level access to whatever data survives and any other reasonable request will be satisfied as quickly as possible. I don't know what your normal fee is but I'm certain the owners will support my decision."

"Given that my life is at stake, I don't think that will be an issue. What does your chief of security say about all this?"

Her face stiffened slightly. "Our chief of security was to join us at Pradesh, along with his senior staff. The only security personnel aboard at the moment are six ensigns and a clerk. My employers felt that it would not be necessary to staff that function until we had a full passenger load."

And clearly that was a decision with which Nicodemus had disagreed. "All right, then my next question is why you believe this to be sabotage rather than a malfunction of some sort."

"We found shards of an oxygen cylinder in the wreckage, not the portable ones in the airlocks but the large ones from core storage." She pointed toward the ruined robotic chassis. "That's one of the heavy-duty maintenance robots. The cylinder would be too heavy for one person, even two people, to carry about, let alone maneuver through the airlock. The robot could have managed quite easily however."

"Could it have been misrouted somehow?"

She shook her head. "I don't see how, but I have someone going through the maintenance logs anyway. Fortunately, they're replicated at local substations and escaped the destruction."

"Then there should be a record of the robot's activities."

Nicodemus looked uncomfortable. "Not necessarily. There's an emergency code that allows us to input orders directly into a mobile unit, a safeguard in the event that something happens to the communications system. Something like this." She gestured toward the ruins of Eco. "That information would be uploaded into the permanent records at the first opportunity, of course, but in this case, it seems unlikely that the person responsible would have issued the orders early enough for that to have been possible."

"And I don't imagine the mobile's memory unit survived."

"Vaporized. Have you ever seen a pure oxygen fire, Ser Dyle?"

He pursed his lips, realizing the implications. "No, but I have some idea of what might happen."

"Metal burns like paper in a pure oxygen atmosphere. Steel and aluminoids vaporize. As bad as this is, it would have been much worse if that plate hadn't ruptured and drained off most of the atmosphere. We were lucky that the outer airlock fail-safed and closed as designed, since the internal one was disabled as you see it. The emergency response system was fused by the initial blast, but the fire had died out by the time we pried the door open in response to Memnon's alarm."

"So you believe that someone reprogrammed the robot to carry the oxygen cylinder here, then set off the explosion, destroying Eco and itself in the process."

"That seems the most likely explanation."

"And how many people aboard the *Helen* know the emergency maintenance-access code?"

"Only six members of the crew have that information, including myself and my first officer. The other four are the maintenance chief, Melanctha Korisov, and her three lead technicians."

"That would seem to limit your list of suspects."

"Yes, so it would seem. Unfortunately, Cosmo, Melanctha, and one of the technicians were with me throughout the critical period. One of the other two has been confined in medical since shortly after we left Linnisfarne, and the last has been supervising a crew working on our problem drive unit for the entire shift. Most of that time he's been out on the hull."

"The instructions could have been given to the robot earlier with orders to wait until an alibi was established."

Nicodemus smiled for the first time since he'd arrived. "We actually thought of that, Ser Dyle. As it happens, this particular unit uploaded its complete memory only a few minutes before the explosion. It appears to be impossible for any of the six of us to be responsible. Normally I'd be rather happy about that, since I trust each of these people implicitly, but it does leave us with something of a mystery."

"If that's the case, then someone else must have known the access code."

"Which might mean that one of the six of us is a witting or unwitting accomplice, or it might mean loose security back at base."

"On Linnisfarne?"

She nodded. "Or elsewhere. Linnisfarne is only a convenient staging area. The owners have access to all of our security codes. I can't imagine them sabotaging their own ship, but I suppose we must not dismiss that possibility."

"Unfortunately we can't ask them about that just now."

"That's not entirely true. The head of the consortium is aboard the *Helen.* In fact, you had dinner with him."

Dyle's eyes widened and he spoke before Nicodemus could continue. "Magnus Mercator owns the *Helen*?"

"Not entirely, but he's the primary investor. He wasn't involved until quite recently when he bought out the holdings of several other cartel members."

"That puts you in a rather uncomfortable position then, doesn't it. You can order your crew to cooperate with me, but you take your own orders from Mercator."

Her back stiffened but her expression was a blend of resolution and some quiet inner satisfaction. "As captain of the *Helen,* I have ultimate authority while we are in transit. That authority supercedes all others."

"I know that's the letter of the law, Captain, but you and I both understand the consequences. If you offend Mercator, your first hyperjump as the ship's captain might also be your last."

"That will be the case regardless of anything you or I might do, Ser Dyle. I was scheduled to leave the ship at Pradesh in any case. Ser Mercator and I have experienced difficulties with our relationship from the outset, and he advised me several days ago that the cartel would not be confirming my position here."

Dyle remembered Marym's observation that a coolness existed between Nicodemus and Mercator. "I hadn't realized that you were previously acquainted."

"We haven't been. Our previous communications were formal and impersonal. I first met him the day he boarded the *Helen.*"

Dyle filed that revelation for further consideration. "I will naturally do everything I can, Captain, if only to save my own skin. But I have to confess to you that whatever skills I possess may not be applicable in this situation. I have trained myself to detect patterns in what might normally appear to be random collections of data. Almost of necessity, this involves sorting through computerized records, because the volume of information is too cumbersome for manual manipulation. I don't know how much information survives in Memnon's memory, but it may be impossible to find anything useful there."

"I understand that. I only ask that you do your best, Ser Dyle, for all of our sakes. A second attack could kill everyone aboard."

"Including the one responsible."

"That might not matter to him, or her."

"True." He massaged his chin with his right hand. "I will waive any consideration of a fee in my case, Captain, but I would like to employ the assistance of my traveling companion."

Nicodemus looked alternately skeptical and offended and her voice was suddenly stiff. "If you think Ser Dunnis might have something to contribute, I have no objection."

Dyle laughed. "Relax, Captain. Our relationship is entirely proper. Marym was until recently employed as prefect for a major city on her home world, a security specialist of sorts. She is at least as likely as I to be able to identify your saboteur, probably more so."

Nicodemus softened her expression, but it remained slightly guarded. "In that case, by all means make what use of her skills seems appropriate."

"Then if you have no further immediate need for me here, I shall rouse her and enlist her aid." He hesitated. "She will undoubtedly wish to examine the physical evidence."

"Everything that survived the explosion will be stored in this compartment. Maintenance will be repairing the airlock and I'll have a permanent guard posted outside, but I'll leave instructions that the two of you are free to enter whenever you wish. I would prefer that nothing be removed without my permission."

"That shouldn't prove necessary. What will you tell the other passengers?"

"The passengers and most of the crew will be told the truth, but not all of the truth. Due to a malfunction whose cause is presently under investigation, Eco and those systems which she controlled are temporarily unavailable. The Mandelbrot drive sustained some minor damage which might prolong the trip, but we are adequately provisioned and still on the proper course. We are also considering alternate destinations to shorten the trip, but I won't announce that unless we decide in favor of a diversion. Life support is unimpaired and other services will be restored once we've had time to link them to the backup AP."

"And what will you tell Magnus Mercator?"

She frowned. "Nothing further, if he doesn't ask. If he does, I suppose I'll have to tell him everything. Should I also announce your involvement in the investigation?"

He shook his head. "Not publicly, not at this point, anyway."

"How will you proceed then?"

Dyle shrugged his shoulders. "I haven't the faintest idea. Perhaps Marym will be able to suggest something."

* * * * *

Marym Dunnis was not one of those people who wake instantly from sleep with all their senses fully alert, as though the interval of unconsciousness had been nothing more than an eyeblink. She was puzzled by the pounding on her cabin door, and recognized its nature only when the flurry of sound had been twice repeated. When she called out for lights and nothing happened, she blinked furiously and searched her memory, then reached down and activated the emergency light beside her bed.

She was out of bed and slipping into a robe while her eyes were adjusting to the pale light and she touched the door release immediately, half expecting to find a uniformed crewperson outside, waiting to direct her toward the airlock. Instead she found Sandor Dyle, dressed with a similar lack of formality, in an otherwise deserted corridor. His eyes were puffy but his expression was a study in neutrality, which Marym found alarming in itself.

"What's happening, Sandor?" She kept her voice low.

"I apologize for intruding, Marym, but we need to talk. May I come in?"

"Certainly."

Her cabin was slightly smaller than Sandor's and the closeness was exaggerated by the subdued lighting. Marym sat quietly while Dyle recounted the facts as he knew them, looking as though she wanted to ask a question from time to time, although on each occasion she avoided interrupting his narrative. His memory was exceptional and he repeated his conversation with Captain Nicodemus virtually word for word. Once finished, he sat back and folded his hands over his chest, waiting for her to respond.

"How was the explosion initiated? Oxygen is volatile but it still requires an ignition source."

"The captain didn't say, but I imagine the robot could have been ordered to trigger it. I examined a very similar unit on my way back here and it was equipped for welding, among other things. A simple spark or electrical short would have accomplished the same thing."

"Who had access to Eco's inner sanctum? I imagine security there was even more stringent than controls over core storage."

"An excellent question, which I failed to ask. Pritchard, of course, and possibly the consultant, Tharmody, although neither of them would have had the maintenance-access code. If we restrict our interest to just those who had security access to both locations, we may be able to find a suspect or two. I imagine Nicodemus and

Paragupta have dual access, although neither of them seems to me a likely candidate."

"Let's leave opportunity aside for the moment. On the face of it, everyone who could possibly have reprogrammed the robot has an alibi, so either there is a wider conspiracy involved or someone else acquired the necessary information through means we cannot even begin to suspect just yet. What are the possible motives for the crime?"

"Mania? An individual with a grudge against a passenger or crew member so intense that revenge would even be worth committing suicide? If that's the case, we certainly have a strong candidate for target if not perpetrator."

"Mercator? He certainly seems to have enemies enough, and I imagine some of them would be happy to sacrifice themselves if they could ensure his death in the process. But I doubt that's the case here. Whoever was responsible seems to have known what they were doing. Eco was targeted specifically and efficiently, while Memnon and the life-support systems were left essentially untouched."

"It was only a matter of luck that the drive unit was not damaged fatally."

She shook her head impatiently. "I doubt there was any intention to interfere with the drive. According to Captain Nicodemus, the hull should have contained that blast. Unless there's evidence that the faulty plate was also sabotaged, I think that was incidental damage."

"Then the saboteur has no intention of dying in pursuit of his or her goal. So what advantage does our mysterious friend gain from having Eco out of the picture?"

"Pritchard said she's a prototype. Could it be a business rival wanting to eliminate a potential competitor?"

"Unlikely. Pritchard is moaning about having lost the improvements he and Tharmody have made, but at worst it costs them a little time. Eco's essential personality is replicated back on Linnisfarne and elsewhere."

"Unless there's been another explosion back there. But I think we're looking at something more specific. What changes aboard the *Helen* now that Eco is gone?"

"The decor has been simplified but I doubt this was a protest against bad taste. Life won't be quite as luxurious, service will be slower, the crew is likely to be short tempered." He paused significantly. "And the surveillance system will be down."

She nodded, having anticipated him. "At the same time security is understaffed and without an experienced senior officer."

"I suppose there are valuables aboard. Most of the passengers are wealthy. But even without Eco, the individual cabins are passively secure with their locks keyed to individual handprints. Even if someone had a method of bypassing the locks, the theft would almost certainly be detected before we reach Pradesh."

"There are undoubtedly many members of the crew who can get around the personal locks. Service personnel, security, housekeeping. Probably even medical staff. But I can't imagine any way to smuggle stolen goods off the *Helen* if external security has been alerted."

"There are ways. Someone in security at Pradesh may have been paid off. Another possibility is substitution. Steal the real Iridian diamond necklace and leave a clever imitation in its place."

"Is there anything aboard valuable enough for someone to go to this much trouble?"

"Unknown. The captain might be able to answer that, but if I was going to transport anything that valuable on a commercial starliner, I wouldn't take anyone into my confidence, not even the ship's captain." Dyle was silent a moment. "There's another possibility. Some items of value aren't physical objects."

"Data files?"

"We could have a bonded data courier aboard. It could be anyone, although probably someone traveling alone."

"We should alert the captain to the possibility."

Dyle sighed. "She won't like hearing it, if she hasn't reached the same conclusion herself. There simply aren't enough crew aboard to post guards in all the likely places."

"And we may have misjudged the motive in any case. It might just be an effort to embarrass the owners. Mercator certainly has enough enemies, and the other cartel members probably aren't universally loved either."

An unproductive silence followed, broken when Marym abruptly stood up.

"Have you thought of something?" Dyle's spirits lifted.

"Yes. I think that I am hungry, and that takes priority for the moment. I'll just change into something slightly more presentable." She started toward the inner compartment, paused and glanced back at Dyle, who had remained seated. "Perhaps you might find other attire more comfortable as well."

He glanced down at his robe as if seeing it for the first time. "Yes, I suppose you're right. I'll rejoin you momentarily."

* * * * *

There were more passengers up and about now even though it was still early by ship's time. It was as though some invisible force was slowly spreading through the ship, telling select people that something was wrong, using each of them as the source of a new sequence of ripples. The few dining places that were open were packed to the limit, their patrons speculating about the cause of the problem or complaining about the lack of amenities. The automated delivery system was down, so runners from each place had to dash back and forth to the galleys, relaying new orders and filling old ones. Dyle and Marym went to the communal dining hall instead and equipped themselves with kaffee and a plate full of delicate pastries after only a minimal wait. They were filling their stomachs and lost in their individual thoughts when a familiar voice startled them.

"Would you mind if I joined you?"

It was Absinthe Mercator, wearing a very plain synthetic outfit that modified its shape to conform to the movement of her body, although it left her breasts uncovered, with her long hair hidden under a turban and her arms circled by a shiny synthetic that slowly changed colors.

"Not at all." Marym responded quickly, nodding toward a seat across from them. "Is the rest of your party around?"

Absinthe shook her head as she settled into the chair, placing a very tall, slender glass—of some drink Dyle couldn't identify—on the table in front of her. "My father and his shadow went off to the fitness room for their daily workout. Callista is a late riser and my sister's internal clock is so skewed she's probably just going to sleep about now. She hasn't been out of her cabin since we returned from dinner last night."

"Is your brother feeling any better?" Dyle was watching her closely, hopefully without revealing his interest.

She shrugged. "Morpheus changes moods the way most of us change our clothing. He says he's sick, but the truth is that he's sulking. Father has him back on a short leash and it chafes him."

"I imagine your father is used to getting his way." Dyle tried to make the tone light, but Absinthe glanced up quickly, catching his eyes.

"Strong wills are a family trait, Ser Dyle. Even Tanith, in her own convoluted fashion. My father can be quite accommodating if he's approached in the proper fashion, but my brother prefers confrontation to compromise. He's been in and out of father's will so many times that we have our own virtual attorney. Have you any idea what's happened? Father was going to stop and see the captain on his way, but I'd rather not wait on his convenience."

"Some kind of equipment failure," he answered casually.

She laughed, but it was short and without humor. "I told him that it was foolish to make so many last-minute funding cuts. I'll bet that's what the captain will blame it on."

Dyle's expression never changed as he pretended ignorance. "I don't understand what your father has to do with the ship's outfitting."

"Absinthe, please. We've been introduced, and I've found it wise to avoid using my family name." She glanced around, as though checking to see that they weren't being spied upon. "The Mercator Trust owns this ship, Ser Dyle."

"Sandor, please," he replied quietly. "Well in that case I'm certain the captain will have explained matters to him. I only hope that the problem is easily remedied."

Marym had remained silent during the exchange, but now she sat forward in a move that was not quite casual. "What brings you all out for this trip? Your father doesn't strike me as the type of man who enjoys himself away from his business interests."

The younger woman raked Marym with a deliberately appraising scrutiny, as though seeing her as a person for the first time. "We have quite a lot of credit invested in the *Helen.*" Marym hadn't flinched, and their eyes remained locked for a few seconds before Absinthe finally turned away, just a few degrees, a reluctant and minimal concession. "But you're right. He only enjoys two things in life—his business dealings and his physical training. When we were children, his bodyguards came and went so fast we rarely learned their names. Then he hired Clout because they both have similar obsessions about exercise and diet. The bond between them is closer than blood now. They even look like each other." Dyle thought he detected a note of resentment, but if so, it was well masked.

"He doesn't seem to have passed the same passion on to his children." It was not quite an insult. Dyle wondered what Marym was trying to provoke but decided to trust her judgment.

"There are other ways to display one's body other than by building muscle mass." She leaned forward to emphasize her breasts in a frank demonstration. "We've all inherited his capacity for passionate involvement in what interests us. Father retains absolute control of the family trust, of course, but there are other avenues for self-expression. My brother has a talent for creating scandals, as you probably know, and my sister is just as obsessed with her body as Father is with his. It takes a different form, of course."

They waited, but she didn't elaborate. "And what is your obsession, Absinthe?" Marym was obviously not done pushing.

"Why sex, of course," she answered cheerily.

Dyle couldn't quite decide whether or not that was a lie, but Absinthe became abruptly less communicative and it was soon apparent that she was through revealing family secrets. They talked sporadically and innocuously for a short while longer, but Absinthe finally excused herself and left. As she walked deliberately and somewhat provocatively toward the exit, Dyle and Marym exchanged pointed looks.

"An interesting family, that one," he observed.

Chapter Five

It had been easy enough to agree to help investigate the destruction of Eco, but it proved to be more difficult to contribute anything positive. Nicodemus was not happy when they suggested the possibility that the explosion was designed to conceal a theft or similar crime which might already have taken place now that the security system was inoperative, but she admitted that the idea had already occurred to her.

"I've impressed some of the crew into temporary security functions, but it's still little more than a gesture." She had invited Dyle and Marym to her private office, a surprisingly small space that was immaculately clean and almost obsessively orderly. She readily provided the list of people who had access to Eco's inner sanctum. Herself and her first officer, of course, plus Pritchard, Tharmody, and two technicians who reported to Pritchard. "Our new security officer would have been given access when he came aboard, of course, but it wasn't considered necessary to include the acting chief, the senior ensign."

Dyle evaded the captain's efforts to learn his plans for the simple reason that he had yet to form any. His talent lay in picking out relevant facts from a mass of apparently heterogeneous information. In this instance, there was a pervasive lack of information, relevant or otherwise. Examination of the wreckage from the explosion had proven to be singularly unproductive, only serving to confirm what had appeared obvious from the outset. A maintenance robot had been ordered to convey an oxygen cylinder into Eco's chamber and detonate it, destroying itself in the process. It was impossible for any of those individuals known to have the authorization code to have given the order, so the guilty party was either a confederate or had acquired the code by some other means.

Nicodemus also told them that she had informed Mercator about their unofficial investigation. "He asked me what I was doing to identify the parties responsible, and frankly I didn't have anything else positive to offer him or a good enough reason to conceal your involvement."

"Considering his apparent disdain of pattern analysis, I can't imagine that was much consolation to him."

The captain's expression was briefly scornful. "What Mercator actually believes is not always reflected in what he says. I discovered that even before he came aboard, and my experiences with him in the flesh have made me even more cautious. I haven't decided whether he is a chronic liar or whether there's some devious purpose at work, but it is not uncommon for him to contradict himself over minor matters. I assume he's more reliable in his business dealings." Her voice gave the lie to this last.

"I suppose we should interview him." Dyle glanced at Marym, whose expression remained neutral. "Just to reassure him that we're actually doing something."

"I suspect that Mercator will be the one conducting the interview, but do as you think best."

"Have you decided what to tell the passengers about the change in our schedule?"

Nicodemus looked, if possible, even more unhappy. "I still plan to tell them the truth, if not all of it. An equipment failure slightly damaged one of the drive units. Although we are in no physical danger, we are no longer able to meet our original schedule." She hesitated. "If we were to continue on to our original destination, Pradesh, the trip would be extended dramatically, so we will be diverting to an intermediary destination where the defective unit can be repaired or replaced."

"How long will all of this take?" It was the first time Marym had spoken since they'd settled into their seats.

"We'll reach Scrimshaw in a little less than a week from now, ship's time. We've sent a message to Linnisfarne requesting that they have a replacement unit and a technical crew waiting for us when we get there, but naturally we have no way of knowing whether or not they can meet our schedule." It was possible for a ship in hyperdrive to send messages, but not receive them. "Replacing and recalibrating a new unit in the array is very time consuming, particularly in the absence of a rigging station, but it shouldn't take more than three weeks. The jump from there to Pradesh will consume another ten days. That's the worst case. If the technical crew can repair the existing unit in place, the delay at Scrimshaw could be reduced dramatically. We won't know until they've had a chance to measure the field displacement."

"Mercator isn't going to like hearing that."

"He didn't. I've already briefed him. But he accepted it as the best choice given our limited options."

* * * * *

The atmosphere aboard the *Helen* had changed dramatically during the past few hours. Despite constant assurances from the crew that the ship was in no danger, the fact that they were harried and short tempered themselves communicated tension to everyone else aboard. The ship's common areas were generally quite well populated, but conversations were subdued and people tended to cluster in small groups. The main topic of conversation was obviously speculation about the ship's status, although a handful confined themselves to complaining about the inconvenience. There was no sign of panic but nearly every face showed strain or concern. Many of the shops and dining places had opened as usual, but service was slow, tempers short, and in most cases the selections were limited. Those personal services still available had to be requested in person, since cabin communication systems were all inoperable. Maintenance workers were installing temporary com in strategic positions throughout the ship, but they were intended for emergency use only.

After a brief conference, Dyle and Marym decided to speak to Mercator immediately. A uniformed crew member with a hand weapon strapped to her waist quietly but firmly barred their way until she confirmed their identity. The Mercator party was lodged in a non-standard luxury module, a comparatively small, self-contained cylinder docked with one of the utility ports on the passenger ring. The lock door was closed, either for security or privacy purposes, and they had to wait while it cycled before stepping inside.

The colorful fittings inside gave them a moment's pause. At first, Dyle thought that Mercator must have his own holographic projection units, because the ceiling above his head was well out of reach, and the corridors were decorated with both static and mobile artwork including elaborate tapestries and even an intricately carved fountain, although the flowing water was holographic. When they stepped inside, he brushed his hand across the bowl of the fountain, which was carved stone. Why settle for illusion when you could afford the real thing?

A thickset young man stepped out into the corridor and glanced in their direction, his expression hostile even before he saw them. "Who are you people?" he asked querulously, pointing at them rudely. "This is a private area. You're not allowed in here."

"My name is Sandor Dyle and this is Marym Dunnis. We're here to see Magnus Mercator."

"Well, he's not here. You'll have to come back some other time." The young man, whom Dyle assumed was Morpheus Mercator, appeared agitated and hostile. His inclination was to withdraw, but Marym forestalled him.

"And just who are you, young man?" Her voice snapped like a whip and Dyle almost jumped himself. Morpheus retreated a step, blinking rapidly. He flushed suddenly and seemed to be on the brink of an outburst when Marym deliberately moved toward him. "Identify yourself, please. We're here on ship's business."

"He's Morpheus Mercator." Callista Dorne stepped out into the corridor almost directly behind the now visibly agitated younger man. He turned to look back at her so Dyle couldn't see his expression, but Dorne shook her head at him. "Go back to your cabin and rest, Morpheus. You know the medication doesn't work as well if you're physically active."

"They shouldn't be here." His voice was low, sullen.

"This is a special case, Morpheus. Go ahead. I'll take care of everything. You need to rest."

He turned back toward Dyle and Marym. Dyle tried to see a shadow of the father in the son, but it was elusive. Morpheus was almost as physically massive as Magnus, but where the older man draped finely tuned muscle over a powerful frame, his son was soft, the flesh hanging loosely, as though he'd been even heavier until recently. It was difficult to tell because of the artificial lighting, but his complexion seemed chalky as well, and one eyelid twitched constantly.

"We're not supposed to be disturbed here," he said so low that they almost couldn't make out the words, but he turned and disappeared through a doorway into one of the cabins. It closed behind him.

Dorne let them see just a hint of weariness before she smiled broadly. "Welcome to our little world. I'm afraid you've met Morpheus at the worst possible time. He's usually much more composed. Please come this way."

She led them to a compartment that had more floor space than three first-class cabins in the main ship. It had been configured as a lounge, with the modern shape-shifting furniture that Dyle passionately hated. A robot attendant rolled forward and posted itself near at hand without being in the way. Dorne gestured toward it. "Can I offer you something to drink?"

"No, thank you. We actually came to see Ser Mercator."

"You've missed him, I'm afraid. He and Gus went down to the fitness center for their daily workout. They'll be at it for a while. You could probably catch them there, but I don't recommend interrupting. Magnus isn't quite the ogre that his reputation would have us believe, but I've known him to discharge long-term employees who imposed on him while he was exercising."

Dyle sat down tentatively, trying not to show his uneasiness as the chair began modifying its shape to match the configuration of his body. Marym didn't hesitate at all, leaning back and allowing the chair to shift rapidly to support her. "Have you known him for a long time then?"

Dorne's eyes were suddenly guarded but her voice didn't betray her. "For some time now. He enjoys my company and values my discretion."

"Then he sometimes takes you into his confidence?"

Dorne gave Marym an appraising look, ignoring Dyle completely. "He told me that you were going to investigating the sabotage of the *Helen,* if that's what you mean."

"Then you wouldn't mind answering some questions."

The other woman sat back abruptly, crossing her legs, and her chair hastily compensated. "I'm not aware that I know anything relevant, but I've no reason not to."

"You are aware, I assume, that Mercator owns the *Helen.*"

"I know that he's one of the investors, and he does refer to it at times as his ship, but he does tend to use the possessive somewhat freely at times."

"I understand that he rarely travels, at least by commercial carriers."

Dorne nodded, but her expression was growing increasingly wary. "He prefers to stay out of the public eye. Magnus has had an active and sometimes controversial career and he has a lot of enemies."

"Perfectly understandable. I'm curious though why he should choose to travel so publicly on this occasion."

"That's a question you would need to put to him."

"Then he didn't tell you the purpose of this trip?" Marym's skepticism was deliberate.

"I didn't say that. I said that you would have to ask him. I told you that Magnus values my discretion."

They were interrupted at that point by the sudden appearance of Absinthe Mercator, who wore only a robe and slippers. Her hair, which had formerly been teased and arranged in a hive atop her head, was now loose and fell down over her shoulders to the middle of her back. She nodded in their general direction but walked directly to the robot, punched an order into its keypad before turning to face them. The robot skittered away behind her.

"I didn't know we were having guests or I would have dressed up," she said casually, her tone making it obvious she considered her social lapse of no consequence.

"We hoped to speak to your father," Dyle answered tactfully. "But apparently we missed him."

"He and Gus went to the fitness center," Dorne explained, but Dyle noticed a brief, silent exchange between the two women. They were both mildly apprehensive about something.

"Well, you won't want to bother him until he's through. Magnus doesn't tolerate any distractions while he's in church."

"Church?" Marym sounded surprised, but Dyle knew her well enough to realize it was feigned.

The robot returned bearing a glass of some dark-green fluid. Absinthe snatched it up and drank deeply before answering. "My father is his own personal messiah, Ser Dyle. His body is his altar and Gus Clout is his chief acolyte. When I was adolescent, he was involved in a minor tubetrain accident. It left a small scar on the back of his right hand, so small that you wouldn't notice it unless it was pointed out to you. But even that was a blasphemy that had to be dealt with through microsurgery. Magnus loves and worships his body, often to the exclusion of everything else." Her eyes flickered toward Dorne for a microsecond. "That's why his children are all warped in one way or another. There wasn't enough to go around."

Dyle knew he was being manipulated but decided to let the game play out the way she intended. "And in what direction does your distortion lie?"

"A callous disregard for the feelings of others and an inflated sense of my own importance." She dropped into a chair and dropped her eyes. "So how is the investigation going?" Her eyes widened in mock surprise. "Oh, I'm not supposed to know that, am I?"

"There's no reason to keep it secret. It just hasn't been convenient to make a public announcement yet." Dyle watched her closely as he spoke. Despite the aura of superficiality, Absinthe seemed the only one of Mercator's children to have inherited his drive and intelligence.

"I don't suppose there's any possibility that it was an accident of some sort." Dorne didn't sound anxious, and Dyle suspected she had only spoken to draw attention away from the younger woman.

"The evidence strongly suggests deliberate sabotage. Whoever is responsible isn't likely to be suicidal, however, and as a precaution the captain has posted guards to protect the ship's vital systems."

Dyle thought he spotted a brief glint in Absinthe's eyes, an indication that she didn't like being upstaged by her father's mistress even in so slight a fashion. But it was gone instantly and instead she reached into the pocket of her robe and withdrew a small electronic device, studying it carefully for a second before depressing the keys to input a code. Her hair suddenly began to move, apparently of its own volition, and Dyle was momentarily startled until he realized she was wearing an electronic brush, microscopic fibers woven in among her natural hair which would respond to a signal to shift into a prearranged pattern. He tried to ignore it, but the slow lifting and intertwining was hypnotic and he waited until it had settled into a tight bun and ponytail.

"You don't mind my showing off, do you, Callista? Wealth doesn't mean anything unless you can flaunt it occasionally."

"Of course not, Abby. There's a little bit of the child in all of us, after all."

The tension peaked then, subsiding when Absinthe abruptly stood up, apparently satisfied that she'd held her own. "I'll leave you to it then. I'm sure Callista can answer any questions about my father as well as I."

But Dorne had little idea of Mercator's plans. "They usually go to one of the cafés once they're done, but it could be any of several. I know that he's meeting someone to discuss business later today. He reserved one of the small lounges. I don't remember the location but I'm sure one of the stewards could find out for you."

That was the best she could suggest and after a few moments of polite conversation, Dyle and Marym took their leave. Dorne seemed briefly reluctant to let them go and Dyle had the distinct impression that she was not entirely happy with her present circumstances. Marym confirmed his opinion once they were back in the Concourse.

"Mercator will be in the market for a new companion before long," she said quietly.

"You think he's growing tired of her?"

Marym shook her head vigorously. "No, I think she's the one who wants to leave. She's just looking for a way to make a graceful exit. I don't imagine Mercator is the kind of man you want as an enemy."

It took them a while to track down Gavin Pritchard because crew communications still had not been fully restored. They eventually caught up to him in an alcove cleverly concealed from passersby in the main shopping area, where he was directing two technicians working on a wall full of exposed circuitry. He looked mildly disheveled and more than mildly annoyed at the interruption, but he masked his feelings well after he'd had a moment to compose himself.

"We're trying to reconnect Memnon to the main ordering circuits so that the concessions will have a direct link to the ship's Stores. At the moment they're sending data in batches in portable units and we've been forced to limit customer choices to simplify things. Fortunately most of the old circuitry is still here, but some of it was added when Eco was installed and the transfer protocols aren't compatible."

"We'll get out of your hair quickly then. I just wanted to arrange a session with Memnon. The captain said you could let us have priority access."

"Yes, I can, but not from here," he fretted, then brightened immediately. "But Dona can take care of you and she's working down at the sepulcher right now."

"Sepulcher?"

Pritchard shook his head. "Sorry. That's Dona's name for Memnon's chamber and the term is contagious. She said it reminded her of the inside of a tomb she once visited. It's located just beyond. . . ." His voice wavered and he looked away. "Just past where the explosion happened. She should be there for a while yet if you want to get it taken care of right now."

They passed two posted guards on their way, both of whom nodded them past without asking them to identify themselves. Captain Nicodemus and her people were clearly efficient and well on their way to establishing orderly if somewhat handicapped services. The airlock to Eco's now destroyed chamber had been at least partially repaired and was closed tightly and under security seal. A few meters beyond, they found another lock, currently open, which led them into a dimly lit compartment, deep and narrow with a high ceiling. Electronic equipment covered every surface of the three facing walls, and the only furniture was a single chair in front of an oversized console.

Dona Tharmody turned as they entered and smiled, somewhat tentatively. "Ser Dyle. Ser Dunnis. What can I do for you?"

"Pritchard sent us down so that you could give us clearance to use Memnon."

She stood up and stretched her arms above her head, probably to cover her uncertainty. "And I imagine you want more than just the normal passenger's clearance."

"The captain told us we could have access to anything we wanted. We're helping with the investigation. We assumed that Pritchard had passed that on to you. If not, I apologize for bothering you."

"No, he hasn't told me anything. Poor Gavin hasn't been himself since his girlfriend died." She cocked her head toward the wall, beyond which lay the ruins of Eco. "But fear not, the captain herself logged in to Memnon and left instructions to that effect. I'm afraid that I can't offer you remote access with that security level but you can ask for anything you want from in here."

"To be honest, I'm not sure what to ask for. If Memnon has been cut off from most input sources, he may not know any more than we do."

"Actually, he knows, or at least knew, almost everything that Eco experienced. His direct access to surveillance and other non-critical systems was severed, but he was interfaced with Eco right up until the end. Virtually every bit of data she received was batch processed through his systems at some point as a safety precaution. His job was to review her performance and analyze for flaws, anomalies, and opportunities for improvement."

Marym made an exasperated sound. "Then why hasn't someone asked him what happened to Eco?"

Tharmody raised her hands as though to calm her down. "You haven't heard the whole story yet. The data is batch processed because most of Memnon's permanent data-storage area was reconfigured for Eco's use. All that he retains is what was cached at the time of the explosion, and even that has random gaps, probably data corrupted when his links to Eco were severed. There would have been a brief surge and I'm not sure that some of it didn't spill past his defenses. One of the first things I did was ensure that whatever data he retained was secured so that it wasn't erased during the next scheduled data flush, but most of what survived is records of transitions on the Promenade, a transcript of our recent dispatches to Linnisfarne, and some housekeeping and stewarding records."

"So what does he know?"

She sighed and leaned back against the padded seat. "I don't think there's much there that can help you. The good news is that Memnon is fully qualified to operate the *Helen* safely. In that respect, he is at least as good as Eco would have been because he has fewer distractions. Yes, I know that an AP doesn't really get distracted, but more data requires more processing time and even though the lapses are imperceptible to human senses, they're nonetheless real. All of the ship's critical data was duplicated and in permanent storage within Memnon, and on a real-time basis, not batched. He assumed control of ship's functions within a microsecond of Eco's destruction, and restored all of the systems available to him very quickly and in the proper order of priority. He retains complete information on the warp drive, on the external monitors, demand and supply within the life-support system although he has limited information about environmental enhancements, and I've recently uploaded stores consumption and some maintenance data from the satellite nodes."

"How about surveillance?" Dyle knew the answer already but felt obligated to ask.

"Not a thing, not even a list of the input locations. We have two teams working on that problem now, but until we reach a competent refitting station, the best we can hope for is to cover a few score of critical spots. The present equipment was installed along with Eco and it's just not directly compatible with Memnon's comparatively elderly architecture. Eco translated the data before sending it through their mutual interface and the translation assembly was destroyed in the explosion."

"But we don't know for sure that he doesn't have relevant information, because we don't know yet what is relative and what isn't." Dyle felt as though he were on more familiar ground. Data, particularly lots of data, was reassuring in itself. Most people were bothered when there was too much information available because the extraneous material distracted their attention from what was important, if it didn't conceal it entirely. Dyle reveled in it, because of his gift for picking out patterns from what appeared otherwise to be chaos. The more information there was, the greater the chance that a pattern would emerge, even if the data itself was meaningless in isolation.

"I'll have to defer to you on that. I can only tell you that none of the surviving data seems helpful to me. You're welcome to poke around in it to your heart's content. I wish you the best of luck. I didn't have Gavin's emotional investment in Eco, but her personality represented a lot of my time and even though I've been well paid, it rankles to have it all go for nothing."

Dyle was about to reply but Marym forestalled him. "Just what exactly were you hired to do, if you don't mind my asking?"

"I specialize in adjusting artificial personalities. The people who create these sophisticated computer systems are usually too close to their subject. They measure success by how the system performs in response to test situations, but since they created the program code with those situations in mind, new systems almost always perform well during initial trials. They don't do nearly as well when faced with the unexpected and they tend to be inflexible.

Even when they deal appropriately under variant conditions, they react like machines, not people. My job is to smooth over those rough edges and create a pattern of responses that more closely approaches that of a human being."

"If you're changing the code, doesn't that defeat the purpose of having an outsider? I mean, don't you just introduce your own prejudices?"

"Obviously I can't be entirely objective, and another specialist doing the same job would create a slightly different personality. But I don't directly affect the programming at all. We put Eco into an enhanced learning mode during our sessions and we interact on a real-time basis. The alterations are subtle and not entirely predictable, just as they would be if I was hired as tutor for a particularly bright but unsophisticated child. You have to remember that these are artificial personalities, not artificial intelligences. No one, human or alien, has yet developed a true artificial intelligence, a machine capable of original thought. At least not that we know of. Artificial personalities are only a mockup of that theoretical possibility."

"So Memnon has a different personality than Eco?"

Tharmody laughed and rolled her eyes. "That's an understatement for you. The two of them are an excellent example of my point, though. Both systems were designed along very similar lines, and in fact many of their base modules are identical. Most of the substantive changes were to allow Eco to process a larger volume of data without increasing response time and some other peripheral modifications. The prime motivator in both cases was pride of accomplishment. Both systems derive pleasure from efficient and accurate performance of their duties, but neither performed exactly as projected. Memnon became a rather uptight perfectionist. During his trial run, he reacted to criticism by sulking. Someone like me was brought in to solve that problem, but Memnon's personality matrix was more volatile than expected. Too much emphasis on self-image, frankly. It's a subtle difference but Memnon became so interested in performing up to his internal standards that it had difficulty processing situations in which practical matters required it to vary from those standards. Eventually it interpreted praise directed elsewhere, even casual interactions among passengers, as criticisms of its own performance. It began experiencing the machine equivalent of a jealous rage during which its actions were often less than optimal."

"Is that why they installed Eco?"

"Not entirely, but it was a contributing factor. Eco is a generation ahead of Memnon, even though he's only four standard years old. She has capabilities that he lacks, and incorporating them now would require so many upgrades that it didn't make economic sense. Besides that, he's an excellent emergency backup system, witness our present situation, and he was already capitalized."

"Do we have to watch what we say around him?" asked Dyle.

She laughed. "It would be a little late for that. He's been listening to this entire conversation." She laughed again when they both twitched nervously, instinctively. "Don't worry. He understands his own problems. He's very human in that regard. Knowing that an action is wrong doesn't necessarily prevent us from indulging in it. He wouldn't do anything to endanger the ship or any of its passengers, and he can't tell a falsehood, but he can be touchy at times."

"What if telling the truth might harm a passenger? If Memnon knew the identity of the saboteur, would he lie to protect them?"

She shook her head. "He's sophisticated enough to distinguish differing levels of harm. It is possible to place him in a position where the conflicts would make it impossible for him to choose between them, but in that case he wouldn't answer at all. He wouldn't lie."

"Then I can rely on him to be truthful at all times?"

"Well, no," she admitted reluctantly. "If you were standing in the ship's infirmary and Memnon judged you to be suicidal, he would probably direct you to a narcotic that would only render you unconscious rather than kill you. Come on, I'll introduce you."

She made way while Dyle edged around to face the console. The chair was a conventional static one so he settled into it, enjoying the fact that it wasn't immediately comfortable.

"He responds vocally, of course, and he can pick you up anywhere in this compartment. Isn't that so, Memnon?"

A gravelly, decidedly male voice responded instantly. "That is correct, Dona."

"Would you explain to Ser Dyle the nature of his access, please?"

"Passenger Sandor Dyle has been granted complete access to all data stores with no restriction. He has also received operational authority at level three."

Dyle spoke up immediately. "What does that mean?"

Tharmody leaned toward him. "It means you can direct the ship's physical operations to a limited extent, including expending ship's stores, requisitioning equipment, and so forth. You can't do anything that endangers the ship or causes more than minor passenger inconvenience, or order a course change, and you can't countermand the orders of anyone else with the same level or higher. And Memnon is just like Eco. He won't carry on a conversation with you or acknowledge your commands until you've addressed him by name at least once to initialize a session."

"Understood. Memnon, in what way does the authority of Marym Dunnis differ from my own?"

"Ser Dunnis has identical access privileges."

"Are you aware of the reason why we have been granted special access?"

"Captain Nicodemus authorized access in both cases, Ser Dyle."

Memnon was apparently more literal than Eco had been. "Our purpose is to investigate the circumstances surrounding the destruction of that part of the ship's infrastructure commonly referred to as Eco. You are aware of the incident which terminated Eco's function?"

"Eco ceased to exist as the result of a contained explosion which destroyed in excess of ninety percent of its physical structure including all core personality modules, temporary and permanent memory, primary communications interfaces, and numerous peripheral systems located in close proximity."

"What was the cause of the explosion?"

"A combustion source within an oxygen-enriched environment."

Dyle hesitated, but it was worth a shot. "Do you know who was responsible for the explosion?"

"I am not able to identify any human agency involved in the incident."

"I tried that already," interposed Tharmody. "Neither Eco nor Memnon would have known who gave the robot its orders, at least not until the remote data cache was uploaded."

"You were interfaced with Eco at the time of the incident, weren't you, Memnon?"

"I was passively interfaced at all times following activation of Eco. Our active interfaces functioned either intermittently as needed, or regularly for scheduled updates."

"What was the last data you received from Eco prior to her destruction?"

"I felt her die."

Chapter Six

Artificial personalities were often designed to mimic human emotions, but they were rarely convincing. In this instance, Dyle could almost have believed that the tones of regret in Memnon's voice were real. "Do you think of yourself as a person, Memnon?"

"My programming array mimics a human personality so to an external viewpoint, I function to a limited extent as an intelligent life-form. Internal problem resolution mandates that solutions be compatible with a human response and expressed in a fashion mimicking human expression. I do not, however, possess an ego and therefore my use of personal pronouns is a convenience to the user. There is no 'myself' in the usual sense."

"Was there anything anomalous in the performance of Eco since the time we left Linnisfarne?"

"Yes. Resupply of the Starlighter was incorrect. Responses to passengers were sub-optimal on one hundred and forty-six occasions."

Tharmody responded immediately. "There was a faulty dataline to the Starlighter, one of the small clubs on the Concourse. It was replaced and the problem was corrected. The passenger interactions were not anomalous."

"How so?" asked Marym.

"Eco and Memnon were not identically programmed, so their responses aren't always the same in ambiguous situations. One passenger asked for recommendations for dinner. Memnon considered several factors, including the individual's stated preferences, her planet of origin, and her ordering pattern during previous meals aboard ship. Eco consulted the same data, of course, but she also had access to a values table that considered the passenger's comments on the meals she had already eaten aboard the *Helen.* Since her response differed from Memnon's, by definition he considers that sub-optimal performance. The other instances are similar."

"I see." Marym's voice was suddenly cool. "I'm not sure that I like the idea of having every word I say recorded and analyzed."

Tharmody hesitated, then nodded. "I can't say that I'm entirely comfortable with it myself. I can, however, reassure you at least partially. All of the surveillance data was securely encoded. Only the captain and her superiors could have accessed it, and everything has been lost now in any case."

Dyle glanced up at Marym. "Any suggestions?"

She nodded. "Memnon, who is authorized to enter this compartment?"

The list was identical to the one for Eco, except that Dyle and Marym were now included.

"Of those names, who have physically entered since our departure from Linnisfarne?"

"Gavin Pritchard, Dona Tharmody, Sandor Dyle, and Marym Dunnis."

"I don't suppose you know who entered Eco's compartment during the same period?"

"From external sources, I am aware that numerous parties have done so within the past several hours, but I believe my information to be incomplete."

"But you don't know who entered before the explosion."

"That is incorrect."

Three heads jerked almost in unison. It was Marym who first regained her breath. "Then you do know who entered the compartment before Eco was destroyed?"

"Yes. The entrants were Captain Lydia Nicodemus, Officer Gavin Pritchard, Temporary Crew Member Dona Tharmody, and passengers Magnus Mercator and Absinthe Mercator."

Tharmody interrupted before Marym could phrase her next question. "Memnon, how did you obtain this data?"

"Under the safe operating protocols, Eco and I were instructed to log details of our physical security and data integrity in permanent storage."

"When did the Mercators visit Eco and who were they with?" asked Dyle.

"Magnus Mercator was accompanied by Captain Nicodemus." Their visit had been short and had taken place almost immediately after departure. "Absinthe Mercator was accompanied by Gavin Pritchard." Their visit had taken place several hours later, and it had lasted for an extensive period of time.

"What was the nature of Absinthe Mercator's visit?"

"That information is not available."

"You have no record of all of their interactions with Eco? That doesn't sound like a very efficient security system."

"Their interaction with Eco was limited to a single exchange, a request for an environmental setting."

Dyle and Marym exchanged puzzled looks, but Tharmody smiled knowingly. "Did they request a holographic projection?"

"That is correct."

"Please replicate the projection here."

The stark, utilitarian surroundings immediately disappeared, replaced by a holographic projection of quite a different location. The three humans found themselves in the middle of a seraglio.

"Oh," said Dyle.

"Aha," said Marym.

"Now I know why he was in such a good mood yesterday," said Dona Tharmody.

* * * * *

Memnon told them the location of the lounge Mercator had reserved but when they found it, there was no sign of their quarry. It was, however, occupied, by an almost painfully thin man and his companion, a ruggedly built woman who watched them alertly as soon as they entered the room. It was large enough to have accommodated a score of people easily, the seats and tables currently distributed in an almost-random pattern although the modular floor indicated that the configuration could be altered quickly, the separate components realigning themselves to any of several preset patterns.

When they entered, the cadaverously thin man half rose. "Ser Mercator?" His companion put a restraining hand on his shoulder and shook her head. Dyle quickly changed course, approaching them directly.

"Hello. I'm afraid I'm not the man you're waiting for. In fact, I'm looking for him myself. My name is Sandor Dyle and this is my associate, Marym Dunnis."

The other man stood up again, smiling tentatively but neutrally, and Dyle noticed the telltale signs of multiple rejuvenation treatments. Judging by his frailty, their utility had decreased to the point where additional treatment seemed unlikely to have any effect. The woman remained seating and didn't smile. Dyle could almost feel her gaze stabbing into his flesh. She was clearly a bodyguard of some sort, solidly built. Insert her between Mercator and Clout and she would not have looked out of place.

"Idrian Caserta, and this is my assistant, Sondra Wong. Are you business associates of Ser Mercator?"

"Not directly. We're acting as consultants and were hoping to exchange information with him. Do you expect him soon?"

Caserta shook his head, looking somewhat downcast. Wong made no effort to disguise her irritation. "I'm afraid I've come as something of a suppliant. I have been negotiating with Ser Mercator to entice him into investing in my merchant fleet. We've had an extended period of bad luck and even though my business is a sound one under normal circumstances, the Tenebrian Conflict has temporarily limited access to some of our best customers. Unless we receive an influx of credit during the interim, I'm afraid I'll have to liquidate a substantial portion of my holdings at a significant loss."

"Magnus Mercator is not a philanthropist, Ser Caserta."

Wong became animated for the first time. "We're aware of Mercator's reputation, and we've insisted on a number of safeguards."

Caserta nodded. "Our alternatives are even less attractive. None of the other major investors I've approached are willing to take the risk. I'd rather face the chance of ruin than the certainty of it."

Mildly disconcerted by the man's frankness, Dyle hastily changed the subject. "When do you expect Mercator to arrive? We don't want to interfere with your own appointment but we would like to arrange a firm meeting time."

"Our arrangements are very informal. Mercator promised to come by as soon as he finished some early morning business, but he didn't specify where or what that was, I'm afraid."

"His morning workout," said Dyle. "He and his, ah, assistant have a session first thing every day in the fitness center."

Wong leaned forward. "Do you know how long they're likely to be there? Idrian has not been feeling well lately."

Caserta shook his head. "I'm just tired, Sondra. You know how I hate to travel these days."

He swayed slightly as he spoke and Wong reached out with her left arm as if to steady him. Her aim was just slightly out of true and Dyle realized the arm was a prosthetic. It seemed likely that Wong served her employer in very much the same capacity as

Augustus Clout, bodyguard and personal assistant combined. Like Clout, she looked as though she'd seen military service of some sort in the past, which might explain the prosthesis. She had scrutinized them both very thoroughly when they arrived, quite openly in fact, and her posture suggested that she was prepared at any time to leap to the defense of her employer.

"I'm afraid we can't be of any help there. We only met Mercator and his party briefly yesterday."

They exchanged a few more pleasantries, but Caserta's enthusiasm for the conversation had waned quickly, nor did Wong seem interested in anything but her elderly and apparently failing companion. Neither of them made even a token protest when Dyle indicated that they would return later in an attempt to arrange a rendezvous with Mercator.

"I wish you the best of luck with your negotiations," he said in parting.

Caserta merely nodded, but Wong glanced up, her expression calm. "I think we've used up our luck long since, Ser Dyle. Mercator's terms are not generous but they are adequate."

Dyle waited until they were clearly out of earshot before speaking. "Caserta may have made some poor business decisions in the past, but he appears to have gained the loyalty of at least one of his employees."

"She's more than an employee." Her voice reflected absolute certainty. "At least in her own view. He might not feel the same way."

He had wondered about that. "There seems to be a considerable disparity in their ages. Are you sure she isn't just concerned about job security?"

"I think it's more than that. She watches him too closely to be strictly professional. You noticed the artificial limb?"

"Yes. It's an inferior type, wrapped in duraplast probably. Which means she didn't lose it in the Concourse military, because they all receive state-of-the-art replacements. Either a mercenary band or a planetary militia."

They managed to corner the maintenance supervisor, Melanctha Korisov, for a brief interview, but the woman was obviously unhappy with the interruption, anxious to get back to supervising the work crews who were still trying to restore some of the ship's lost functionality. She made no effort to conceal her impatience as she confirmed what they already knew about the maintenance robot and the way in which its activities were logged into the system. There were at least a half dozen ways the robot could have triggered the explosion and no, it would not have required any particular expertise to convince the comparatively simple machine to destroy itself and damage the ship.

"They're little more than voice-operated automatons. We can program them to perform routine maintenance tasks without supervision, and they can even demonstrate very limited discretion under some circumstances, but there is no reason to give them even a rudimentary personality. In my experience, the simplest tools are usually the most reliable."

A steward caught up to them a short while later with what appeared to be positive news. Although virtually all background data on the passengers had been lost along with Eco, there were a few exceptions. Eight passengers had been treated in the medical section since departure, and their files had been replicated in that facility's specialized and isolated data system. It also contained medical profiles and summary personal histories of every member of the crew. One of the eight passengers was Morpheus Mercator.

Dyle felt a totally irrational surge of optimism. He thought it unlikely that the younger Mercator was involved, but there was a strong possibility that a crew member was responsible. Whoever had plotted the destruction of Eco must have possessed more than a casual familiarity with the *Helen*. Extracting information by interviewing individuals was time consuming, uncertain in its results, and did not lend itself to his particular talent, the ability to find order where others perceived only chaos. When the steward offered to escort them to the medical section, Dyle agreed at once, but Marym shook her head.

"I'd just distract you. I think I'll walk in the gardens for a while."

In Medical, a technician explained the unfamiliar console display to Dyle and left him on his own. His initial elation dimmed somewhat as he examined the first few files. The passenger profiles were extracts that lacked most of the information he might have found useful. As he expected, Morpheus Mercator was being treated for stim withdrawal, as well as some related physical damage to the stem of his brain. The other seven passengers were suffering from various minor ailments, with one exception. Idrian Caserta had not actually received any treatment, but he had filed a formal request for non-revival if he should experience a terminal event during the course of the voyage. Apparently his weariness was more than just physical.

The crew data was more extensive and Dyle spent a considerable time sifting through it, scanning individual profiles that fit particular criteria, then manipulating the data to detect trends and anomalies. He studied the profiles of each person who had access to either Eco or Memnon, everyone who worked in maintenance and security, and anyone who had been added to the crew during the last ten days before departure. Although nothing leapt out of the data and demanded his attention, he wasn't disappointed. He knew from experience that it was unlikely that he would find anything during his initial pass. If there was a pattern there, it would emerge gradually until he could recognize it.

And he did in fact find a few items of interest, although they were probably irrelevant to his investigation. One of the two Lysandrans aboard, Safronel, worked in maintenance as a warp-drive technician. The other, Pylandris, was the steward they had already met. They were the only two non-humans among the crew, although there were at least a half dozen alien passengers, mostly Merseki, which he knew through direct observation. There was still some lingering resentment among fringe elements of the Lysandrans following their defeat but neither Pylandris nor Safronel had served in the military and their records were spotless. Cosmo Paragupta had applied for the position Lydia Nicodemus currently held, which might explain his warmth toward Mercator, probably encouraged by the latter's unhappy relations with the *Helen*'s current captain. Two thirds of the crew had worked aboard the ship before its recent conversion; the remainder were new. It was not an unusually high attrition rate for a ship that had just come out of an extensive drydock. In fact, it was lighter than he had expected. All records of disciplinary action would have been filtered out before the files were transferred to Medical, so he wasn't surprised to find nothing there. Dyle made a mental note to ask the captain, who might well have private records off-line, but he didn't expect anything to come of it.

Anyone whose service was questionable would have been discharged while the ship was being refitted.

When Dyle was done, he was surprised at how much time had passed. He exchanged a few words with one of the meditechs, who assured him that the data would be uploaded to Memnon as soon as a connection was reestablished, then headed back to the passenger area, wondering if Marym was still wandering the gardens. Dismissing the temptation to go look for her, he went instead to the lounge where Caserta had been waiting for Mercator, but it was empty now. Either Caserta had given up and left or Mercator had kept and completed his appointment. He was actively hungry so he bought himself a tray of meat pastries from a morose young man in a tiny eatery and washed them down with a tube of what claimed to be "natural" water, but which was probably recycled.

Against the odds, he did find Marym a few minutes later, spotting her as he crossed the Atrium. She was speaking to someone whose back was to Dyle, and he hesitated, uncertain whether or not he should join them. Marym noticed him a moment later and waved him over. Her companion half turned and Dyle recognized the rugged, hook-nosed profile of Abraham Baxter.

"Your friend here has been reassuring me that you're on the trail of the culprit and his apprehension is only a matter of time."

It was not the greeting he had expected and he exchanged a quick glance with Marym, whose expression showed surprise and a sudden wariness. His own face must have betrayed the same because Baxter abruptly barked a short, unamused laugh. "Don't worry, Sandor. Marym has been the soul of discretion. Captain Nicodemus has quietly been informing some of us that the event which has deprived us of most of our luxuries was not an accident as previously reported. She was most discreet about your involvement, but I have known Lydia Nicodemus for several years and she would not have overlooked the fact that you were aboard. That woman has one of the most organized minds I've ever encountered, rivaling your own in her way. She's the most competent ship's captain I've ever met."

Dyle saw no point in denying Baxter's conclusion, but decided against confirming it. "Magnus Mercator doesn't seem to share your opinion of the captain's abilities. I understand she's leaving the ship when we reach Pradesh."

Baxter's eyes narrowed slightly but his expression was otherwise unchanged. "Mercator has misjudged things in the past."

"And no doubt will do so again in the future. I don't suppose you know why they're at such odds?"

Baxter averted his eyes. "Lydia has mentioned something of the matter."

"I'm sorry. I would not want you to betray a confidence."

The other man shook his head. "It's mostly a matter of style, and in his case, economics. The *Helen* is already behind schedule, and over budget. Lydia wasn't satisfied with the state of the Mandelbrot drive containment, the understaffing, or the original decision to allow Eco to run the ship's infrastructure without constant real-time monitoring. She gave in on the first two but refused to take the ship out until essential services were restored to Memnon."

Marym gave an exasperated sigh. "It looks as though she should have held out on the other two as well. The damage to the drive system would have been avoided, and if we had a full crew it would be easier to deal with the present situation."

"In hindsight, I imagine even Mercator might agree with you, but in his defense, the run to Pradesh was designed to point out the ship's flaws under a mild strain, and a full crew and refitting facility are waiting for us there. If we get there, at least. I suppose you know that we're probably going to be diverting to a closer port."

"Captain Nicodemus did mention that they would be investigating that possibility." Baxter was a friend of sorts but Dyle still resisted the temptation to let slip what he had been told in confidence. Politicians ferreted out information from force of habit, and rarely through straightforward means. If he was quietly fishing for details, Dyle was determined to avoid the hook.

"Well, even if you're not going to admit that you're involved, I'll still offer to help in any way I can. Personally I find these omnipresent surveillance systems intrusive and annoying, but I'd have to admit I'd feel safer if I didn't suspect that Eco's eyes disappeared along with her voice."

Dyle kept his expression neutral, then nodded. "I don't suppose it's general knowledge, but most of Eco's functionality was lost." All of it, actually. "There's no immediate cause for alarm. The emergency backup system is functioning as designed. At worst we'll be greatly inconvenienced."

"So long as there's no repeat performance by the guilty party, of course. No, don't say anything. I'll keep my forebodings to myself, but I did have a piece of information, probably of no significance, that I wanted to pass on. You know that I have had something of a personal interest in the Mercators these past few years."

"Yes, of course."

"Seeing him again, unexpectedly, after all these years was a bit of a shock, actually, even without that shaggy hairdo of his. Mercator lived for a time on a lightly settled world called Percussion, named for its nearly constant thunderstorms as I recall. They were forced to leave after Magnus made a sizeable contribution to the planetary development board. The donation was to compensate them for the destruction of a traffic-monitoring substation and protect the member of his family who rigged the explosive device."

"Morpheus, I assume."

Baxter raised his eyebrows. "The boy? No, Morpheus seems content to destroy himself. It was the daughter, Tanith. She was apparently under the impression that the monitors were secretly watching everything she did and she didn't like being spied on. I can only imagine what she must have thought about Eco."

* * * * *

Dyle and Marym sat in one of the privacy cubicles after Baxter left them. "I would feel considerably more at ease if there were fewer Mercators aboard this vessel," Dyle admitted. "Magnus had access to the codes which could have been used to program the robot, and although no one has said so, I imagine he could also have arranged to have access to Eco, and he could have passed on that information to one or all of his children. Absinthe had the opportunity to scout the layout during her assignation with Pritchard, although she appears to have no motive. Tanith, on the other hand, appears to have a motive, however irrational, but may not have had the opportunity. Morpheus had neither motive nor opportunity, insofar as we know, but his medical records indicate he is being medicated because of suicidal impulses related to stim withdrawal."

Marym made a disgusted sound. "My family chooses not to acknowledge one another, but at least we remain free to pursue our individual happiness. The Mercators seem determined to destroy themselves, individually or as a group. Whatever happened to his wife? Their mother?"

Dyle shrugged. "I have no idea. I believe Morpheus' mother died before they left Cathanor. The daughters were born later, and there's no record of their mother either."

"Well, at least we have suspects. That's progress."

"Yes, and another interesting though possibly irrelevant fact to throw into the stew. The Mercators at one time lived on Percussion."

She looked at him blankly, waiting for him to explain.

"I've just been going through crew profiles and Percussion is the home world of First Officer Cosmo Paragupta."

* * * * *

Most of the other passengers seemed to have developed their own theories about what had happened, some wildly fanciful, some disturbingly close to the truth. Dyle didn't know what official version Nicodemus had decided to adopt or how widely it had been disseminated, so he decided their best choice was to say nothing at all. They stopped by the captain's office to check in with her, only to learn that she was personally inspecting the repairs to the outer hull and could be reached only by radio.

For lack of a better plan, they returned to the Mercators' private module where the posted guard, not the same one as they had encountered earlier, told them that to the best of his knowledge, Magnus Mercator was not currently in his quarters. "I haven't seen him either coming or going." One of the daughters had headed toward the common area a short while ago, but he didn't know which one it was. "But it wasn't the Dorne woman because I know her by sight."

Since she was the only one of the party who had been at all helpful in the past, Dyle decided to risk imposing on her again. They found her in her own cabin this time, although her door was open. She was sitting in a multiform lounge chair, listening to music of a form Dyle didn't recognize, but which seemed subdued, almost ethereal. She greeted them with what appeared to be genuine warmth, inviting them into a compartment that was surprisingly Spartan.

"I hope you'll excuse yet another imposition but we're still trying to locate Ser Mercator."

"I told Magnus you were looking for him, but he was not in a good mood the last time I saw him. The training program aborted in the middle of his routine and by the time he and Gus managed to override the fault, he'd lost his rhythm. He's obsessive about his exercise regimen, and I'm afraid Absinthe teased him about it and made matters even worse."

"Everyone is entitled to be irrational on one subject."

She turned a surprisingly appraising glance in his direction. "Do you really think so?"

"Of course. It's a gift, not a burden. The creative impulse originates in irrationality. If we thought exclusively in rational terms, we would devote all of our time to practical matters rather than waste it on things like art or literature."

She laughed lightly. "You and Magnus might want to compare notes. He said something very similar recently. He's a brilliant man in many ways, but he has a tendency to focus his attention so tightly that he misses much of what is happening around him, and he dismisses the argument out of hand if you try to convince him to take a broader view. He has no time for the arts and doesn't understand why others don't feel the same."

"I never said I don't appreciate the fruits of irrationality. I simply observe the nature of their origin."

"Well in that case, Magnus is exclusively a carnivore."

"Is he about? We would really like to speak to him."

"I mentioned your earlier visit and that you'd be back, but Magnus doesn't wait for anyone. Other people wait for him, except possibly for the captain."

Dyle remembered Idrian Caserta waiting patiently in the lounge and felt a momentary sympathy. "Then we will simply have to track him down. Do you know where he's gone this time?"

"Yes, but I'm not sure that will help you. He took care of some business matters and then went back to the fitness center."

"To complete his program, presumably."

"No, he'll have to run through the entire regimen again. He believes that the whole is greater than the sum of the parts. I would not recommend interrupting him, particularly this time."

"Then we'll just have to wait until he's through."

* * * * *

They took their time. The sanitized version of recent events was percolating through the passengers, who seemed no less prone to speculate but with considerably less alarm. A small group of children were playing an informal game of some sort in a section of the garden, and several adults were watching them idly. There were several possible routes so they chose a path that wandered toward their immediate right until they saw a sign for the fitness center and the free-fall gymnasium. The latter was a large chamber where the artificial gravity was turned off. The former was through yet another airlock, which debouched into an anteroom. Six separate antechambers radiated off this hub, apparently identical in configuration. Two of them were presently occupied, one with a privacy screen up. They glanced through the second but the occupants were two women jogging on a treadmill. Prior to Eco's demise, they would have been able to choose from among numerous holographic landscapes, but at the moment they were surrounded by undecorated metal walls.

"They must be in the other module." Marym gestured toward one of several pair of padded seats distributed around the periphery of the hub. "Shall we wait?"

"As much as I would enjoy returning the man's snub, I doubt that he would even notice, and wouldn't care if it was brought to his attention. If we had any other potentially profitable course to follow"—he lifted his hands expressively—"but we don't."

While they waited, they reviewed everything they had learned, which didn't take long at all, and the avenues of investigation still open to them, which unfortunately consumed even less time. Dyle summarized what little he had gleaned from the medical files, even those details which had no obvious bearing on the case, and that took longer, but not a great deal.

They had fallen into an awkward silence when Marym suddenly surprised him. "Tell me about Abraham Baxter."

"Baxter? I can't imagine him being involved in this."

"Nor can I. That's not why I'm interested. Is he married?"

"No, never has been. There were rumors of a liaison with another Senator a few years back, but she had a lifetime contract with her husband, and if they were involved it was a passing thing. Abraham rarely had time for anything outside his career, which is why I find his premature retirement particularly puzzling."

"Perhaps he just decided that it was time to live for himself rather than for his job. He's an attractive man. I don't suppose he would have any difficulty finding attentive company."

"I imagine not."

Another silence followed, longer this time, broken mercifully by the sound of the privacy shield lifting from one of the fitness chambers. To Dyle's immense relief, it was the one they were watching. Mercator emerged first, followed closely by Clout. Both men wore waist sashes and slippers only, carrying their other clothing loosely in their hands. Their almost artificially smooth, hairless skin seemed almost to shine, evidence that they'd both used the sonic shower before emerging.

"Ah, Ser Dyle and Ser Dunnis. I hope you didn't have a long wait." Mercator didn't sound as though he cared either way.

"Time spent in reflection is never wasted," he answered easily, without rising. "Your pardon, but I believe you are bleeding."

Mercator immediately glanced at his right shoulder, where a thumb's-length cut was slowly oozing red. "Oh, that. I must have opened it up again during this session. The power cut out without warning earlier today and I would have been seriously injured if the safeguards had not operated properly. As it was I scratched myself, but it's entirely superficial."

"If you would like to defer our conversation until you've had it attended to. . . ."

"No, not necessary. It'll scab over quickly and I'll have it treated later. I've had considerably worse injuries in my time. Captain Nicodemus has briefed me about your efforts on our behalf. We have some privacy here. How can I help you?"

Dyle waited for the two men to seat themselves, but they remained standing. He considered doing the same, then decided it had been done deliberately to provoke just that reaction. "I understand that the *Helen* belongs to you."

"Only in part. I bought shares in a cartel that owns this ship and two others."

"But you own the largest share."

"Yes. What does this have to do with our current problem?"

"Excuse me for being blunt, but you've made more than your share of enemies during your lifetime."

It was Clout who answered. "Magnus has never shied away from making unpopular decisions. Most people are unable or unwilling to make difficult choices and they resent those who don't share their shortcoming."

"Are you suggesting that this was an attempt on my life?" Mercator didn't sound concerned. "If so, it was a particularly inept one. It's my understanding that the only reason we are experiencing more than minor inconvenience is a fault in the ship's exostructure that couldn't possibly have been part of this individual's planning. And while it is true there are a great many people who would not be unhappy to hear that I'd died, very few of them would be willing to sacrifice their own lives in the process."

"We're aware of that." Marym's voice crackled with authority. "We don't believe this was an attempt on your life, but it could certainly be an effort designed to harm you in other ways. Financial ways."

Again it was Clout who responded. "We are insured."

"Against damage, certainly. What about loss of business? If the *Helen*'s maiden voyage is a disaster, how much do you stand to lose?"

Mercator and Clout exchanged looks. "All right," Mercator replied at last. "I accept the possibility. Do you have any idea yet who is responsible?"

Dyle shook his head. "Vague suspicions, but nothing I would put into words, not even informally. At least not until we have good reason to do so. That's why we're here."

"All right, I suppose that's fair. So what can I do for you?"

"Well, to start with, you can tell me about your daughters."

Chapter Seven

The environmental controls might have been as stable as Captain Nicodemus claimed, but the psychological temperature in the compartment suddenly dropped perceptibly. Mercator's face moved but he remained silent and it was Clout who finally broke the silence.

"What do the young ladies have to do with your investigation?" Clout sounded both angry and apprehensive. If Mercator was in fact involved in an unhealthy relationship with one or both of his daughters, Clout must necessarily be aware of that fact. And since his employer was by reputation a difficult man to fool, he in turn could not possibly fail to know that his bodyguard and his mistress were similarly entwined. In fact, Dyle would not have been surprised to learn that their relationship had his active support. Dorne might well be camouflage designed to divert attention from a relationship that would be acceptable on only a tiny fraction of the worlds populated by humans. He had felt even at their first meeting that Dorne was concealing something, and that she was uncomfortable with the deception.

"We don't mean to be unnecessarily intrusive, but neither can we just pretend that certain facts don't exist. There has been a similar incident in your past, I believe."

Mercator nodded slowly. "You know about Tanith's episode on Percussion."

"Only superficially. We were hoping you could elaborate."

Mercator began pacing back and forth. "It's a subject I find distasteful and I don't like talking about it."

"We wouldn't ask if we didn't think it might be important," said Marym, her voice superficially sympathetic. Dyle knew her well enough to know it was her professional voice. Marym disliked Mercator intensely and had from the outset. "We will respect your family's privacy absolutely unless it proves impossible."

Mercator stopped pacing, facing the bulkhead, apparently lost in thought. A few seconds clicked by before he spoke again, resignedly this time. "Tell them, Gus. You know as much as I."

There was another pause as the bodyguard gathered his thoughts, or perhaps decided upon the degree of candor required.

"Tanith and Absinthe are fraternal twins. It was a difficult time for their mother because of the occupation. Cathanor was bombarded more heavily than any other human world, you know. By both sides. We managed to get her offworld just before the capitulation, and that was the last time any of us ever saw her. She died of complications a few days later. The unborn infants were saved, although both suffered from some minor physical defects, all of which were treated surgically and through cell therapy. It wasn't a particularly advanced world, the technologies available were less sophisticated than in most places, and not everything the medicators attempted was a complete success. Absinthe developed normally but her sister displayed occasional physical anomalies with the onset of puberty. The war was over and we'd moved them to some place where they could be given the very best treatment by then, but some of the damage was irreversible."

Dyle resisted the temptation to ask for specifics. Clout seemed to be finding this almost as difficult to talk about as did his employer, or perhaps he was just being careful about how much he revealed. "You were working for Mercator already then?"

Clout seemed surprised by the question, but nodded. "Unofficially and irregularly. I didn't join him permanently until he was in exile."

"You were a mercenary, I take it?"

"Sometimes. I did a lot of different things back then."

Clout was clearly uncomfortable talking about his past, so Dyle didn't press the issue, despite his curiosity. "Tanith's problems were physical, or psychological?"

"Both. Her body chemistry is volatile and affects her mind. Her behavior became erratic, occasionally self-destructive, with frequent violent rages, periods of deep depression, and delusions of persecution. Fortunately, the worst of this could be alleviated by medication designed to compensate for the changes in her hormones. Her late adolescence passed almost without incident, except that she fell prey to her own success."

"She decided she didn't need her medication any longer." Dyle had known what was coming. "So she has a mediator."

Clout nodded. "The first few occasions were dismissed as anomalies, but eventually she fell into a pattern. For several weeks she would take her medication quite docilely, but then there would be an unpleasant incident, sometimes violent. Most of that has never appeared in the public records. A mediator seemed the best solution."

Mediators were inserted directly into the patient's brain. They manipulated certain elements of the body's chemistry to achieve the same results as conventional treatment, and could also control a subdural vial to release measured doses of tailored medications. The vial would need to be refilled periodically, but the procedure was simple and could be performed by anyone after a few minutes of training.

"What happened on Percussion then?"

"The mediator malfunctioned." It was Mercator who answered. Dyle turned in his direction, but that seemed to be all he had to say.

Clout resumed the narrative. "It would have been bad enough if it had just failed. Tanith would have reverted and we would have known something was wrong in time to deal with the problem. Instead of neutralizing her difficulties, it started to reinforce them. She disappeared one morning without saying a word, was missing for several days, at the end of which she planted an explosive device which heavily damaged a traffic-monitoring facility she believed was being used by some mysterious organization to spy on her." He laughed unpleasantly. "Ironically, she was identified and later apprehended thanks to surveillance data accumulated by that very same facility."

"An unfortunate accident."

"No, Ser Dyle, it was no accident. Tanith's paranoia wasn't entirely unjustified. The mediator had to be calibrated at regular intervals, not only to correct any potential internal fault but because perfectly natural shifts in her body chemistry as she aged required slight programming changes. A subsequent examination of the device revealed that it had been deliberately altered to subvert its original purpose. The technician who performed the calibration had already left Percussion, and efforts to locate her have failed. So far." There was promise rather than anger in the last two words.

"The young lady seems to have led too innocuous a life to have acquired such sophisticated enemies."

"No, she was simply an innocent bystander. The blow was aimed at the father, not the daughter."

"That's what concerns us as well." Marym addressed herself to Mercator, who had turned around toward the end of the story, hands clasped at the small of his back. "The destruction of Eco may well have been designed as an indirect attack on you, on your financial interests if not your life."

"I accept that possibility. But I still don't see how my daughter could be involved. She no longer has a mediator. Members of my party ensure that she takes the proper medication and we watch her constantly. She hasn't been without supervision since we came aboard." He fumbled with the clothing draped over his arm and removed a small, oblong device from a pocket. "This is a proximity monitor. It is triggered by either of two transmitters, one embedded in Tanith's mastoid, the other in her heel. She knows about the one in her heel. She cannot leave our compartment without the two of us," he nodded toward Clout, "knowing about it. Her sister as well, when Absinthe deigns to carry her telltale with her."

Clout produced his own. "The only time she's left the module since we docked was to attend the First Jump Banquet. We seal the lock when we sleep. There's no possible way she could have gotten out without our knowing about it."

"Could she have had contact with anyone else aboard without your knowledge? A crew member perhaps."

Mercator shrugged. "I don't see how. Gus looks after the family's security and he's very good at his job."

Clout nodded, smiling tightly. "No surveillance is foolproof, but I'm reasonably sure there has been no unusual contact between Tanith and anyone else aboard."

"But the same isn't necessarily true of her sister, is it?" Marym's tone was deliberately provocative.

"I'm not aware of any reason why you should be interested in Absinthe's activities." Mercator's voice contained more than a hint of warning.

"Anyone who arranged unauthorized access to Eco in the hours leading up to the explosion is automatically suspect." She gave no indication that she had noticed his change of tone.

Mercator hesitated, glanced at Clout, who was in turn staring thoughtfully at Marym. "Would you care to explain that?"

"Absinthe spent a considerable length of time in Eco's inner sanctum in the presence of one of the ship's officers."

Clout digested that, with some apparent distaste. "I see. Another of her assignations, I imagine. It would have to be Paragupta or Pritchard. Not the former, I think. He's too interested in forwarding his career to risk offense, unless he hoped to enlist her influence on his behalf. No, he's not brave enough to risk it. Pritchard then. He'd be easy enough prey for her. The only other possibility is Nicodemus, and while I wouldn't put it past Absinthe, I doubt the captain could be swayed from her duty even by her wiles."

"I can't confirm or deny the identity of the other party."

"That's all right. Absinthe won't be coy if asked. She prefers to flaunt her liaisons. I imagine this unidentified crew member—let's call him Pritchard for the moment—wanted to minimize the risk of discovery. Would it help if I told you that Absinthe has a long and colorful history of such dalliances?"

Dyle glanced at Mercator, who had remained silent. "What we are now is an accumulation of those things which we have been in the past. We're not far enough along to differentiate between what helps us and what doesn't but the more we know, the more likely it is that we will eventually understand. I would not presume to judge where I know little and understand even less."

Mercator didn't look at him. "It is not the lifestyle I would have chosen for her, and I would prefer that she demonstrate rather more discrimination than is often the case, but she is an adult and chooses her own diversions."

"Might I ask why she is still living with you? She strikes me as too independent to submit to another's will, even her father." It was Marym again. This time the question sounded almost casual, but Dyle suspected otherwise. The relationship between Absinthe and her father had to be more complex than that. If Mercator was involved sexually with one or both of his own daughters, as they suspected, Absinthe's promiscuity was almost certainly her way of dealing with the power disparity between them. It was entirely possible that the conflict was expanding and growing more dangerous.

"She does so only intermittently. On two occasions she has attempted to start a new life under an assumed name. Both efforts failed when her identity was exposed, once by an enterprising media scout who unearthed her secret quite accidentally, once by an anonymous party whose motives were no doubt similar to those of the technician who sabotaged Tanith's mediator. I expect her to try again."

Marym seemed content, at least for the moment, but Dyle had one more question to ask. "I imagine you make some effort to monitor your enemies, Ser Mercator."

"Those I can identify and who have the power to act. Yes, certainly."

"Are any of them aboard the *Helen*?"

Mercator shook his head, but Dyle thought he might have hesitated for a second first, exchanging a quick glance with Clout. "None that I know of."

"How about Idrian Caserta?"

It was a wild shot, and it missed completely. Both men burst out laughing. Mercator seemed to find it particularly funny. He settled down into one of the seats and crossed his legs.

"I think you can safely leave Caserta off the suspect list." Clout began to dress, shedding his sash without any indication that he felt awkward doing so in front of an audience. If anything, he was actually posing a bit provocatively, perhaps to see what kind of reaction he could provoke. Dyle knew that public nudity was virtually unknown on Tashista, Marym's home world, but she displayed no visible reaction. "He is, or at least was, a competent entrepreneur. Built a small trading firm from nothing, expanded cautiously but steadily, made very few mistakes. The shooting war between Tenebria and its neighbors flared up unexpectedly and even though he managed to save all of his assets, it cost him most of his available credit. Until the shooting stops, he'll be lucky to break even on everyday operations, and he has nothing left to cover maintenance and other unusual expenses. If he was younger and healthier, he could probably salvage things by moving into another market and displacing someone less competent, but he's dying and he knows it. His company is his only family and he wants it to survive him."

"Are you going to give him what he wants?" Dyle addressed the question to Mercator, who seemed to be daydreaming.

"For the most part, with some restrictions. His operation fits nicely with my own interests in that region. He retains his title for as long as he wants it, but his health is failing rapidly now and he won't use extraordinary measures to prolong his life."

"Some might interpret that as taking advantage of a dying man." Dyle remembered Sondra Wong's intense and obvious devotion to Caserta and wondered how she felt about matters.

"They'd be wrong." Clout sounded actively angry. "Magnus isn't the monster he's often made out to be. He makes difficult decisions, and that inevitably creates enemies. It always has, and it always will. A certain degree of ruthlessness is necessary to succeed commercially. We could have demanded terms much more favorable than we did and Caserta would still have had no choice but to accept them. We knew it and he knew it."

Mercator sat forward. "When we had our meeting today, Caserta's secretary was bristling with animosity, Ser Dyle, but she was positively amiable by the time we were done. The last thing Idrian Caserta wants right now is any disruption of my finances, believe me. He's going to get almost everything he asked for and far more than he expected. And no, I haven't grown soft. I expect to recoup any lost income many times over in the long term."

* * * * *

Dyle and Marym found a secluded nook in the gardens where they sat and compared notes, a procedure which took a depressingly short time. Paradoxically, they simultaneously had entirely too many and too few potential suspects. Since the destruction of Eco could have been designed to mask some unspecified illicit activity of whose existence they were currently unaware, anyone aboard could be responsible. Virtually anyone among the passengers or crew could be involved in something illegal, and at least some undoubtedly were. At the same time, the number of people who were known to have possessed the necessary information to complete the sabotage was small, and all of them appeared to have solid alibis. Even if the damage was definitely intended to impact Mercator's credit balance, the list was not significantly altered. A survivor or relative from Cathanor, human or Lysandran, native or from among the intervention forces, might have lingering resentments from the war, or a business rival might seek secretive redress for old wrongs. The perpetrator might be working on his own or through an agent with no personal motive at all.

"Even the steward, Pylandris, could have a credible motive," said Marym disconsolately.

"I don't think motive is going to help us. We have to concentrate on opportunity." It wasn't the first time Dyle had said something similar. "We have three options there, none of them very helpful. Everyone with legitimate access has an alibi for the critical time period, but that doesn't mean they didn't provide the information—knowingly or not—to a third party."

"But since only two people had authority both to enter Eco's chamber and to redirect the robot, we either have to narrow our focus there or accept a much more complex conspiracy involving lapses by two separate crew members."

"None of which feels right to me. The second possibility is that the leak comes from Mercator or one of the other members of the consortium who were privy to that information back on Linnisfarne."

She nodded. "Which makes everyone in Mercator's party a significant suspect."

"Including Magnus himself. I suppose there might be some elaborate insurance scam or other angle that we're missing."

"So what's the third possibility?"

"Systems failure. Security might have failed or been subverted to allow someone not officially authorized to program the robot and provide it with the right security code to access Eco. For that matter, we've been told that the security system would have prevented an unauthorized human from entering, but not a maintenance robot proceeding under what were apparently legitimate instructions. Are we certain that loophole really exists and, if so, is it a common failing, or was it specifically shaped to allow this kind of attack?"

"Good question. That would assume that this was in the planning stages long before we left Linnisfarne. We need to pursue that."

The balance of their conversation was unproductive and the silences grew longer. Dyle was curious about Marym's impressions of Mercator and asked her what she thought of him.

"He seems less dynamic than his reputation suggests."

"He's considerably older than he looks. I wouldn't be surprised if his uncharacteristic sympathy for Idrian Caserta is at least partly because he sees his own future in a dying man's eyes."

"At least he has a family."

"Such as it is. But do you really see any of the three carrying on their father's business?"

"No," she admitted. "Possibly Absinthe, if she decided she wanted to. They'd be better off putting Clout in charge. He seems to be made of much the same mold as his boss."

"But apparently lacked the drive, or the opportunity, to distinguish himself."

"Perhaps he's happy to be a power behind the throne. He gets to travel around in a luxury compartment, carry on with his employer's beautiful consort, and probably draws a sizeable salary."

"I'm sure he earns it. There have been at least a half dozen attempts on Mercator's life since he left Cathanor, and I wouldn't be surprised to learn that there were that many again that never reached the public eye."

"So where do we go from here?"

Dyle shook his head. "I need to think about something else for a while. Let's have a quiet meal and pretend that we're still on a leisurely trip to Pradesh. Afterwards we can try to track down Pritchard and find out if the security arrangements for the robot were out of the ordinary and then check in with Captain Nicodemus."

"That sounds like an admirable plan to me, Ser Dyle."

But like most plans, it soon went awry.

* * * * *

Their dinner was excellent. Some of the dining places had jury-rigged the local holographic projectors to restore some semblance of their former decor, and the connections to the ship's stores were in much better shape. They talked about matters unrelated to Eco's destruction; Dyle reminisced about his childhood on Hazard and, after some prodding, Marym speculated about her future. Her background as a prefect would not translate readily to law enforcement on another world, whose laws and cultures would have to be studied before she could hope to pursue her former career. Fortunately, she had run one of her family's businesses for several years while building up the credit necessary to buy a higher profile position, and was reasonably familiar with the regulations governing trade among the Concourse's member worlds.

After indulging themselves with a tray of delicate sweets made from a sweetened paste twisted into helical shapes and flash cauterized, they reluctantly decided to renew their efforts to locate

Pritchard, but before they were able to do so they noticed a clearly agitated Callista Dorne moving through the milling crowd in a side passage. She was advancing in their general direction, and Dyle was curious enough to suggest they intercept her.

She didn't seem to recognize him for a second or two, then gave him a rather nervous smile. "My apologies, Ser Dyle. I was preoccupied. Did you want something?"

Her eyes skittered past his shoulder, searching the crowd to his rear.

"You appeared to be in some distress and I thought perhaps we might help."

She blinked and looked at him as though seeing him for the first time. Dyle could almost hear the thoughts racing through her head. Would she trust him or not?

"I'm sorry, but I'm trying to find someone. I don't suppose you've seen Tanith Mercator anywhere about? Her father needs to see her and it's rather important that we find her quickly."

"So much for Clout's efficiency." Marym spoke under her breath. "How did she bypass the monitoring system?"

Dorne looked more confused than ever, her eyes switching back and forth between the two. "How did you . . . ?"

"Mercator told us about the implanted warning system. I gather she found a way to disable it after all."

After a momentary hesitation, Dorne apparently decided to trust them. "She didn't disable it. The alarms went off as soon as she entered the airlock. I know she seems docile most of the time, but she's actually very quick-witted and she's a genius when she's working with mechanical devices. Magnus and Gus were out somewhere but Absinthe and I were both wearing telltales and we should have been able to stop her." She reached into her pocket and half withdrew what Dyle recognized immediately as a narcogun. "I've used it once before. But she anticipated us, triggered the emergency lock release."

"That should have trapped her between the two doors."

She nodded. "It did. She cut off our communications and then talked the outside guard into using the manual control to let her out. Magnus didn't want the guards to know that she was being restrained because it would have been all over the ship. And she hasn't tried anything like this for months. We thought she had finally begun to accept that it was for her own good."

"Can't you track her through her implants?"

Dorne shook her head. "They're triggered by proximity. We would have to be close enough to see her."

"Where would she have gone? Does she follow a pattern when she gets away?"

"It doesn't happen often enough for there to be a pattern." She sounded breathless now and was obviously anxious to pursue her search. "We have to find her before she does something we can't smooth over. Magnus has everyone out looking, even Morpheus."

"We'll help if we can," offered Marym. "Where are the others?"

"Morpheus is supposed to be checking with the security people to see if she went into the crew area. Gus went to the gardens; Tanith likes being out in the countryside. Absinthe said she'd look in the other passenger modules and I think Magnus is still somewhere else in this section. He thinks she might be trying to hide in the crowds because she knows we'll look for her in the park."

"What if she goes back to your module while you're all out here?"

"The guard is still there. Magnus told him that she'd had an adverse reaction to a new medication she was taking and might be hallucinating. It's pretty close to the truth."

"All right, let's see if we can find her."

The Promenade, shops and restaurants for the most part, was laid out roughly on a three-level grid. Dyle suggested that they work as a unit, one person posted at an intersection to make sure she didn't slip past them while the other two moved along the adjacent passageway, peering into the interiors or even entering some places to make sure Tanith wasn't concealed behind an obstruction. Dyle paused when they reached the first restaurant, thwarted by a handful of privacy shields, but Dorne immediately produced a very illegal passthru, studying the image that appeared on the tiny screen for a few seconds before shaking her head. "She's not in there." Dorne turned away and Dyle followed.

"I have the impression this isn't the first time you've had to do this."

At first he thought she was going to ignore his comment, but when they reached the next cross passage, she spoke without looking at him. "She escaped twice before since I've been with them. The first time she had only the single unit in her heel and it took us three days to find her. She used a pair of scissors to cut the transmitter out of her foot. The second time she jumped from a second-story balcony into the bed of a passing cargo crawler. Magnus paid dearly for that one. He pressured the local authorities to throw a cordon around the entire city but it still took almost a week to find her."

"A very resourceful young woman."

"She's a monster." There was no mistaking the animosity in Dorne's voice. "If it were up to me, she'd be locked up someplace."

"Magnus appears to have strong family feelings."

She shook her head. "It's his sense of duty that's the problem. He knows his children are all badly warped. He feels responsible."

"Absinthe appears reasonably normal."

Dorne made a disgusted sound. "She's the worst of the lot, but at least she performs well in public." But then they were starting the next leg of their search and the conversation ended.

They made their way methodically through the entire shopping area, row by row, level by level. Dyle noticed Dona Tharmody in a kaffe shop, sipping something green and steaming, and one of the two Lysandrans aboard the *Helen* passed in the crowd, moving quite hurriedly. Dyle couldn't tell if it was the steward, Pylandris, or the maintenance worker, but he did notice the bulky package held tightly in the Lysandran's arms. He turned his attention back to the matter at hand, glancing quickly through the interior of a souvenir shop that specialized in jewelry. "She doesn't appear to be here," he said at last. "And these shops mark the end of the Promenade."

"Unless she's come in since we started." Dorne sighed dramatically. "She must have realized that with the surveillance system inoperable it would be difficult to find her."

"But she can't get off the ship. It's only a matter of time until she's located."

"That wouldn't matter to her. Tanith has a truncated time sense. Events more than a few days in the past or future are outside her frame of reference."

"It's possible that someone else has already found her."

"Yes, I suppose it is. But I've been worried about her ever since we came aboard. Sometimes her withdrawal is calm, resigned perhaps, but for the past couple of days I've sensed that her mood was changing. I told Magnus that I thought she was planning something, but he was convinced that there was no way she could know about the implant behind her ear and that she couldn't get away again."

Marym met them at the end of the row, her face expressionless. "We don't have enough sets of eyes to do this properly," she said quietly. "She could have switched levels or arrived after we started and there's little chance that we would have seen her."

"I know." Dorne seemed calmer now, perhaps satisfied that she'd at least done everything within her power. "I'm sorry if I've wasted your time in a pointless effort."

"Not at all," Dyle reassured her. "The diversion is a welcome one."

"Perhaps if we enlisted the help of the crew?" suggested Marym. "The guard must already know most of what's going on."

Dorne shook her head. "I would rather let Magnus make that decision." She glanced at her chrono. "We're all supposed to check back shortly. Thank you again for your assistance."

Dyle and Marym exchanged glances and he silently indicated that he would defer to her judgment. "We'd like to help, unless you'd rather Magnus not know that you've told us."

Dorne was obviously torn, but she resolved whatever internal struggle might exist quite quickly. "I'm not sure how much I care about what Magnus knows any longer. Yes, I would appreciate any help you might offer, if only to bring this episode to an end. I should warn you that Magnus gets very angry when things don't go the way he had them planned. I doubt he'll show you any direct discourtesy, and maybe this time he'll actually welcome outside involvement. He has expressed considerable respect for your abilities, Ser Dyle." Her eyes flashed toward Marym and she hastily amended her statement. "I'm certain that he will have a similarly high regard for yours as well."

Marym nodded politely, indifferent to Mercator's opinion, expressed or otherwise.

The guard was still on duty when they reached Mercator's private module, although he looked considerably less sure of himself than during their last visit. He glanced at Dyle and Marym but addressed his remarks to Dorne, informing her that there had been no word, and that she was the first to return from the search. "I really should report this," he said uneasily. "I'm sure the captain would be happy to help search for the young lady."

"I'm sure that Ser Mercator will take care of that in due course, if he hasn't already." She turned to her companions. "Would you like some refreshment while we wait?"

They were sitting in the same small lounge they'd used during their previous visit when Absinthe Mercator joined them. She was rather overdressed for a search party, wearing an ankle-length body stocking, scarlet with white feathers—possibly real ones— around the collar, waist, and wrists. "No sign of her," she reported brightly. "Not that I expected otherwise. She's too canny to be caught that easily. I suppose she might have seduced another passenger and concealed herself in his compartment."

Dorne glared at Absinthe, her expression openly hostile. "I thought seduction was your specialty."

Absinthe seemed amused rather than offended. "Is that a professional observation, Callista?"

Dorne's face betrayed simmering emotions, but her voice remained calm as she stood up. "If you don't mind, I'm feeling a bit restless. I think I'll stretch my legs." She nodded to Marym and Dyle, then walked to the airlock and disappeared through it.

"Well, it looks like I'm nominated to play hostess." Absinthe sat back, crossing her legs, and the multiform chair reconfigured itself quickly and smoothly. "I gather Callista has explained our little problem?"

"The immediate one, yes. Your father had previously told us about your sister's difficulties."

"I'm surprised, and you should be flattered. He rarely talks about her, even to his closest associates. He's not actually ashamed of her, but it is awkward. Whatever responsibility my father bears for the inadequacies of Morpheus and I, he's blameless in her case, though more through lack of opportunity than ability. Perhaps that explains why she's his favorite." Although neither of her companions showed any sign of discomfort about the frankness of her remarks, she followed up with an insincere apology. "I'm sorry. I shouldn't talk about family business, should I? I was forgetting my manners."

"I doubt that there's any problem with your memory." Marym caught and held the younger woman's eyes for a moment before Absinthe turned away with a light laugh.

"We all rebel against our father in our own ways. I prefer flamboyance and a touch of decadence to self-destruction."

"Take care that you haven't chosen a longer road to the same destination."

Absinthe and the conversation were both somewhat subdued after that. Dorne didn't return but Morpheus Mercator stormed in after a few minutes, having already berated the guard outside. Ignoring the two strangers, he stood over his sister, gesticulating with both hands, his face working furiously.

"It was all just a waste of time. If we needed further evidence that the crew was incompetent, we have it now. No one has seen her and no one is willing to go look for her either."

Absinthe reached out and grabbed her brother's wrist, pulling him down toward her. "They can't leave their duties without instructions and Father doesn't want any official notice taken unless it's absolutely necessary. You know that."

"But the ship is too big for us to search it by ourselves," he complained petulantly. "You know how hard it is to find her if she doesn't want to be found."

"Yes, I know. Isn't it about time for you to take your medication?"

"I don't need it anymore." His voice altered again, sounding much younger. "You know it makes me sick."

"Just a little dizzy and it only lasts for a little while. Why don't you go and take it now so that you'll be feeling better if we have to go look for her some more."

There was a sound from the direction of the airlock. Hoping to be rescued from the necessity of taking his medicine, Morpheus pulled his hand away from Absinthe and moved to where he could see who was coming. "It's Father," he said.

But it wasn't. It was Augustus Clout. He gave a slight start when he saw Dyle and Marym, then turned to Absinthe.

"There's been an accident," he said.

Chapter Eight

Absinthe Mercator was on her feet so suddenly that Dyle could almost have sworn that she'd teleported into an upright position. Her hands were at her sides but her fingers were curled into tight fists. He was only mildly surprised by this suggestion that her feelings for her sister might run deeper than the superficial disdain she had shown so far.

"What happened to her? Is she all right?"

Clout shook his head. "It's not Tanith. We still don't know where she is."

Dyle could no longer see Absinthe's face, but he suspected her confusion mirrored his own.

"What is it then?"

"It's. . . ." He paused, glanced at Morpheus, then back to Absinthe. "It's your father," he said tonelessly. "I found him lying in the gardens. He's dead."

The words were startling enough that for the next few seconds Dyle was less than usually attentive to his surroundings. The death of Magnus Mercator would send ripples through civilized worlds, and some of the uncivilized ones as well. Absinthe stood where she was, silent and motionless. Morpheus stepped back as though he'd been struck, then incongruously he laughed, a nervous reaction in all likelihood. He spun on one heel and strode quickly out of sight, back toward his cabin.

"How did it happen?" Marym's voice was steady and unemotional. "You said something about an accident."

Clout answered her, but his eyes were still fastened on Absinthe. Dyle had assumed that Clout was involved with Dorne, either with his employer's approval or behind his back. There had been no hint of an emotional involvement with the daughters, intimate or otherwise. At least not until now. He filed this observation with the others he'd been mentally accumulating.

"Not an accident. From the looks of the wounds, someone attacked him from behind and beat him to death."

"Have you told anyone else?"

Marym's firm voice broke Clout's concentration and he glanced toward her. He stared quietly for a second or two, as though noticing her existence for the first time, then nodded. "I found a maintenance technician and told him to report to the captain. I waited until help arrived. A security team was erecting a privacy screen around the site when I left."

"Did you see anyone else in the vicinity?"

"There were a few people strolling in the gardens. No one I recognized and none of them came near the body while I was there." He glanced around. "Where's Callista?"

"She was here earlier but left again." Absinthe's voice seemed calm, perhaps unnaturally so. "We still have to find Tanith."

"I know." Clout sounded suddenly weary. "Discreetly if possible."

Dyle decided to intercede. With Magnus dead, the lines of authority here were unclear. Morpheus was technically the oldest of the three children, but he was emotionally if not intellectually unreliable. "I think it would be best to tell the captain. I'm sure she has no more interest in causing a sensation than do you."

Absinthe turned in his direction, her expression completely neutral. "I would prefer to honor my father's intentions in that matter, Ser Dyle."

But Clout put a hand on her shoulder and bent toward her. "Under the circumstances, I think that Ser Dyle's suggestion might be best. I'm not sure what her reaction might be if she were to hear of your father's death while beyond our reach."

Her head bobbed, just once, to indicate her acceptance of the situation. "Perhaps you might do us that service, Ser Dyle? That would allow the rest of us an opportunity to resume the search."

"I would be happy to serve you in that fashion," he responded formally, rising to his feet.

* * * * *

As it happened, they didn't need to find the captain, because Captain Nicodemus already had the stewards out looking for them. They were spotted almost simultaneously by two of them, one of whom explained rather breathlessly that the captain urgently requested that they join her in the formal gardens. Dyle was not greatly surprised.

"One major crime aboard the *Helen* insulted her professional dignity. A second one is not going to improve her mood."

They allowed themselves to be escorted by one of the two stewards, a young woman who could provide no information they didn't already possess. "I know the spot," she admitted. "It's surrounded by flowering trees. You could pass right by and not notice a sizeable party of people just out of reach, if they didn't make any noise."

An armed security officer was waiting at the turnoff from the main path. He was clearly uneasy and moved to bar their way until the steward interceded. "The captain asked for them," she explained. "I was told to bring them directly here."

"Is that Dyle?" The captain's voice was readily identifiable, although as described, the dense thicket of flowering shrubs completely concealed her. "Send him in."

They passed through, without the steward, and an abrupt turn took them to an open area surfaced with a common strain of durograss. A small but elaborate fountain gurgled contentedly on the opposite side of the clearing. Nicodemus and Paragupta were both there, standing slightly away from a team of four technicians clustered around the now lifeless form of Magnus Mercator. He was lying prone, one arm stretched above his head, the other at his side.

Nicodemus greeted them curtly, her face dark with anger. "We've had another incident, a murder."

"Magnus Mercator. Yes, we heard." Nicodemus' face darkened even further, so he hastily explained. "We were with his daughter when Clout arrived with the news. The other daughter, Tanith, is missing and they're concerned that she might have had some adverse reaction to her medication. We were coming to ask if you could alert the crew to be on the lookout for her."

"We're not a child-care facility," she replied shortly, then visibly calmed herself. "I'll have it taken care of. But we have a more immediate problem, obviously. At least now we know why Eco was destroyed. With the surveillance system inoperable, we have no record of passenger movements. Anyone could have struck the man down and returned before the body was discovered, which leaves us almost a thousand potential suspects."

"It's not quite that bad," Marym reassured her. "In many cases we should be able to ascertain passenger movements by cross-checking their stories with their companions. It should be even easier to eliminate the vast majority of the crew." She frowned, suddenly realizing the scale of the investigation she was suggesting. "Of course, that would require considerable time and resources."

"Mercator certainly had no shortage of enemies." She glanced toward the body. "We're making a complete holographic record and securing anything that might represent physical evidence."

"If the blow was struck from behind, there may not have been any other physical contact with the assailant."

"There were multiple blows, Ser Dyle, from various angles."

"A crime of passion then," suggested Marym. "The killer hated the victim enough to continue the assault even after death."

"Or intended that we think exactly that," amended Dyle. "May we look?"

The body was lying on his side in a fetal position. Mercator had been savagely attacked well after he must clearly have been dead and the back of his skull was almost completely flattened. There was surprisingly little blood. He was still wearing the sleeveless shirt he had donned after his workout and Dyle noticed that the angry-looking scratch on his shoulder, the one he'd received in the fitness center, was still untreated. That was the least of Mercator's troubles now. Dyle's stomach churned.

Marym seemed unaffected by the carnage, walked carefully around the perimeter of the scene to examine the body from every angle. "He hasn't been dead very long," she observed. "There are drops of blood leading over to the fountain. His assailant probably cleaned up before leaving."

"The medicators will be able to tell us something once they've examined the body. They're on their way now." Captain Nicodemus seemed restless. "May I assume that you will make this a part of your investigation?"

Dyle turned toward her. "You do realize that the two incidents might be completely unrelated?"

"I accept the possibility, but it seems highly unlikely. Eco's destruction made this attack possible. If our surveillance system was still operational, it would only require a simple query to find out who was responsible. Do you really believe that this is some bizarre coincidence?"

"I have reached no conclusions in either direction. I simple acknowledge the possibility that this was a crime of opportunity."

"But you will look into it?" There was a hint of desperation in her voice and Dyle hastened to reassure her, but only to a point.

"Of course. But we share your handicaps, Captain. It may be necessary to wait until we reach Scrimshaw and allow the local authorities to use their resources to question everyone aboard."

Nicodemus shook her head. "Scrimshaw is a frontier world, Ser Dyle. I seriously doubt that anyone there will be able to offer substantial help, even if they're willing. This is not, after all, their responsibility." She took a step away, then hesitated and turned back. "I understand that I am asking a great deal, and that I have no right to do so. There was no affection between us, and the fact that he died while in my charge is likely to stir some tongues. I have neither the right nor the power to delegate any of that responsibility to the two of you. I can only appeal to your sense of justice. Magnus Mercator's reputation is well known and he may have deserved to die, but not in this fashion, and not at the whim of any individual, no matter how wronged."

"We appreciate your position, Captain. Please feel assured that we will do everything we can. But I must caution you that reputations can sometimes be misleading. At the best of times, my talents are constrained by circumstances. My successes are remembered, but not my failures. And in this case, I am deprived of my greatest asset, information. Obscure patterns may be ferreted out; invisible ones remain hidden."

"Fair enough. I'm returning to the bridge. I'll pass the word to the crew about the Mercator girl. Cosmo here will see that you have anything you wish." And with a last, brief glance at the body, she turned and left.

First Officer Paragupta hadn't spoken since their arrival. He was standing back at the very edge of the open space, his face ashen, eyes wide, hands trembling. Although he had turned away from the sprawled body, he kept glancing in that direction, then averting his eyes, as though repulsed by the sight but simultaneously drawn to it. He stepped forward now, nodding acknowledgment, but his voice was trembling.

"I am at your service, Ser Dyle."

Marym was still on the far side of the clearing, had crouched low to stare at the ground, letting her eyes move slowly over the crime scene. Dyle hoped she might notice something he'd missed, because he'd seen nothing at all that was useful.

"We'll need to know the time of death, as accurately as possible."

"Medicator McCoy will be handling the body personally. He's the senior officer in the medical section."

"It would be best if this location was kept isolated even after the body has been removed."

"I'll issue orders to that effect. Should we post a guard or will a barrier shield suffice?"

"A guard shouldn't be necessary. Are there any forms of data collected in this area? Something that might operate independently of the ship's overall systems?"

Paragupta hesitated, then nodded. "There are instruments that record environmental data, humidity, temperature, possibly soil acidity. Most, if not all of them, are passive and isolated. Are they important?"

"Probably not," he admitted. "But I would like to have their data uploaded into Memnon so I can manipulate it. There might be something useful there."

"I'll have it done. Anything else?"

Not that Dyle could think of, but he was spared having to confess to that by the arrival of the medical team.

They were very efficient and Dyle didn't even notice a reaction when they first saw the condition of the body they'd been sent to retrieve. Medicator McCoy supervised, an irascible but very efficient individual who was clearly impatient with anything less than absolute concentration on the task at hand. Dyle felt increased confidence that no pertinent information would be overlooked due to slipshod procedures. Several tissue samples were taken on the spot, after which two technicians flash froze the body as it lay. The affected area included the soil directly under the ruined skull, and McCoy himself wielded the laser that cut out the adjoining section of turf.

They had brought a carryall whose general shape and purpose couldn't be well disguised, but it was completely enclosed and unmarked and would probably attract little attention unless someone was specifically watching for it. The entire procedure was completed quickly, quietly, and with only minimal criticism from McCoy. The latter waited until the body had been wheeled away before turning to Paragupta.

"The postmortem shouldn't take very long. Obviously I can make a fair guess at the cause of death already, unless something unusual turns up."

Marym moved around to face him. "Can you estimate the time he died?"

McCoy glanced at her, then at Paragupta, without saying anything. Paragupta said, "Ser Dunnis and Ser Dyle have the captain's authority to conduct an investigation."

McCoy made an inarticulate, ambiguous sound. "I'll have a more precise answer for you shortly, but based on the body temperature and the state of his blood, I'd say no more than two standard hours, probably a little less."

"And did you notice anything unusual about the wounds?"

"Other than their number, no. But I can tell you one thing. Someone did not like this man. Not even a little bit."

McCoy's departure left them with Paragupta and two technicians who were recording the scene again now that the body was no longer present. Dyle had been massaging his chin for several minutes, a sure sign that he was agitated. He straightened up suddenly.

"Some time ago, Captain Nicodemus offered us the exclusive use of one of the lounges for our investigation. I'd like that arranged as soon as possible."

"I'll have it done immediately, Ser Dyle." Paragupta's color had returned with the departure of the body, and his voice was steady again.

"I'd also like a linkup to Memnon. It takes too long to run down to the other end of the ship every time I think of something I want to ask."

Paragupta hesitated a second this time, then thought better of it. "I will tell Officer Pritchard to make it a priority."

Dyle glanced at Marym. "Can you think of anything else? Memnon will have duty rosters, credit transfers from all the shops and diners, and other data that might eliminate some of our suspects."

"We need to have our status made official. We're going to have to start questioning people with the weight of the captain's authority behind us."

The first officer looked uncomfortable. "I'll speak to the captain about it. She may not want the rest of the passengers to know about this yet. They're edgy enough about the sabotage."

"The Mercator party already knows, and we were probably overheard by the guard posted there when Clout made the announcement. I suspect it will be all over the ship within the hour regardless of whether or not we admit it officially. We could pretend that we're just investigating the sabotage as a possible attack on Mercator's financial holdings, but we can't ask relevant questions without leaving enough clues to suggest that something else is wrong."

"I understand. I'll convey your sentiments to the captain and let you know what she decides."

Dyle and Marym left while the technicians were erecting a heavy-duty privacy barrier around the clearing. "You do realize the odds we're facing," said Marym.

"Because this is a crime of opportunity, you mean?"

"Among other things."

"Of course I do, but what choice do we have? Should we have told Nicodemus that she'd have to find someone else?"

"I suppose not," she said resignedly. "She expects you to pull something out of your wizardly pattern-analyst hat, you know."

He sighed. "So how would you have approached this back on Tashista?"

"I would have delegated the authority to one of my detective teams who would have hired a data contractor to go through traffic records, financial transfers, and everything else recorded electronically."

"Well, all we're missing here is the team of detectives, the contractor, and the records." She didn't laugh. "You do agree that this was not premeditated, I assume."

"Not in an immediate sense. Unless Tanith Mercator bludgeoned her father to death, there's no way the killer could have known that he would be in the gardens alone at this particular hour, and it's a stretch even for her. It's more likely that whoever it was seized on the chance when it offered itself, acting impulsively. The same party may or not be responsible for the earlier sabotage, may have simply gotten lucky while waiting for a chance like this. It might be the first time Mercator was out without Clout at his side."

"And the killer just happened to find him alone in the gardens?"

"Might have followed him from somewhere else. Dorne said that he was searching in the Promenade when she last saw him. Anyone could have seen him there."

"They were all out and about by themselves at the time of the murder. Any one of them could be responsible, even Clout. He found the body, after all."

"Dorne was with us for most of the critical period."

"But she left after the tiff with Absinthe. And that was just about the time of death as near as I can tell."

"She would have to have gone directly to the garden to have killed him."

"I didn't say it was likely. I said it was possible. She might have run into Magnus as he was returning to check in, told him that Tanith was still missing, and accompanied him to the garden, supposedly to continue the search."

"And Absinthe could have done the deed just before that."

"As could Clout, or Morpheus, or any of several hundred other potential suspects. One thing we don't lack here is motive. The only one I can think of aboard who didn't have a reason to kill Mercator was Idrian Caserta."

She laughed softly. "If this was a holovid, that would make him the prime suspect."

"Well, we'll check his alibi. Maybe Mercator decided to back out at the last minute. But Caserta doesn't look strong enough to have inflicted that kind of damage."

"His secretary could have managed it."

"We still have a problem with motive there but she's certainly a possibility. We have lots of possibilities, Marym. Too many."

"And we don't have a murder weapon, or any idea of what it might have been."

"Hopefully, Medicator McCoy will be able to suggest the solution to that problem."

* * * * *

But he couldn't. His report was terse and unhelpful. A blunt object but with a smooth surface. There is no evidence of tearing in the wounds. There were at least twenty blows, probably more."

Marym asked about residue, slivers of metal, bits of cloth, but McCoy was equally discouraging on that score. "Traces of foreign organic matter, probably from the foliage at the scene. Nothing that might help you, I'm afraid. The weapon, whatever it was, may have been sheathed in one of the more durable synthetics."

The data transferred from various recorders and instruments in the gardens didn't cast any light either. With commendable alacrity, Pritchard had set up a console linked to Memnon in a small lounge, evidence that Captain Nicodemus had already lent the weight of her authority to Dyle's requests. Marym watched silently as Dyle manipulated the data in a remarkable variety of ways, looking for anything anomalous, any change in pattern that might help them. He felt more at ease with this abstract world of information and kept at it even after he had privately concluded that there was nothing there to help them.

"You know what we're going to have to do," Marym said gently when he finally cancelled the last display and turned away from the console.

"Yes, I'm afraid so. The two of us can't possibly question all of the potential suspects. Nicodemus might loan us a security person or two to help, but she's understaffed there anyway and the current situation aboard ship makes their presence elsewhere every bit as important."

"So we prioritize. We start with the more obvious candidates and work our way down until we run out of time, breath, or patience."

"We could cover twice as many if we conducted the interviews separately."

But Marym shook her head. "Double a smidgeon and you still only have a pinch. We'd still have to compare notes afterward, and one of us might fail to pick up on something the other would have noticed right away." She smiled. "You're a very perceptive person, Sandor, and so am I, but our perceptions aren't always the same. Remember our reactions to the dinner party the first day we were aboard."

"All right, point taken. So who goes on our list? Everyone in Mercator's private party, obviously."

"Including Tanith, if she ever turns up."

"All right. And I suppose Idrian Caserta should be included even though he appears to be the only one aboard who is likely to mourn Mercator's passing."

"We'll have to consider the captain as well, although tact suggests we do so less formally."

"Possibly, but I suspect she'll volunteer for the process. She admits openly that she detested Mercator and she'll want to clear the air and avoid any suggestion that she was trying to inhibit the investigation. Anyone else for the first wave?"

"Paragupta."

Dyle raised an eyebrow. "Why him? He was fawning on Mercator earlier."

"Intuition. I don't think the image he projects is a true reflection of his personality."

"All right. Anyone else? I was thinking about the steward, Pylandris."

"The Lysandran? Why him in particular?"

"Because he passed us on the Promenade while we were on our way to Mercator's quarters. He was coming from the right direction, in a hurry, and he was carrying an oblong object of some kind."

"What kind of object?"

He shook his head. "Unknown. It was wrapped in some kind of cloth, a blanket possibly."

"Very observant of you."

He grinned at her. "I don't always find my clues in data displays."

"All right, he's in. That makes eight people, not counting the captain. When do we start, and where?"

"As soon as possible, and here. Let's leave the captain aside for the moment, and we obviously can't speak to Tanith Mercator until she's been found."

"You're certain the captain will back us on this? We might ruffle a few feathers."

"The only person aboard the *Helen* who might have pulled enough weight to interfere is dead," Dyle said evenly. "At least until we reach Scrimshaw, Captain Nicodemus makes all the rules."

* * * * *

They decided to see Clout first because it was he who had found the body. A steward had been assigned for their exclusive use as a runner, or more properly as an escort. Her name was Feykirk and she had one of the few functioning remote communicators aboard the *Helen*. "I can only reach the captain, medical, and security right now. The other units are being used for repairs on the outer hulls. The captain said to tell you that I'm alert and discreet." She accompanied that announcement with an exaggerated smile.

Dyle liked her immediately but her obvious high level of energy made him feel old and tired. "We need to have the captain make a general announcement about our status. There's no possible way to pursue the investigation without revealing that Mercator has been killed. I would prefer that she not mention our involvement with the sabotage. It's not clear yet that the two are directly connected, and even if they are, it might be best if we didn't let it be known that we were looking into both matters."

"If we ask questions about it, they'll likely guess," said Marym.

"Probably. We'll just have to feel our way."

"The captain has already taken care of that, Ser Dyle. There are notices being posted in the Promenade and other common areas, and I know that she informed Absinthe Mercator personally."

Dyle turned to Marym. "It sounds like the young lady has become the de facto head of family, at least unofficially. I wonder if anyone aboard knows what provisions Mercator had made for the disposition of his estate."

Feykirk cleared her throat. "Your pardon, Ser Dyle, but as it happened I was with the captain at the time and it appeared to me that Ser Mercator was deferring to her father's secretary."

"Clout?" He nodded to himself. "Force of habit, probably. I suspect that he spoke with his master's voice in the past. Once the reality has set in and the estate is settled, I doubt that Absinthe will allow anyone else to supersede her now that her father's dead."

Marym made a noncommittal sound. "Could you fetch Ser Clout for us?"

"Of course." And without another word, Feykirk vanished down the corridor.

Since Marym had more experience with formal interrogations, they agreed that she would take the lead. "I don't think we'll be able to shake Clout if he doesn't want to cooperate. If he doesn't want to cooperate, there's not a great deal we can do about it."

"As far as we know there's no reason for him not to. This is going to reflect badly on his professional credentials. I know officially he was only Mercator's personal assistant, but it's pretty obvious that his primary purpose was to serve as his bodyguard. Unless he's in line to receive part of the estate, I can't suggest any motive for him."

"You're forgetting his suspect relations with Dorne."

"Ah yes. Should we confront him about that, do you think?"

"Not yet, unless the situation demands it."

It took longer than they expected and Dyle was quite restive before Feykirk returned, with Augustus Clout a few steps behind her. "Ser Clout was searching for the missing young woman," the steward explained.

"Any luck with that?" asked Marym.

Clout, whose expression betrayed his impatience, shook his head. "She has proven to be very difficult to find in the past. I really should be out there. I'm very familiar with her habits, her preferences. It would be tragic if she hurt herself. Or others," he added belatedly.

"We won't delay you any longer than is absolutely necessary. Won't you take a seat?"

Marym had specifically requested that the multiform furniture be removed, leaving only static, utilitarian seats and a single broad table. If Clout was surprised or annoyed by what might have been construed as discourtesy, he hid his reaction, settling on a straight-backed, solid-looking chair that had probably come from the galley. Marym sat across the table from him while Dyle, feigning restlessness, began slowly walking around the room, staying at the periphery of Clout's vision or just outside it.

"Could you tell us the circumstances under which you found the body? Please don't leave out any details. At this point, we don't know what may or may not be relevant."

"There's little enough to tell. We were all out looking for Tanith, as I should be now. I made a quick pass through the Atrium and Promenade while Magnus went directly to the gardens. I hadn't entertained much hope of finding her out in public, but it was possible that she realized that and acted contrarily to her previous escapades. She tends to hole up some place quiet whenever possible, and the gardens seemed the most likely place. She couldn't have entered the crew areas without someone at least having seen her even if they didn't question her presence."

"Callista Dorne said that you were supposed to be searching the gardens while Mercator joined her in the Promenade."

Clout looked flustered, but only for a split second. "That's right. I'd forgotten. Originally that was what we planned, but Magnus was certain she'd gone to the gardens and we swapped locations just after we left the others."

"So you reached the gardens at what time?"

Clout responded with the hour. "I'm sorry but I can't be more specific than that. I wasn't wearing my chrono."

"Then it seems that he may still have been alive when you first reached the garden."

He appeared to be considering the ramifications and it was a few seconds before he spoke. "I thought it must have happened sooner than that. Given the state of the body, I mean. It must have taken a while to inflict that much damage."

"Surprisingly little if you're properly motivated. What happened when you first reached the garden?"

"Magnus had told me the approximate search pattern he was planning to use. I started at the opposite end and began working my way back. I expected to meet him halfway and when I didn't, I thought he might have found her and broken off the search. Just to be thorough, I continued anyway, and a few minutes later I found his body."

"Did you see anyone else in the vicinity?"

He shook his head. "I could hear someone talking down by the reflecting pool, but the conversation seemed casual. From that clearing, you can't see anything outside the immediate area."

"Nor can you be seen from anywhere else. Did you touch the body?"

"No, of course not."

"Then how did you know he was dead?"

Clout gave her a sardonic look and didn't answer aloud.

"All right," she admitted. "Silly question. When were you employed as a mercenary, Ser Clout?"

That seemed to take him by surprise and it was a few seconds before he answered. Dyle interpreted that as meaning he was about to lie, or at least tell only a partial truth. "I have been associated with military units, but properly speaking, I've never actually been employed as a mercenary."

Which might mean he'd worked for one of the quasi-legal militias for hire rather than a licensed operation.

"What were the nature of your duties as Mercator's personal assistant?"

For a second, it seemed that he might not be prepared to answer. He stared directly at Marym, whose return gaze never wavered. "I don't see what relevance that has to the situation," he said slowly and calmly.

"Is there a reason why you won't answer the question, Ser Clout?"

The clash of wills was almost electric. Clout leaned back and crossed his legs, normally a sign of submission, but Dyle knew better. If he answered, it would be because he chose to do so, not because he was intimidated.

"My duties were rather complex, but essentially what I was paid to do was to run his life for him. For some time now I've made all the major decisions for Magnus Mercator, both financial and personal."

Dyle was standing directly behind Clout when he asked his very first question. "Did you suggest that he invest in this ship?"

"Of course." Clout continued to look straight at Marym. "The trust owns several commercial vessels, but they're all cargo haulers. The real profit comes from carrying people and that's the direction the trust should take in the future."

Chapter Nine

"That's a pretty sweeping statement. I wonder if the Mercator siblings will agree with your assessment. It is their decision, ultimately, isn't it?"

Clout tried to keep his voice neutral, but there was a smug, knowing undertone that was unmistakable. "Oh, I think you'll find they agree with me, and that they will continue to defer to my judgment." He hesitated for a second. "Or at least as far as they've deferred to their father in the past. I admit that they do have very different ideas at times."

"I won't ask you if Mercator had any enemies because we all know the answer, but I will ask if you believe any of them are aboard the *Helen*?"

"Well, there's obviously at least one." No one laughed. "The straight answer is that there are probably several people aboard who hated him enough to wish him dead, and perhaps more than one who would have acted if given the opportunity. We screened the passenger and crew lists before arranging this trip and there are no obvious candidates, but Magnus led a controversial life. Most of his enemies are anonymous strangers. That's why he so rarely appears publicly. In retrospect, this trip was obviously ill conceived, but sooner or later, I expect, someone would have found a way to kill him."

Marym tried to find out why Mercator had chosen to travel publicly this time, but Clout wouldn't oblige. "I can't see any relevance to the murder and I still consider myself an employee of the family. I won't betray their confidence without good reason."

"How well do you know Ser Dorne?"

"Callista? She joined us just over a standard year ago. She's become surprisingly sophisticated since then. We found her on a backwater planet while considering an investment opportunity there. It didn't work out, but she proved to have a variety of talents and Magnus decided to hire her as paid companion."

"How would you describe her relations with Magnus Mercator?"

Clout laughed. "He was never dissatisfied with the services she provided."

"Then she is no more than an employee like yourself?"

The man's amusement was obvious and inappropriate, but he didn't seem to care. "Oh, not like myself. She has no real authority, and their relationship was always most informal. They had an understanding, of course, but there has never been any sort of formal arrangement."

"Does she get along with the other members of your party?"

"Morpheus seems mildly fond of her, when he's in the right mood. She and Absinthe clash at times, but they respect one another. I have no real idea what goes on inside Tanith's mind." He seemed genuinely saddened by the last. "She's had a very difficult life."

"How about yourself?"

"Me? I get along with everyone. It's one of my greatest assets."

"Pardon my frankness, but are you on intimate terms with Callista Dorne?"

There was an uncomfortable, prolonged silence during which Clout's expression never changed, but it was obvious that he was considering his answer closely before responding. His belated response left them no better off than they had been.

"Callista is a very scrupulous person, Ser Dunnis. I cannot imagine any circumstances under which she would betray the trust of a patron."

"But her patron's wishes are no longer at issue, are they? Given that she's no longer under any obligation to Mercator, she is free to make other arrangements."

"And you wish to know if those arrangements might involve me."

She let his statement stand without comment. Dyle thought they might have reached a standoff but Clout finally broke the silence. "I'm not convinced that this is any of your business, but the answer is yes, I certainly hope to continue my acquaintance with Callista Dorne on at least its present level of intimacy."

And that was all he would say on the matter. They asked him a few more questions, mostly designed to lull him before they threw in a variation of an earlier query, but he remained calm and consistent throughout. When they finally told him he was free to resume his search for Tanith, his manner was polite but not cordial.

"What do you think?" asked Dyle, as soon as he was beyond earshot.

"He's a very intelligent man, very much in control. Most of what he told us was the truth. The rest I'm not sure about. He's certainly withholding things, which may or may not be relevant, and he might have lied outright. This sort of exchange amuses him, I think, so he may be better at it than it appears. I begin to understand why Mercator employed him."

"I thought he was telling the truth about Dorne."

"So did I. There's an attraction there, and it's mutual. She may have held him at arm's length."

"I'm not so sure. I mean, I don't think she was unfaithful to her pact with Mercator, but I don't think she had to fend Clout off. He seems to value self-control and I don't think he'd have risked alienating Magnus. There was a rapport between them."

"He doesn't seem particularly broken up by his loss."

"If he was, we wouldn't see it. But I think the attachment was intellectual rather than emotional. If I'm reading Clout correctly, he has a strong sense of duty, useful in a mercenary if that really is part of his past. If I had access to the public datanet, I could probably tell you more than you want to know about him." His frustration was audible toward the end.

"Crimes were solved before there was such a thing as a datanet, you know." She smiled to take the sting out of it.

His face lightened. "But it's so much easier when you can let a machine do the boring parts. So what's your opinion of Clout as a suspect?"

"Mixed. He obviously had opportunity, and possibly two separate motives. I'm skeptical that Dorne's favor would be sufficient, but that coupled with the increased influence he appears to be gaining with the heirs is certainly suggestive."

"To say nothing of what he may have inherited directly. Even Mercator's detractors admit he was loyal to his supporters and generous to anyone who gained his favor."

"So he goes on the short list."

"Right at the top."

But the list would not be nearly as short as they hoped.

* * * * *

Absinthe Mercator arrived a few moments late, pushing ahead of Feykirk to enter the room. Dyle was a well-traveled man and was familiar with a wide range of customs and styles of attire, but even he was momentarily taken aback. Mourning wear varied considerably from world to world, but it was almost always conservative, subdued, even drab. Partial nudity was not uncommon in some cultures, although traditionally the more controversial portions of both the male and female anatomy were kept covered on commercial vessels out of consideration for the mores, or at least the aesthetics, of fellow travelers.

Absinthe seemed determined to violate both traditions on a grand scale. The sleek body wrap that clung to her body was both quasi-fluorescent, and internally animate. Differing patterns and gradual color changes chased each other across her body, or at least that part of her body which was actually concealed. Her left leg was covered down to the ankle, but her right leg was bare all the way to her hip. Similarly her right arm was concealed from neckline to palm, but her left was completely uncovered, as was the adjoining breast. Her long hair had been braided and arranged so that it fell down across her sternum, then curled up to underline and emphasize the exposed portion of her chest.

"You wished to speak to me," she said curtly, her eyes unfriendly. She looked directly at Dyle, ignoring Marym.

"Please accept our condolences for the death of your father," said Marym. "Would you please take a seat?"

"I'd rather stand." Her eyes remained locked on Dyle, who found it mildly disconcerting, although he gave no visible sign of his reaction.

Marym was determined not to let Absinthe define the terms of the conversation in any detail. "Please take a seat. We'll try to get this over with as quickly as possible."

"I question your right to have me summoned here. You have no official authority and I'm not required to answer any of your questions."

"Captain Nicodemus has requested that we conduct this investigation. Her decision carries the weight of law."

"Nicodemus works . . . worked for my father. As his primary heir, I stand in his place." She still hadn't turned toward Marym, but her eyes were slightly averted now, looking past Dyle.

"That may be true after the terms of his estate are adjudicated, but even if he were still alive, his wishes would remain legally subject to the captain's decisions." There was an awkward silence for a few seconds, then Marym continued, her voice softening, but only slightly. "We're only trying to discover who was responsible for your father's death. We won't detain you any longer than is necessary."

Conflicting emotions chased each other across the younger woman's face, anger, resignation, apprehension, and what might just possibly have been a flash of amusement. Dyle suddenly wondered whether or not this show of indignation had been genuine. Absinthe spun around suddenly and dropped into a chair, crossing her legs so quickly that her costume's response time lagged, fluttering unsupported for a second before settling back into place.

"All right. What do you want to know?"

"How did you learn that your sister was missing?"

"My father told me. He gathered us all up and gave us our assignments. I was sent to peek into each of the passenger modules, in case she was huddled in a corner somewhere. She used to do that sometimes when she was a child, but I knew it was a wasted effort. Tanith isn't stupid, and obviously she's found herself a good hiding place again."

"Was that the last time you saw your father?"

Her eyes moved away from Marym's face and it was obvious that she was avoiding a direct answer. "I left with Morpheus. My father was still giving instructions to the others. I did what I'd been told to do and then returned. I believe you were there when I arrived."

"Were you in the gardens at any time today?"

"No." It was said firmly. "In fact, I've never been there. Rustic scenery clashes with my wardrobe."

"How long has Augustus Clout worked for your father?"

Absinthe moved restlessly and her clothing compensated. "I don't know. It seems like forever. Several standard years at least. When you've lived on as many different worlds as I have, you begin to feel disconnected from time."

"Were relations between them cordial?"

That brought a short, barking laugh. "They were so close it was sometimes hard to tell them apart. Clout knew exactly how to play on my father's vanities because he shared an almost identical set. The daily exercises weren't a duty for him; they were a perquisite. He wasn't quite as fanatical about physical perfection as Magnus, but he was a very close approximation."

"What is his status now that your father is gone?"

"If I'm named as the new head of the family trust, I'll find a place for him. Mercators always reward loyalty. For the present, we've agreed that he will handle routine family business."

"We?"

"Well, Morpheus and I. He's never shown any interest in where the credit comes from so long as it's always there. We can't ask Tanith even if we knew where she was because she's not competent to decide."

"And Callista Dorne?"

Absinthe shrugged. "She's not exactly an employee, but she has been faithful. Provision will be made for her if necessary."

Dyle had been hovering just out of direct line of sight, silently, but now he asked his first question. "Do I understand you to say that you don't know the terms of your father's estate?"

Without turning to look at him, Absinthe responded levelly. "That is correct, Ser Dyle. My father never volunteered the information and I was never interested enough to ask."

That was a lie. Absinthe knew they didn't believe her and apparently didn't care. Her response to a question about her father's potential enemies brought a sarcastic laugh and no help.

Marym waited to see if Dyle would follow up, then asked her own question. "Did you have any reason to believe that this trip was particularly hazardous?"

"Any time my father risked public exposure he was in danger. But he was particularly proud of the *Helen* and wanted to be aboard for her first flight. He originally planned to stay aboard until Yahboo, but Clout convinced him to have the yacht meet us at Pradesh."

Dyle was curious about the relationship between Absinthe and her father. If there was in fact anything incestuous there, Absinthe seemed to be taking the loss extremely well. He sensed tension, of course, but no grief. Whatever her relationship with the dead man, her emotional reaction was strangely muted.

They asked a few more questions, but without learning anything new. Marym thanked her for coming and again expressed her regret about the circumstances. Without another word, Absinthe rose, flashed a cryptic glance at Dyle, and swept out of the room.

Feykirk came in on cue but Marym shook her head. "No more today, I think. No one is going anywhere, and I'm hungry and tired. Unless you think otherwise, Sandor."

"No, of course not. We can resume tomorrow." They conferred briefly and decided to start early, but not too early, and Feykirk promised to make herself available.

"The captain has assigned me to this duty for as long as you want me."

Dyle suggested that they try one of the fancier dining places, particularly since the captain had told them all of their meals and other reasonable expenses would be charged to the *Helen*'s administrative account as partial recompense for their professional services. That required a change of clothing so they returned to their individual cabins, agreeing to meet at the airlock when they were ready. Marym was already there when Dyle arrived.

"We may have to alter our plans," she said quietly.

"How so?"

She held up a message cube. "I found this stuck to my door. It's an invitation to dinner from Abraham Baxter."

His eyes widened. "Apparently you've made a friend."

She shook her head. "It's for both of us, and he says it's very important."

Baxter was waiting for them in the Minstrel's Glen, which would normally have been thick with holographic shrubbery. Actual human musicians drifted among the widely scattered tables, playing subdued tunes on miniharps, vibroflutes, and other instruments, generally without catching the attention of the customers. They didn't see Baxter anywhere, but when they inquired, a hostess dressed in a filmy, elfin costume conducted them to one of three tables masked by privacy shields. It flickered off when she touched the control on her belt, then reappeared once they had stepped across the insubstantial barrier. Dyle consciously suppressed his usual mild claustrophobia, telling himself repeatedly that the barrier was insubstantial, that he could pass through it with only a mild shock if necessary.

Baxter was alone. He stood up, smiling, and invited them to be seated. "The selection here is excellent. One might almost imagine that it had its own kitchen." The various restaurants all drew their food from the ship's extensive common galleys, of course. The only variation was in the choices offered and the decor, and much of the latter had been rendered irrelevant by Eco's demise.

They looked over the selection and touched the icons on the table to indicate their choices. Almost immediately the privacy screen, which appeared as a soft blue shell from the inside, darkened to indicate it was about to drop. Dyle had expected a robot, but their drinks were delivered by another costumed human, a slender young man this time, who nodded to acknowledge their thanks and left without making a sound. The screen sprang up immediately he was gone.

"As much as I enjoy your company, Senator," said Marym, "I have to ask why you couched your invitation in such urgent terms."

Baxter appeared to be relaxed, but Dyle knew that he was a consummate actor. It was almost a prerequisite for the professional politician. "The two of you are investigating the death of Magnus Mercator, are you not?"

News of the killing and their official effort to determine who was responsible had already spread throughout the ship, so the question was rhetorical. Dyle thought he knew his old friend well enough to judge his moods accurately, but there was something odd going on behind those deep-set eyes at the moment. "Are you trying to tell us that you know something relevant, Abraham?"

"Potentially, and indirectly. May I ask how you intend to proceed?"

Dyle and Marym exchanged looks but Baxter leaned forward, gesturing dismissal with his hands. "My apologies. I have no right to ask that. I can imagine the difficulties, however. Killed in a public place, presumably with no witnesses. And the man had no shortage of enemies aboard ship, as I'm sure you've already discovered."

"Mercator was a controversial and unpopular figure," admitted Dyle. "You didn't invite us here to belabor the obvious."

"No, I didn't. How long have we known each other, Sandor?"

"I met you briefly when you were serving as a page in the Concourse Senate. I was barely grown myself at the time. I don't suppose we were actually acquainted until you were elected to your first term."

"Twenty standard years then."

"That sounds about right." He considered prodding, then decided to let Baxter choose his own pace.

"You knew that I served in the military for a while."

"Yes, indeed. You and your twin, Cecily, enlisted together. You were involved in peacekeeping missions and minor police actions, rose slowly but steadily through the ranks, but resigned your position after Cecily was killed. Two years later you made your first successful run for the Senate." He paused. "Cecily died on Cathanor, didn't she?"

Baxter nodded. "While we were storming the capital. I was wounded in the same action, but not significantly."

"Are you suggesting that as a motive for killing Magnus Mercator?" asked Marym.

"No, only as a predisposition. There's more, unfortunately. You know that I retired from political life recently."

Dyle nodded. "A terrible waste of talent, if you don't mind my saying so."

"That's debatable, I suppose. I would like your promise that what I'm about to say remains among the three of us. I promise you that it has no relevance to the death of Magnus Mercator, although it might seem that way."

Dyle looked at Marym who nodded to indicate she'd follow his lead. "If that's the case, we'll certainly respect your confidence."

For a few seconds, it seemed Baxter might yet balk, but he seemed to come to some internal decision, sat back in his seat, his interlaced fingers resting against his chest. "My decision not to seek another term was not entirely voluntary. My influence on the Interworld Commerce Committee had become something of an obstruction to the interests of Magnus Mercator and some of his associates and they decided that the Senate would be more amenable to their views if I was no longer a member."

"I can't believe that you'd allow yourself to be frightened into resigning."

Baxter laughed, but without humor. "No, he knew better than that, though I have no doubt that Mercator would have tried that approach if he'd thought it might work. He was much more clever than that. He laid his groundwork carefully, bided his time, and then sprung his trap. If I'd been younger, I might have suspected something, but I've grown soft, in body and in mind."

"Blackmail," Marym suggested softly.

He nodded. "I haven't led a blameless life, but I've always been open about my failings. If you choose to pursue a public career, you have to assume that you're surrendering the right to keep secrets. I've never been married, I contributed generously to the support of the two children I've fathered, and I'm on good terms with both their mothers. I've never accepted a bribe, never sold my vote, never knowingly broken whatever law applied to me wherever I found myself. I made the mistake of thinking myself untouchable, and perhaps I was guilty of arrogance because of that."

"So how did they get to you?" asked Dyle.

"Through Kumi, my daughter. She's a sweet girl, but her mother protected her too much. She's gullible and easily manipulated and she lives on Cathrax."

Dyle shook his head. "Never heard of it."

"One of the older worlds, heavily populated. Nominally a republic but it's effectively run by an entrenched bureaucracy. The laws are rigidly enforced and the punishments are generally quite harsh by Concourse standards. Their voting rights were suspended for a year once because they fell below the minimal human-rights provisions of the Concourse charter."

Dyle could already see where this was going. "They enticed her into committing a crime and they're holding that knowledge over your head. You were told to resign or watch your daughter go to prison."

"She had no idea what she was getting into, thought it was a legitimate project that would finally make her independent of her mother's purse strings, and mine too I guess. But they didn't want me to resign. They just wanted me to change my position on a few subjects. I resigned preemptively to deny them that influence, and made it clear that if Kumi was arrested, I would resume my career."

"Couldn't you get her offworld?"

He shook his head. "Her status was the equivalent of material witness. She wasn't under arrest but she couldn't leave Cathrax."

Dyle made a disgusted sound under his breath. "I can see that you had good reason to hate Mercator, but if anything the circumstances would provide a disincentive to killing him. With the equilibrium upset, anything could happen."

Baxter's face changed and he suddenly looked much older. "You don't understand. Just before I boarded the *Helen,* I received a message from Kumi's mother. Kumi tried to leave Cathrax under a false name. It was a foolish attempt; they have very sophisticated port facilities and identified her immediately. She must have panicked, tried to run for it. She's dead."

Dyle closed his eyes briefly. "I'm terribly sorry, Abraham."

Marym also expressed her sympathy. "I'm surprised you were willing to sit at the same table with him under the circumstances."

"At the time I thought it might serve a purpose. I hadn't seen Mercator in a very long time and I needed to know how his appearance had changed."

"I'm sure we both appreciate your telling us this, Abraham," said Dyle. "But I've known you a long time and I could never seriously suspect you of doing something as contrary to your disposition as to kill a man in cold blood."

"Oh, it wouldn't have been in cold blood. You're right about that. But I needed to know what Mercator looked like because I intended to ensure that he never left this ship alive."

An awkward silence followed during which time itself seemed momentarily suspended.

"Oh, I didn't do it. I promise you that. But I might have if . . . when the opportunity presented itself. Mercator was a monster. It's only now, when he's actually dead, that I realize I couldn't possibly have gone through with it. Or maybe I could have, but I would have hated what he'd made of me even more than what he was himself." There was another interruption as their food was delivered, a human assisted by a robot servitor, or perhaps it was the other way around. Baxter waited until the shield was back up. "I'm sure I've earned a place on your list of prime suspects. I apologize for burdening you with this, but I didn't feel comfortable concealing the truth from you now that it no longer matters."

Dyle didn't know what to say but Marym responded immediately. "We appreciate your candor, Senator." Her face was neutral but Dyle noticed that she had reverted to calling him by his title. Former title, actually. They had been on a first-name basis the day before.

"Please eat. I trust I haven't completely routed your appetites."

They turned to their food with universal relief. Eating made immediate substantive conversation impossible, and gave them all an opportunity to think about what had just passed among them. Intellectually Dyle knew that his Hibiscan flowershrimp had been prepared expertly but he had difficulty enjoying it. This was a side of his old friend he had never known before, never even suspected, and he was having difficulty reconciling the old with the new.

Baxter's appetite seemed unaffected and he was done long before his companions, pushing back from the table after ordering another drink. His face seemed more relaxed now, as though he had somehow transferred the burden of his guilty thoughts simply by putting them into words. And perhaps that was the case, because Dyle and Marym remained subdued.

"I know you won't want to hear this either, but I rather hope that this is one of your rare failures, Sandor. Whoever killed Magnus Mercator deserves to get away with it."

"You don't mean that, Abraham."

The older man nodded. "No, I suppose I don't. If I had killed him, I would have turned myself in. I believe that there are rare circumstances in which it is ethical to act contrary to the law, even a good law, but I also believe that such an act should not be undertaken lightly and should not go unpunished. I won't be sorry in this case if the balance isn't kept."

"But you have no personal knowledge of the crime?" asked Marym. "None whatsoever?"

"Happily, no. But I feel obligated to tell you that I have no alibi for the time in question. I was alone in my cabin, brooding for the most part."

"Under the circumstances, there's no longer anything preventing you from running for your old seat during the next election," Dyle observed.

"I know. I've thought about it. But I'm not sure that I could ever approach the job again with quite the same degree of enthusiasm and confidence. I feel irrationally guilty, by association if not by deed. Even resigning was a partial capitulation to an external pressure, and I'd prided myself on my independence throughout my career. And in the days since I learned of Kumi's death, I've learned things about myself that came as rather a revelation. I haven't closed that door permanently yet, but I'm not ready to walk back through it."

"Then what will you do?"

"I plan to leave the *Helen* at Ambergris and return to Aragon for a while. I haven't visited the family estates in more than a standard year. I hope to persuade Dahlia to visit if she can get leave from her job. She's my other daughter and I don't see her nearly as often as I'd like." His eyes were suddenly clouded and he glanced back and forth between his two companions. "I've lost a great deal recently. I hope this confession has not cost me two friends as well, one old and one new."

Both hastened to assure him otherwise, and Dyle made a bad attempt at a joke that still managed to break most of the tension. By the time they placed their final order for drinks, she was calling him Abraham again and they were all in good spirits. But Dyle knew that although their friendship remained intact, it had changed its shape forever.

Marym was obviously sleepy and left the other two to finish their last drink alone, announcing her intention to retire for the day. Baxter followed suit a short time later but Dyle was feeling restless and decided to walk for a while, which he did, so lost in thought that he was briefly disoriented when he discovered he was deep in crew territory. The posted guard must have recognized him and let him pass without challenge. He was, in fact, very close to the sealed chamber where Eco had once been housed, and beyond which lay Memnon's inner sanctum. Although none of the information in Memnon's storage banks appeared to be helpful, he found the manipulation of large quantities of data subtly soothing and decided to pay a brief visit. He waited for the local security system to identify him, then stepped through the doorway into the gloom.

"May I be of service, Ser Dyle?" Memnon's voice seemed slightly richer, more human, than it had previously.

"I thought you were prohibited from initiating contact except in an emergency."

"As a redundant system, that was true. Since I am now primary, certain of my behavioral restraints have been removed or modified per standing instructions and subsequent modifications made or authorized by Chief Systems Officer Pritchard."

Dyle slowly advanced toward the padded chair that faced the console. "You are aware of the death of one of the passengers, I assume."

"Captain Nicodemus made notes to that effect in the ship's log. I also have access to orders from First Officer Paragupta establishing a security zone at the scene of the event, and complete records from the medical section including the results of the postmortem. I was also notified through the scheduling module that Lounge 1138 has been reserved indefinitely for the use of passengers Sandor Dyle and Marym Dunnis for the purpose of conducting an investigation into a criminal act resulting in a human fatality. As further corroboration, there are subsidiary reports within the security module, maintenance, stores, and housekeeping which together imply substantially the same situation."

"Can you extrapolate any further data on the basis of what you know?"

"Creative extrapolation is beyond my capacity."

Dyle was only mildly disappointed. He had yet to see any useful results from an intuition module. "All right. I want to open the files pertaining to the destruction of Eco which I was working on this morning."

He sidled around to the front of the chair and was about to sit down when something attracted his attention. He bent forward very slowly until he could see the small dark smear on one corner of the padding, at just about the spot against which a large man might rest his upper arm and shoulder. It looked like dried blood.

"Memnon, has anyone been in this physical location during the past ship's day?"

"Yes."

"Identify all such people, please."

"Office Gavin Pritchard. Passenger Sandor Dyle. Passenger Magnus Mercator."

Dyle nodded to himself. "At what time was Passenger Mercator present?" Memnon told him and he quickly matched that to his mental time chart. Mercator had visited Memnon for almost a full hour, and had left only moments before Tanith's escape from their private module.

"Please display the working file created by Passenger Mercator during this work period."

"Unable to comply. Passenger Mercator secured the file with a personal encryption code, then ordered me to erase the transaction record from permanent and flash memory."

"All right. Display a list of all files consulted by Mercator during this session other than those he created himself." If Mercator was thorough and knowledgeable enough, he could have concealed that trail as well, but Dyle was lucky this time. A lengthy list of files appeared, all involved with internal ship's operations, and virtually all dated subsequent to Eco's termination. As far as Dyle could see at first glance, they had been selected randomly.

But no human activity was truly completely random, and it only took a short time for him to discover what they had in common. Each and every one of them reflected in some way on the performance of First Officer Cosmo Paragupta.

Chapter Ten

In the morning, Dyle told Marym about his discoveries while they drank kaffee at a quiet place on the Promenade, but she didn't attach as much significance to it as he had expected, given her earlier suspicion of the first officer. "We already knew that Mercator was planning to replace Nicodemus at Pradesh. It stands to reason that he would want to evaluate a potential replacement."

Dyle shook his head. "I can't believe that a man as thorough as he was would have left that decision until so late. I'm sure that the *Helen*'s new skipper is waiting at Pradesh."

"I realize that's likely the case, but it might be no more than an interim appointment. Or it might be that he was considering replacing the first officer as well. Paragupta certainly doesn't strike me as the kind who could assume a major command. He's too tentative."

"And a bit too anxious to please. I agree. A captain needs to radiate authority and self-confidence and he's deficient in both areas, however technically adept he might be."

"And if we noticed it so readily, Mercator did as well and decided to dig a little deeper."

"Possibly. But the depth of his search puzzles me, as well as some of his findings. Back at Linnisfarne, Paragupta occasionally relieved the stores officer during loading. In itself, that's not surprising given that they were behind schedule and had to work round the clock to finish in time for departure. But the pattern of his activities is odd. The duty roster survived because it was considered essential to the ship's safe operation and was replicated within Memnon, but the actual transaction records in Stores were not. There's a perpetual inventory maintained locally but only a limited number of actual transactions, so all of the historical data was lost with Eco. Memnon also confirmed that Mercator tried to examine the records of one Lars Volkrung, master of stores, but was unable to do so. Officer Volkrung resigned his position the day before we left Linnisfarne. The acting master of stores is someone named Ganelon, who was brought aboard as a last-minute replacement. The officer who approved his posting was Cosmo Paragupta."

Marym stirred. "Now that's suggestive."

He nodded enthusiastically. "There's more. Among the first officer's duties is a routine inspection of Stores, which is to occur no less frequently than once in every five ship days. Under the present emergency circumstances, I imagine that requirement might be temporarily relaxed in favor of more pressing matters. Paragupta apparently thinks otherwise, since he has visited Stores a minimum of twice per ship day."

"He's smuggling something."

"That seems likely. At a minimum he has brought something unauthorized aboard, something important enough or valuable enough that he paid off Volkrung or arranged for an accident to get him out of the way."

"Do you think Mercator confronted him or brought this information to the captain's attention?"

Dyle shook his head. "I don't think he had the chance to do either. Tanith made her escape just about the time he closed out his files and left Memnon's chamber."

"Should we tell the captain ourselves?"

"Not yet, and it may be unrelated. We do know, however, that our first officer is a more resourceful person than he appears. I also found out that he had previously instructed Memnon to inform him if certain patterns of inquiry were pursued, and Mercator triggered the alarm. Paragupta certainly knew what Mercator was doing, and may have known early enough to have followed his victim and killed him. He would have been notified while Mercator was still at work, and had more than enough time to intercept and follow him when he left that location."

Marym's face hardened. "You haven't set yourself up as bait, have you? If he knew about Mercator, he'd be aware of your query as well."

Dyle shook his head. "No, because I didn't look at the original records; I examined Mercator's sealed copies. Then I locked my file and the record of my queries and edited Paragupta's watchdog program so that it ignores activity by the two of us. Only the captain can override us, and she'd have to know the encrypted data existed before she could do that. I may decide to unlock the data later in order to see how he reacts, but not at the moment." He glanced at his chrono. "So who is first on our list today?"

* * * * *

They found Feykirk waiting outside the lounge. Dyle found her relentless cheerfulness a bit wearing, but he managed to respond in something approximating her manner before sending her off to retrieve Pylandris, the Lysandran steward. Marym asked if Dyle would do the questioning this time. "I'm not xenophobic, and the Lysandrans never came near Tashista, so I don't have any prejudices on that score, but I wouldn't know how to read his body language and I think that would put me off my game."

Pylandris was typical of his race. He would have been tall for a human, but not dramatically so. Although roughly humanoid, Lysandrans had unusually long necks and a comparatively small head, perched atop a gracefully curved body covered with a light fur that looked like feathers. It was not surprising that they had been dubbed "swans" during the war, and that term still persisted unofficially. Lysandrans varied in coloration much as did humans, and Pylandris was a golden brown. Dyle had visited one of their colony worlds and had stayed long enough to learn to recognize many of their physiological features. He judged Pylandris to be comparatively young, though well past their equivalent of adolescence.

They had not thought to arrange for one of the bucket-shaped seats his race preferred, but he settled into one of the chairs without complaint.

Dyle introduced himself and Marym and confirmed that Pylandris understood the purpose of the interview.

"You wish to question me regarding the death of Passenger Magnus Mercator."

"Correct. But I'd like some background first. You are from Plesnia, I believe?" Dyle had read what survived of the steward's personnel file in considerable detail.

"That is correct, although I was born on Listeray." Lysandran voices were very humanlike, but there was always an undertone, a soft moist echo, that Dyle found distracting.

"This is your second posting aboard a human-operated ship?"

"I was previously employed as a galley assistant on the *Manchu*. We carried freight and passengers in the Hidalgo Cluster and sometimes into nearby regions." Marym had taken Dyle's role from the previous day, hovering just out of the line of sight, although neither of them knew whether or not Lysandrans reacted similarly to humans. She frowned very slightly now, and quietly walked over to the console that connected them to Memnon. Neither Dyle nor Pylandris could see the screen and she tapped the key for visual only.

Dyle was intrigued but returned his attention to the matter at hand. "Why did you leave your last ship?"

"My present assignment is more remunerative and will provide a wider range of experience. There was also some question about the continuity of my previous employment."

If this had been a human, Dyle would have asked if his former employers had been unhappy with his performance, but Lysandrans would consider this a serious insult. Pylandris had been living among humans for a considerable period of time now and would probably have reacted placidly, but on some level he would still be offended. "What was the nature of this uncertainty?"

"Local conditions had reduced the level of commerce making continued operation a marginally profitable enterprise."

"Can you be more precise about those conditions?"

"There was armed conflict between several human colonized worlds."

"The Tenebrian Conflict?"

"Yes."

"You've lived among humans for how long?"

"Seven of your standard years."

"So you can distinguish among us fairly easily, I imagine."

The Lysandran's head bobbed in what would, in a human, have been a nod but was more likely a sign of impatience. "It is a necessary skill for performance of my duties."

"You must pardon me if I seem to be asking unnecessary questions, but it is a requirement of the human investigative process and it assists me with the organization of my thoughts."

"It is not necessary to explain this procedure. My duty is to serve my superiors as primaries and all passengers as secondaries. It is not my place to question the nature of those requests."

"All right. Did you know Passenger Magnus Mercator by sight? Would you have recognized him if you encountered him in a passageway?"

"Yes. It has been my duty to attend to him on two occasions."

"You served us at the captain's table at the First Jump Banquet. What was the second occasion?"

"He requested my assistance in subduing a second passenger under his charge while he administered medication."

"When was this?"

The time Pylandris mentioned was approximately two hours after the dinner party for First Jump had broken up.

"How did it happen? Was it a chance encounter or did he specifically ask for you?"

"My personal presence was requested through Eco. I proceeded directly to the private module, received my instructions, and left as soon as I was dismissed. Passenger Mercator ordered me not to repeat any of the details of my time there."

"Your personal presence. Mercator asked for you by name?"

"He requested that the Lysandran steward attend. He was not cognizant of my name."

Dyle could guess why. Despite their fragile appearance, Lysandrans were physically quite strong, stronger than humans of the equivalent size. Mercator could have called security, but then the incident would have been officially logged. Lysandrans had a high regard for lines of authority—excessively high by human standards—and would have acknowledged Mercator's authority to physically subdue members of his own party. Pylandris would also have been much more discreet than most humans, particularly if told not to talk about the incident. Lysandrans did not gossip.

"You understand that I have Captain Nicodemus' implied authority to conduct this investigation, do you not?"

"All crew have been ordered to cooperate with you and Passenger Marym Dunnis."

"And the captain's authority supersedes the instructions of any individual passenger?"

"That is my understanding of human customs."

"Then tell me what happened when you responded to Passenger Mercator's summons."

"I was met by Passenger Callista Dorne, who may have been distraught. I still have some difficulty interpreting human emotions with some facial types. She informed me that one of Passenger Magnus Mercator's children, Tanith Mercator, was subject to violent, irrational episodes which required forcible medical treatment. I suggested that an appeal to the medical section would be more appropriate but was told that this was not an acceptable solution."

"Who told you that?"

"Passenger Magnus Mercator, after I had entered the module and evaluated the situation."

"All right. Go on."

"A female passenger had armed herself with an edged weapon and was standing in an alcove between one of the cabins and the lounge area. Passenger Augustus Clout was confronting her and speaking in terms which I believe were designed to lessen her distress. Two other passengers whom I knew to be Passenger Magnus Mercator's remaining children were watching from a safe distance. I believe their emotions were excitement rather than alarm, but once again I am not confident of my interpretation."

Marym completed whatever query she'd initiated and stood up, her face neutral. Dyle waited for her to give him some kind of sign, but she simply resumed her quiet pacing.

"How did you proceed?"

"The human female was unskilled. She was overpowered quite easily. Passenger Magnus Mercator administered medication subcutaneously."

"And Tanith was all right after that?"

"There was no detectible change in the condition of Passenger Tanith Mercator after the medication was administered."

Dyle frowned. "That seems odd. Do you have any idea why not?"

Pylandris moved his head in a gesture that Dyle knew was a sign of amusement. "No medication was administered to Passenger Tanith Mercator. Although the individual whom I restrained was identified by that name, I knew this to be false. The medication was administered to Passenger Absinthe Mercator."

Although Dyle was usually good at keeping a straight face, he was caught so completely by surprise that even an inexperienced Lysandran might have noticed. "You're certain of that?"

"The two individuals are quite easily distinguished."

Dyle paused, collecting his thoughts. "Let's move on. At the time of Mercator's death, you were off duty, I believe."

"That is correct."

"Do you mind my asking where you were and what you were doing?"

"We do not share the human obsession with privacy. Although I have not been told of the precise moment of Passenger Magnus Mercator's death, I am reasonably sure that I was either in the hydroponic gardens at the time, or on my way to it from the stewards' lounge or back to my personal quarters following my visit."

"And what were you doing there?"

For the first time, Pylandris hesitated. "Are you aware of the dietary differences between humans and my species?"

"I think so. There's a surprisingly large degree of compatibility. I've lived on Lysandran food for several days." It was by his standards exceedingly bland, but nourishing.

"I also can consume most human food with no ill effects. However, there are certain enzymes that are missing. A prolonged deficiency would affect my health adversely. To avoid this problem, the captain has designated a small portion of the hydroponics for the use of myself and a second member of my species who serves in the crew. We cultivate a few of our native foods there, enough to make it unnecessary to take a corrective supplement. We also find your food rather soft." Pylandris opened his mouth to display the serrated ridges of his jaws that served the purpose of teeth in humans. "I harvested a mature zyloti rind and took it to my quarters."

"Did you see Mercator or anyone else whom you recognized while you were in or near the gardens?"

"I saw Passenger Rudolf Kreuk near the reflecting pool, and Crew Member Tilda Ashiri, who tends the hydroponics. There were other passengers present but none with whom I was acquainted. My path did not take me near the site of Passenger Magnus Mercator's death, nor did I see anyone acting in a surreptitious or hasty manner."

Dyle asked Feykirk to have the zyloti retrieved from the Lysandran's quarters so that he could examine it, apologizing to Pylandris for the necessity.

"It is not a matter of concern. As I have said, the human obsession with personal privacy does not apply in my case." Dyle had just about run out of useful questions to ask when a second steward arrived, slightly breathless, carrying the cylindrical zyloti, a tuberous plant the length of a man's arm, tapered at both ends. It was certainly heavy enough to have served as a club, but the smooth outer rind appeared completely undamaged except for a small piece that had been cut out with a sharp-edged instrument of some kind. "I sampled it to ensure that it was sufficiently aged," explained the Lysandran.

Dyle was satisfied, at least for the moment. He returned the zyloti to its owner, and thanked Pylandris for his time.

"It is a part of my duties to respond to the requirements of the captain and designated passengers."

When he was gone, Marym and Dyle exchanged significant looks, each waiting for the other to speak. She was the first to find her tongue. "Is it true that Lysandrans cannot tell a lie?"

He shook his head. "It's exceedingly rare. They consider it dishonorable. They've gotten much better at it since the war, one of the less admirable things we've taught them."

"Do you believe his story then?"

"The general cast of it, yes. The zyloti just about the right size to explain the parcel I saw him carrying. He would have kept it wrapped because exposure to sunlight, even artificial light, accelerates the softening of the outer integument. Yes, everything he said is perfectly plausible." He paused. "On the other hand, it would serve quite well as a bludgeon and, if he'd wrapped it with duroplast, it wouldn't leave any traces behind. I still think he's an unlikely candidate, but I'm not ready to let him drop off the bottom of our list of suspects just yet."

"We might want to promote him a step or two. I checked Memnon's astrographical database. The Hidalgo Cluster is right in the middle of the contested region in the Tenebrian War. How much would you like to wager that Pylandris is a former employee of Idrian Caserta?"

Dyle caught his breath, then let it out slowly. "Well, it's a small universe, isn't it?"

* * * * *

They were supposed to interview Callista Dorne next but Feykirk returned empty handed. "Apparently the missing young lady has been located and the family summoned."

"Why would that be? Is she all right?"

Feykirk looked unhappy for the first time since they'd met her. "I couldn't say. I've had no word of it myself, but the guard posted there told me that the entire party except for Morpheus Mercator had gone off with one of the ship's officers. Would you like me to see what I can discover? I could call the captain." She indicated the communicator on her belt, but was clearly hesitant about using it.

"Yes, please do. No, wait. Perhaps Memnon can help."

Memnon could indeed. Tanith had been discovered concealed in one of the ship's ventilation shafts. "At the present time, I have no other information about her status."

Dyle asked for and received the corridor number. "Feykirk, can you take us there?"

"Certainly. If you'll come this way."

Feykirk led them to a part of the ship they had not previously visited, deep in its bowels somewhere along the utility corridor that separated Stores from Security. They passed a bored-looking crew member early on, a much more alert one shortly before reaching their destination, a major corridor junction crowded with people. They heard Clout's voice before they saw him, although they couldn't distinguish the words, but the first recognizable faces they spotted were Absinthe Mercator and Callista Dorne, standing together at the fringe of a crowd of uniformed crew members. Captain Nicodemus was there as well, along with a substantial representation of security and maintenance personnel, and a few wearing the neutral pale tassels of general administration, which included Stores.

A large grill had been removed from one of the massive ventilation shafts scattered throughout the ship. Clout was standing at the opening, talking animatedly to Nicodemus, who looked as though she were experiencing considerable difficulty controlling her temper. Portable lights were being set up to better illuminate the interior of the shaft.

"If you'll wait here a moment, I'll try to find out what's going on." Feykirk was obviously enjoying this variation from her normal duties. Dyle suspected that no one would interfere if they asked the captain directly, but decided not to spoil the steward's fun. They watched as she spoke to one of the security people, who was clearly irritated at her first approach, but whose expression softened after a glance in their direction. The exchange of information didn't take long.

"The young woman is barricaded in a control nexus about thirty meters in. She has a clear view of both approaches and is threatening to do herself harm if anyone comes within reach. She refuses to talk to anyone except her father, which is obviously impossible, but Passenger Clout feels that he can convince her to come out of her hidey hole. The captain isn't so sure and wants to use narcogas, particularly since it might be possible to severely damage the atmospheric distribution system in this portion of the ship if there was a physical struggle. No one knows how she got in there; the vent here hadn't been tampered with so she must have found a point of entry elsewhere."

"How did they locate her?" asked Marym.

"Memnon reported an anomaly in the ventilation patterns. Maintenance thought it might be a faulty aileron and sent a technician in to calibrate them."

Dyle glanced toward the center of the confusion. "Looks like the captain is having her way."

A security officer had appeared carrying an oddly shaped weapon whose projectiles were arranged around the exterior of the barrel, which in this case was merely an aiming and balancing device. Dyle had seen them in use before, during the riots on Alembia and during a rescue operation against kidnappers on Haniker. The capsules contained an odorless, invisible gas which was released by any significant impact after they were armed and launched. Unconsciousness was virtually instantaneous and there were minimal aftereffects. The gas itself became inert very quickly. The shooter would probably have nose filters installed and since the gas was relatively heavy and non-volatile, its effects would be limited to a very small area, particularly in the confined ventilation shaft.

Clout was obviously protesting again, but his voice was lower and it was clearly pro forma now. The captain had made her decision and it would be carried out. The shooter climbed into the ventilation shaft a moment later and the babble of conversation stopped as though someone had turned on a dampening field. The next few seconds crawled by. Dyle thought he might have heard a distant, muted pop, but it might also have been his imagination.

Everyone remained silent, even when a figure emerged from the shaft.

"She's down," he said clearly. "You can go in for her now."

Clout was the first to move, obviously surprising those around him. Two medicators, one carrying a good-sized field kit, and a burly security operative followed almost immediately. The wait was longer this time, and some conversation revived. The captain and the shooter were speaking quietly together. Marym nudged Dyle's shoulders and inclined her head toward Dorne and Absinthe. He nodded and followed her lead.

"We've just heard." Marym's voice reflected genuine sympathy. "I'm sure she's going to be all right."

Absinthe's eyes were unfriendly, but she responded politely if somewhat shortly. Dorne seemed genuinely pleased to see them, but she was still tense. "I hope she hasn't hurt herself. She doesn't usually, but we never know what she's going to do when she has one of these episodes. Or what she might say." She and Absinthe exchanged glances briefly.

"She won't be saying anything for a while. The narcogas won't wear off for some time. They'll have her in the medical center by then."

"We'll take care of her ourselves," Absinthe answered testily. "The medicators can't do anything for her that we can't do as well. My sister has had these spells for most of her life. We're used to dealing with them."

"I'm not sure the captain will agree to that," suggested Dyle mildly.

"She has no right to hold her!" Absinthe was growing visibly agitated.

Dyle might normally have backed off, but he decided to probe instead. "Your sister has threatened ship's personnel, damaged or at least interfered with life-support systems, and trespassed in regions closed to passengers. I doubt very much that Captain Nicodemus would be willing to risk a recurrence, particularly in view of recent events aboard ship."

For a moment it looked as though Absinthe might explode. Her face worked furiously, her color was up, and her hands had clenched into fists. Dyle remembered Pylandris' testimony that she had been forcibly restrained and medicated and wondered if he had gone too far. But the moment passed, her tension faded, and her voice was calmer, though no less determined when she spoke again. "We'll confine her to her cabin for the balance of the trip if that's what it takes. And there's always a guard outside the airlock. They shouldn't be fooled a second time."

There was a sudden flurry of activity near the ventilation shaft. One of the medicators emerged first, turning immediately to help guide the leading end of a pressure stretcher out of the opening. Several other crew members moved forward to help ease the now unconscious and contained Tanith Mercator out into the open.

"Clout and I will deal with this, Callista," Absinthe said dismissively. "There's no need for you to involve yourself." She hurried off then, without a word to Dyle or Marym. Dorne was visibly shaken and uncertain, and Marym obviously wanted to take advantage of the situation.

"It appears that we're all supercargo at the moment, Ser Dorne. Perhaps this would be a good time for us to have our little talk. Things will have sorted themselves out by the time we're done."

Dorne looked back and forth between the now rapidly disappearing clot of people and her immediate companions. "All right, I guess it's best to get it over with."

They made their way back to the lounge, Feykirk in their wake, saying little along the way. Dyle tried to make casual conversation to make their companion feel less threatened, but Dorne was obviously distracted and not listening closely. She seemed positively surprised when they reached their destination, and took a seat obediently when told to do so, clasping her hands in her lap and suddenly looking much younger than she had previously. Dyle had guessed her to be a few standard years older than the Mercator sisters, but now he was less certain.

Marym resumed her role as primary interrogator. She walked Dorne through her past, her meeting with Magnus Mercator and their subsequent liaison, nothing of which seemed immediately relevant. Her questions were tactful and Dorne grew noticeably calmer, but Dyle suspected Marym was deliberately trying to get the young woman to drop her guard before asking more significant questions. Dorne admitted without shame that her relationship with Magnus had been primarily an exchange of physical and social services for credit and that she had accepted his offer of an ongoing relationship as a way to escape her impoverished home world.

"That's not to say that I don't . . . didn't like Magnus. He was a hard man to deal with at times, but honorable in his way. And never cruel, despite what they say about him. He didn't regret his past, even though he knew that he'd made some poor decisions. The only people who never make mistakes are the ones who never act in the first place. I can't tell you how many times I've heard him say that."

She had originally contracted to be his companion for one standard year. The contract had expired without formal renewal but they had gotten along well as a couple and stayed together informally, although she had been thinking recently about striking out on her own. "I know my way around now and I've made a few contacts. Magnus was always in motion. He changed residences the way some people change hairstyles. No, that's an exaggeration. But the longest we've stayed on one world is less than half a standard year and I'd really prefer to settle down someplace."

"Had you mentioned this to him?"

"I have never concealed my feelings on the matter. Magnus never felt the kind of deep emotional attachment for other people that would prevent him from letting me go."

"Not even for his children?"

"No," she said with absolute certainty. "His loyalty to them is another aspect of his sense of duty."

"How much did you know about his business dealings?"

"Very little. He didn't hide things from me, not in general anyway, but I wasn't interested. I didn't even know that he owned the *Helen* until after we came aboard."

"Did he ever mention anything involving security passwords or access to Eco?"

"No, not that I can recall."

"Was his mood at all unusual since departure? Did he seem apprehensive, or act secretively?"

She shook her head. "He's been somewhat moody, but I think that was because he was fighting with his son more frequently than usual. Morpheus has flashes of his father's inflexibility and when the two of them were at odds, it was always tense."

"Augustus Clout was employed as his personal assistant?"

"That was his title." Her voice was slightly strained now.

"But he was actually a bodyguard, wasn't he?"

She nodded. "But he was an able assistant as well. Magnus told me that Clout could have been a formidable rival if he wasn't so lazy. Lazy is a relative term, of course. I've never met anyone with such constant intensity as Magnus."

"Please tell us again what happened from the time Tanith disappeared until you were told that Magnus was dead. And don't leave out any details, even if they seem inconsequential."

Dorne did so, her account varying not in the slightest from what she'd previously told them and adding no new information that helped. She was clearly calmer and more at ease by the time she finished, and Marym decided that her guard was down as far as was possible.

"What is your relationship to Augustus Clout?"

Initially Dorne seemed more puzzled than alarmed. "I don't understand. We know each other, of course. In a sense, I suppose we're co-workers. We've always been pleasant to one another but I wouldn't describe us as friends. If anything, Clout has even less capacity for human warmth than Magnus."

"Then you were never intimate with him?"

Dorne straightened in her chair and her voice was indignant. "Of course not! There may not have been any insistence upon exclusivity in my arrangement with Magnus, but it would have felt like a betrayal of trust."

"I beg your pardon then, Ser Dorne. You understand that we must ask these questions, however unpleasant?"

Dorne slowly settled back, clearly only partially mollified. Her outrage had seemed genuine to Dyle and he found it hard to believe that she wasn't telling the truth. She probably had not acted upon the attraction between the two of them, but that didn't mean it wasn't there. It didn't give her a motive to kill Mercator though. If their arrangement was informal, she was free to dispense her favors and amuse herself with anyone she wanted. On the other hand, might Mercator not resent a liaison, even a potential one, between his mistress and his bodyguard? Could one or both of them have decided to avoid potential retribution by eliminating its source?

Marym reverted to innocuous questions, soothing Dorne's outrage. When she sensed the woman's guard was as low as it was likely to drop, she probed again. "I understand you were present during the episode in which Absinthe Mercator was forcibly medicated."

Dorne stiffened. "You mean Tanith Mercator, don't you?"

Marym's face was neutral. "I may have misunderstood. I was under the impression that both sisters used mood-controlling medications."

"Tanith is the one with the problem." Dorne's voice was even, but she was no longer meeting Marym's eyes. "I'm not aware of any drugs her sister might be using." That was transparently a lie, and Dorne must have known that she wasn't fooling them. "Magnus rarely discussed his children's medical problems in my presence. He found the subject distressing."

Marym let the ensuing silence stretch uncomfortably far.

"Where did you go when you left us with Absinthe just before Mercator's body was found?"

Dorne relaxed slightly. "She does get under my skin occasionally. She does it deliberately and I know it's just a game for her, but I can't help reacting occasionally. I went out for a walk, as you know. I was so mad I couldn't think at first and then I bumped into someone in the Atrium and came to my senses. After that I told myself I was looking for Tanith again, and I walked to the far end of the Promenade and back, but I wasn't really looking for her. When I got back, you were all gone and the guard told me what had happened, or at least as much as she knew."

"And you didn't pass anyone else you knew either coming or going?"

"I don't think so, but like I said, I wasn't paying all that much attention to what was going on around me."

"All right, I think we're done for the moment. Thank you very much for your cooperation."

Dorne stood up, but she didn't move toward the door. Marym pretended to be examining the notes she'd entered into the tabletop transcriber, waiting for her to break the silence if she wanted to. Dyle called up a random display on Memnon's console and bent forward as if to study it.

"Do you have any idea who did it? Who killed him, I mean?"

Marym deliberately made an entry before answering. "We're not at liberty to discuss the possible results of our inquiries just now. I'm sure you understand the need for discretion."

"Yes, of course. But I was just concerned. I mean, what if whoever is responsible decides to kill again?"

Marym sat back. "For what reason? If the killer was, as seems likely, one of Mercator's many enemies, then they've succeeded in what they set out to do."

"But might the killer not wish to continue his revenge, against other members of the family, possibly?"

"Captain Nicodemus has a guard posted at your module at all times. If you feel that additional security is necessary, you should address your concerns to one of the ship's officers."

"Yes, of course. I'm sorry. It's just been so unnerving lately." She glanced nervously toward Dyle, then shook her head, turned, and left.

Feykirk appeared immediately, but Marym waved her off. "Take a break, Feykirk. Ser Dyle and I are going to eat before we talk to anyone else."

Chapter Eleven

Except for their general body type, Morpheus and Magnus Mercator had not resembled each other closely. They both had powerful frames, but where the father had been fit and heavily muscled, the son carried his weight loosely and out of balance. He was ungainly where his father was graceful. There was a softness about him that went beyond poor muscle tone and conditioning, almost a systemic flaw. His short, black hair seemed somehow unkempt even when, as now, it was neatly combed into a suggestion of his father's famous and now absent mane, and his complexion was blotchy, a common reaction to the more advanced drugs used to treat stim addiction.

Morpheus clearly resented being summoned and flounced down in a chair without being asked and without speaking a word. He folded his legs and stared at some imaginary object on the blank wall behind Marym, pretending indifference, playing at indignation. Dyle turned away to hide his amused grin, but Marym played her part to perfection. She was perfectly willing to wait him out, pretended to be entering data into her notes, or perhaps she really was. Sandor would not have been surprised if that was the case. The tableau held, a silent and invisible contest of wills, but the outcome was never in doubt. Morpheus uncrossed and recrossed his legs a few times, cleared his throat softly, then more loudly.

"If you weren't ready for me, why are you wasting my time?"

Marym made one more deliberate entry before sitting back and meeting his eyes. "My apologies, Ser Mercator. I thought you needed the time to collect yourself."

"It's just Morpheus. I don't use my father's name. And I am perfectly collected, thank you. Shall we get this over with?"

"I gather relations between you and your father were not entirely amicable."

"Have you any idea what it is like to have someone overseeing every detail of your life, as though you were applying for a job as his son?" His manner was petulant and a bit sly, Dyle thought, but it was partly an act, an exaggeration designed to leave a false impression. Perhaps more of his father's personality had been passed on than was immediately apparent.

"I'm sure that we've all had our share of difficulties in the past, but it is more immediate problems that concern us right now. Your health has been a source of some concern lately, I understand."

"My father overreacted. I had an adverse reaction during a stim session which he chose to consider more serious than it actually was. It was just his latest effort to exert control over my life."

"But you are being medicated."

"It does no harm so it wasn't worth arguing about." Morpheus was clearly on the defensive. "I don't see that this is any of your business."

"No, I imagine you don't." Marym's tone implied that she hadn't the slightest interest in his opinion. "Your sisters are also being medicated, aren't they?"

Morpheus was even less adept at concealing his reaction than Dorne had been earlier. "Tanith has been ill for most of her life. That's never been a secret."

"But Absinthe's problems aren't as obvious, are they?"

There was a lengthy pause, but Morpheus wasn't to be lulled so easily. "I have no idea what you're talking about."

Marym sighed theatrically. "All right, let's move on to the events surrounding your father's death. You don't appear to be devastated by the loss."

"We were never close," he said defensively. "Magnus never had time for personal entanglements. I regret his death, of course, but I won't pretend to be distraught about it."

"I imagine you stand to gain something from his estate."

Morpheus responded so quickly and tonelessly that Dyle was certain he'd rehearsed his answer beforehand. "The family assets are all controlled by a trust. There is provision for certain individual disbursements in the event of my father's death, but the bulk of the credit will still be jointly held. Control is split equally among my sisters and I, with a fourth share administered by a small board of governors chosen by Father. Absinthe and I retain voting rights, but Tanith has no say in business decisions."

"You seem much better informed on the subject than your sister was."

Morpheus made a dismissive sound. "Absinthe knows the setup just as well as I do. She just enjoys being difficult."

"I see. Does this board of governors derive any income in compensation for their duties?"

"They draw a stipend for their services, and some of them are on the payroll for other reasons."

"Are any of these individuals aboard the *Helen*?"

"Yes. Clout is on the board. And Idrian Caserta will be once the acquisition is official."

"When your sister bolted, your father asked you to help look for her, didn't he?"

"Father didn't ask. He issued instructions."

"How did you proceed?"

Morpheus worked his face to indicate that he was bored. "I checked with the crew people who were watching the two entrances to the ship's interior. Neither of them could remember seeing Tanith at all that day, and both were certain she hadn't passed them. I found the first to be rather insolent, but the other suggested that I try the stewards' accessway in the concession area. That exit was supposed to be locked at all times, but apparently under the present circumstances, there's been some laxness in security. It was open when I got there, as a matter of fact, and unattended. My father was not happy to hear of it."

"Your father? But I understood that you never saw him after the search began."

Morpheus jerked slightly and Dyle could almost hear him thinking. "Only for a moment. He was making a quick pass through the Promenade and asked me what I'd found out, so I told him. We spoke for only a few seconds. I was supposed to follow up while he went to the gardens, which he thought was her most likely hiding place. As it turned out, he was wrong."

"What did you do after that?"

"I followed the passageway and got hopelessly lost, as a matter of fact. It's like a maze in there and the junction markers were no help at all. I finally found a stubborn young woman who refused to listen to me and insisted on taking me to security. There was only a clerk there, because everyone else was on duty. She wanted me to wait for someone in authority to return, and refused to give me directions back on my own. I finally walked out on her, but as you've probably surmised, I got lost again. By the time I finally found my way back, the body had already been found and no one was interested in helping to look for Tanith."

"And you have no idea who might have killed your father?"

"Of course not. I would have said so immediately if that was the case."

"How did you get along with Augustus Clout?"

Morpheus shrugged. "He likes to throw his weight around and he sometimes forgets that his position is that of an employee rather than an equal. My father encouraged him in that, I'm sorry to say."

"I understood that your father relied on him a great deal."

"He has his uses." Morpheus smiled at some inner joke. "Now that Father is dead, he may get a chance to prove his value after all."

"Did he get along with the rest of the family?"

"Absinthe was particularly fond of him." The sly tone was back.

"Were they intimate?" Marym shot back immediately.

Laughing, Morpheus nodded. "I'm not betraying any family confidences. Absinthe tries to bed anyone who looks even remotely interesting, and usually has her way. She even tried her luck with me once or twice, and I've had my suspicions about her and Tanith since we were kids."

The balance of the interview was less productive. Morpheus became increasingly sullen and less communicative. Sudden mood changes were common during stim withdrawal. Dyle was struck by the waste the young man was making of his life. He had inherited an intelligence that might even rival that of his father, but he lacked self-discipline and focus. Perhaps now that he was out from the shadow of the overwhelming personality of Magnus Mercator, the inner man might emerge, but Dyle thought it might be too late, that the potential Morpheus had wrapped itself in comfortable and possibly impenetrable insulation. Marym did get him to let slip that he knew his father was not happy with Captain Nicodemus, but he didn't react to the first officer's name, either positively or to the contrary, and his ignorance seemed genuine.

Dyle and Marym were debating whether or not to ask for Paragupta next but Feykirk entered with news that changed their plans.

"Excuse me, but I received word that one of the passengers has asked to meet with you as soon as possible if it's convenient."

"Which passenger?" asked Dyle.

"Ser Idrian Caserta. He sent a steward to say he'd be holding a table in the Domino if you could join him."

They still hadn't decided whether or not to reveal to Paragupta what they knew about his suspicious activities in Stores, and this would allow them to put off deciding. Feykirk offered to escort them once again, but they dismissed her, since they knew the way as well as she did.

Life aboard the *Helen* had normalized, although it was not exactly as it had been when Eco was functioning. Most of the restaurants and shops that had been open before were open again, although stripped of their exotic scenery and paraphernalia. Their links to Stores had been repaired and were working properly, so menus and stock were no longer limited. The murder was still a major topic of conversation, but the apprehensive expressions that had been common ever since Eco's demise were almost completely gone. People strolled about singly or in small groups, and no longer congregated in intense discussions about their personal security or the ship's status. The captain had posted announcement of the diversion to Scrimshaw, and most interpreted this positively. Children were present without supervision again, and the crew looked tired but considerably less harried.

The Domino was on the top level of the Promenade, both physically and figuratively. Customers paid a premium to have pretty much the same food they could have been served more cheaply elsewhere delivered by humans fitted with repulsor belts that allowed them to float around inside the spherical dining space. The tables themselves were similarly equipped and programmed to slowly rearrange themselves in intricate, shifting patterns. They were greeted by an attendant wearing gauzy wings that were material rather than projections, but equally non-functional. He guided them through the maze to Caserta's table and left without speaking.

Caserta greeted them warmly although his face looked even more drawn than it had when they'd first met him. He asked if they'd like a privacy shield, but Dyle suggested that it was unnecessary for the moment. "Unless you have reason not to be overheard."

"None at all. Please order yourselves some refreshments." They did so, and chattered lightly about the restaurant's decor until the drinks arrived. Dyle was surprised not to see Sondra Wong and said so.

"Sondra is having her prosthesis repaired. It's been giving her trouble lately. I'm taking advantage of that fact by asking for this meeting, because I didn't wish her to be present, and that's been a rare situation of late. Sondra has added the duties of a nurse to her job description recently, despite my assurances that she need not concern herself."

"Why did you ask us to meet with you?" asked Dyle.

"Mercator made a comment during one of our sessions which I thought might be of significance and I wished to pass it on. But I also have a very selfish reason, I'm afraid, but I'm dying and I don't have time for the usual niceties." He raised a hand to fend off the anticipated protest, but neither of his guests had any intention of contradicting him. It had been obvious from the outset that Caserta had little time left to him. His body was worn out, and further rejuvenation treatments would not extend his life another day. He might last another standard year or even two, but certainly no longer than that, and probably a good deal less.

"You're concerned about the status of your business arrangement," Dyle said quietly.

"That is my preoccupation, yes. My company is the only child I will ever have, you see, and I am determined to ensure that it has a future. I have been assured by the Mercator family that the terms of the original agreement will be honored despite the tragedy, but it is easy to promise something when it is expedient and act otherwise from a distance."

"I'm sure we both appreciate your problem, but I don't see that there's anything we can do."

"No, of course not. I just hoped that you might be able to advise me in general on one aspect of the manner." He hesitated, visibly uncomfortable. "I only wished to inquire as to the likelihood that Magnus Mercator was killed by a member of his immediate family. If one of the heirs was forced to forfeit his or her share of the trust, the balance of power would shift dramatically and it would be much easier to repudiate a transaction that had yet to be formally consummated."

Dyle chose his words carefully. "We are not in a position to say, Ser Caserta. At this point, no one in Mercator's private party has been definitely eliminated, but neither is there reason to believe that any one of them should be the focus of our investigation. He had a great many enemies, as I'm sure you know. Unless you have some evidence you wish to share with us?"

Caserta shook his head. "Just an observation, possibly of no consequence. During our negotiations, Mercator's man Clout briefly excused himself. Magnus was uneasy and evasive until his return, and we were unable to make any significant progress during his absence. I sensed it was not just because he relied so heavily on Clout's financial acumen. He made an offhand comment, which he immediately dismissed as a joke, but it seemed rather odd at the time, and doubly so considering what has happened since."

Their dinners arrived, and Dyle waited impatiently until their conversation could resume. "You were saying. . . ."

"Sondra asked him for some details about the continuity of management clauses, but Magnus put her off and it was quite obvious that he was waiting for Clout to return. Patience is not numbered among Sondra's virtues and she pressed the point, even going so far as to ask him if there was a reason why he was unwilling to answer. He dismissed that notion immediately, saying that he was just concerned about his assistant's prolonged absence. Then he added a curious comment to the effect that he and Clout thought there might be a stowaway aboard the *Helen*."

"That seems rather unlikely, doesn't it?"

"Oh, he made a joke of it himself and changed the subject, and then Clout returned and we were back to business. I had completely forgotten about it until a few hours ago. Sondra was trying her best to reassure me that everything will go ahead as we expected, and I think she truly believes that's the case, but I still have my doubts and she can read my moods. She seems absolutely convinced that none of Magnus' children is responsible. I wished I shared her confidence."

"We can't add anything to what we've already told you," Dyle responded. "For that matter, it's by no means certain that the truth will ever come out. But Mercator was an astute businessman. Whatever the outcome, it seems to me likely that his successors would be inclined to look favorably upon any agreement which he had embraced."

"Yes, that's what Sondra keeps trying to tell me. I suppose you're right, and in any case there's nothing I can do to influence matters now. I hope that the excellent food compensates you for this waste of your time."

"Time spent in good company is never wasted," Marym replied graciously. "And we thank you for taking the trouble to pass on your information."

They remained some time longer, but it became obvious that Caserta was growing fatigued so they excused themselves, using the not-untruthful excuse that they needed to resume the interviewing process. Although they offered to see him back to his quarters, Caserta waved them off. "I'll summon a steward with a scooter and ride back in style. Thank you again for indulging my anxieties."

By mutual consent, they didn't discuss anything substantial on their way back to the lounge, but once there they exchanged looks indicating they had both come to the same conclusion. Dyle was the first to put it into words. "That's why Mercator was so interested in the first officer's secret. It may have been something that Paragupta said or did that made him suspicious, or he may have been alerted in some other fashion. He was looking for signs of smuggling or some other illegal activity, and that led him to Paragupta."

"But how could there be a stowaway on board? It just doesn't seem possible given the security precautions. How could he have hidden another passenger from Eco?"

"If he did it, then it's possible. With his authority, he might have been able to order Eco not to reveal his secret. Only Nicodemus could have overruled him, and she would have had no reason to look into the matter." A thought suddenly occurred to him. "Memnon, do you have visual access to the Stores area?"

"I have direct surveillance of Central Stores Processing, but not of subsidiary locations."

"How about the storage area itself?"

"Since access is limited to authorized personnel, that would not be considered a priority."

"Did Eco monitor the storage area?"

"Original specifications included universal coverage of all common areas, secured or otherwise. Implementation of surveillance in specified areas within Stores, Maintenance, and Hydroponics was inhibited by budgetary revisions during the final stages of construction. I have enhancements including an official objection and disclaimer from Captain Lydia Nicodemus and the responsive confirmation of variance from Chairman Magnus Mercator, acting for the Trendways Consortium."

Dyle nodded with satisfaction. "He probably decided it was an unnecessary expense. Memnon, do you monitor atmospheric changes in all areas of the ship?"

"Yes. Atmospheric monitoring is one of my prime responsibilities."

"Can you determine whether the consumption of oxygen in Stores is consistent with the level of human traffic in that area?"

"Yes, I can make that determination. The answer to your implied question is that consumption of oxygen in Stores has been inconsistent with monitored human traffic since shortly before our departure."

"Inconsistent in what way?"

"Consumption has been approximately thirty-one percent higher than can be accounted for by monitored human traffic, with a range of error of two point five percent."

Marym didn't look particularly surprised. She anticipated Dyle's next question. "Memnon, how do you account for the discrepancy you just described and why hasn't it been reported to the ship's officers?"

"The data does not reveal any reportable discrepancy."

That caught them both by surprise, and Dyle resumed the dialogue. "Explain why the higher rate of oxygen consumption is not discrepant."

"Additional consumption is not inconsistent with the presence of logged non-human oxygen breathers in the Stores area."

Marym was visibly startled. "I thought that the only non-humans aboard were the two Lysandran crew members and a handful of passengers."

But Dyle supplied the answer, since she hadn't phrased it as a question. "Livestock. We're transporting animals, pets perhaps. Memnon, are the non-human oxygen breathers intelligent beings or animals?"

"Passengers cannot be domiciled in Stores, therefore, all mobile non-human life-forms are by definition animals. Enhancement is available."

"Can you provide us a list of these animals, and their owners of record?"

The console screen immediately changed, displaying data in orderly rows. The list wasn't long and they didn't need to scroll through it. Most entries were the property of individual passengers, probably pets. The remainder included an exotic paratiger en route to an exo-zoo on Minotaur, a breeding pair of fuzzilopes sold to a farmer on one of the fringe worlds, and an unspecified experimental animal that belonged to a laboratory on Pradesh. None of the contact names, owners and escorts, meant anything to Dyle or Marym. But the final entry aroused Marym's curiosity because it was the only one to have been logged after the change in cargo masters. The escort was listed as Adrian Sypher, a passenger.

"Memnon, what is Adrian Sypher's cabin assignment?"

"There is no passenger with that name aboard at this time."

She exchanged looks with Dyle. "Why is that, Memnon?"

"I have no information which would satisfy that question. Most passenger information was retained exclusively in Eco's memory."

"So who's been taking care of this experimental animal if Sypher isn't aboard?"

"I have no information which would satisfy that question. It is possible that an anecdotal explanation might be available through Stores personnel."

"I might be able to save us some time," interrupted Dyle. "Memnon, can you display a list of all passengers who have physically entered the Stores area since departure?"

"That information is not available as it was stored in Eco's memory. I can provide an abridged answer covering the past ship's day."

"All right, let's see it."

The list appeared instantly. It only took a few minutes to determine that all of the visitors were either among the named owners or escorts, or a member of those individuals' parties. "Then it has to be a crew member," said Marym triumphantly.

"Not necessarily. If I wanted to mask my visits in this situation, I would have brought a pet along as well. While visiting my official cargo, I could easily arrange to make provision for my unofficial one as well."

"So what's next?"

"What do you think?" he answered brightly.

"I think we should take a look at this lab animal for ourselves."

It took them a while to find their way, even with directions, and Dyle regretted that they dismissed Feykirk for the rest of the day. Eventually they found themselves in a reception area where an irritable clerk failed to think of a good reason for denying them access but was scrupulous about making sure they logged in and that they understood the rules governing passenger behavior within Stores. "There are monitors all over the place in there so we don't miss much," she lied.

Only a small portion of the livestock holding area was in use. Most of the pets were in transparent, shielded cases, but a few were opaqued, including the paratiger and the container they were looking for. It was taller than they were, and large enough to have held a small hovercraft. Marym glanced at the locking mechanism that secured the hatchway. "Ship's issue," she said.

"Excellent. Memnon, are you there?" There was no reply and Dyle sighed. "Well, I thought not but it was worth a try. One of us has to go back for an override. They'll have one in reception for use in an emergency. I should have thought of it when we first arrived."

Marym sat down on a cage containing three slurricats, who scampered around enthusiastically to investigate this new stimulus. "I don't mind waiting," she said lightly.

It took longer than he expected, because even with his authorization from Captain Nicodemus, he couldn't convince the receptionist to give him the override. A younger woman of higher rank answered her summons, looked equally displeased with the irregularity, but begrudgingly handed him the small device. "Will you require any further assistance?"

"Not at the moment." Dyle was himself rather annoyed by now, but more interested in looking inside the sealed container than in rebuffing a petty irritation.

"In that case, my staff cannot assume responsibility for any harm that might come to the cargo, or to your person, in the event that something happens down there."

"I'll take my chances."

Marym didn't appear to have moved since he'd left her, but she slid down to her feet as he approached. The override neutralized whatever personal coding had been entered into the lock's internal memory. There was a faint click as the physical restraints withdrew invisibly.

"If it's dangerous, whatever is inside is probably further restrained to allow entry and maintenance, but let's be on guard anyway." Her expression didn't change, but he sensed that she'd become more alert. Very slowly he grasped the handle and gave an experimental tug. It shifted, very slightly, and with almost no sound. He nodded once to indicate he was ready, then pulled the hatch to the side, where it retracted into the double hull of the container.

They could see almost the entire interior from where they stood. There was a table and three chairs, a self-contained data unit and console, two bunk beds, and a small, walled-off area in the far corner that was probably a sanitary facility. There were two humans inside, one sitting at the table, the other lying in the upper bunk bed.

Both of them were children.

Chapter Twelve

Dyle was caught completely by surprise, and in retrospect realized that they'd been very foolish acting as they had. The stowaway might have been a dangerous fugitive rather than two apparently innocuous children.

Both children were watching them, curious but showing no obvious signs of fear or even concern. Dyle stood frozen at the entrance, but Marym stepped inside, smiling broadly. "Hello, do you speak standard?"

They did, and quite well once they were over their initial shyness. The boy was Jossi and the girl, his sister, was Lanelle. They were both very polite and only slightly apprehensive because they'd been told to stay very quiet and not let anyone except their uncle know that they were aboard the ship. Their uncle visited them regularly, but he was late today and they wanted to know if he had sent Marym and Dyle in his place.

Their makeshift quarters were very well equipped. The enclosed area included all the sanitary facilities they needed and their uncle took away their dirty clothing and brought it back clean. They had a small stock of self-contained rations, which warmed themselves when the right sequence of icons were touched on the colorful packaging, a working data console and holo unit, not connected to the *Helen*'s systems, and a few physical games and puzzles. Dyle judged both children to be on the brink of adolescence, the boy slightly the elder. They weren't at all secretive now that they'd been discovered, but they were clearly wary of the consequences. Efforts to convince them to discuss their background or the reason for their clandestine voyage inevitably resulted in silence or "Uncle told us not to talk about that."

Neither would they identify their uncle by name, but that was hardly necessary.

Marym stayed with the children while Dyle trudged back to the reception area. This time he ignored the woman on duty completely, who reciprocated by pretending that she didn't notice him. "Memnon, please provide the present location for First Officer Cosmo Paragupta."

"The first officer is presently off duty in his quarters."

"Excellent. Can you reach him there?"

"All executive officers have been provided with portable communicators for emergency use. Additionally, my monitoring capacity has been restored in the quarters of senior officers and staff."

"All right. Please advise the first officer that I would like to see him in the Stores area as soon as possible. Tell him we need to discuss some unusual cargo."

There was barely a pause. "I have advised him. He has indicated he will join you immediately."

"Excellent. Now tell security that I need two armed operatives here promptly."

"They have been dispatched."

"I'll wait for them."

The security personnel arrived first, two men who looked enough alike that they could have been brothers. Dyle led them back through the maze of equipment and supplies, posting them at a spot some distance from the children's container, where they could watch the area adjoining the entrance without being able to see inside.

"The first officer is coming down to help us deal with the situation. The condition of one of the experimental animals requires some intervention. We hope to deal with the matter, but there remains the possibility that it might escape and pose a danger. If that happens, we want you to stun it so that we can resecure it."

"We'd be in a better position to do something if we were closer, Ser Dyle," protested the senior of the two.

Dyle shook his head. "I appreciate that, but there is a confidentiality agreement covering the situation. Unless there is a clear emergency, the exact nature of the animal cannot be revealed."

The security man didn't look happy, but he nodded.

Paragupta showed up only a few seconds later, and the expression on his face told Dyle much of what he needed to know. Marym was still inside, talking to the children, but Dyle intercepted the first officer near the entrance, speaking in a low voice.

"Before we proceed any further, I want you to glance over to your right. They've been ordered to keep their distance, but they'll be watching you."

Paragupta saw the security people and blanched, but his voice was surprisingly steady. "I'm not ashamed of this. I'd do it again if I had the chance."

"Do what again? What is this? Kidnapping?"

He shook his head. "No, nothing like that. I'm letting them have a chance, the only chance they're likely to get."

"They're related to you?" There was absolutely no family resemblance. Paragupta was dark-skinned with black hair, tall and slender. The children were fair and blond and the boy a bit pudgy. The girl was slim but surprisingly small for her age.

"No. We told them I was their uncle but that was just to make them feel a bit easier about leaving. They were sad about that, despite everything. How much do you know about Linnisfarne, Ser Dyle?"

He searched his memory. "Not very much. We were only on the surface for one night before we boarded, and we never left the transient area. It was a lost colony, wasn't it?"

"Yes. Only Albemarle was out of contact with the rest of the human race for a longer period of time. It was settled by dissidents from Tenerife, just before the civil war that nearly destroyed that colony as well. The few who knew where the emigrants had gone either perished, forgot about it, or chose to forget. They had been on their own for more than two hundred standard years when an enterprising commercial explorer poked into their system looking for prime real estate. During the intervening years, they had developed a rather idiosyncratic culture, based on the dominant religious group among the original settlers. Linnisfarne is currently a constitutional theocracy which practices a number of customs which the Concourse Senate prefers to call 'questionable.' Their membership was delayed for several generations after rediscovery because of some of these customs, and they have been suspended from time to time in response to current conditions."

"Are you telling me these children are political refugees?"

"In a manner of speaking. We both know that the Concourse isn't really a government and intervenes only in extreme cases and after much hand-wringing and debate. The children are orphans of heretics who committed suicide rather than submit to reindoctrination. Voluntary euthanasia is legal on Linnisfarne as it is on most worlds nowadays. The children would have been taken into state care."

"Unfortunate as that might be, it hardly makes them political refugees. If everyone who lived under a system with which they disagreed was declared a political refugee, they'd probably be in the majority."

"I realize that, but you don't understand the implications for a child of heretics on Linnisfarne. To start with, they'd both be sterilized."

Dyle's lips thinned. "That seems extreme."

Paragupta nodded enthusiastically. "They'd be forbidden to ever marry, even childlessly. The only jobs they can hold would be menial labor and they'd be denied the consolation of the Church. That last doesn't sound so bad until you realize that all medical treatments are administered by the Church. And that's not the worst of it."

Dyle sighed silently, waiting for the final blow.

"Only ten percent of heretical children taken into state care live for more than a year. The official reason is despair at having been sundered from God, and despair there is in plenty. But the truth is that they are systematically mistreated and quietly denied the supplements that allow the colonists to survive on the native food sources. The Senate suspects that's the case and has sent observers periodically, but it's hard to prove and the Senate itself is very reluctant to move against a member world without clear evidence."

"So you decided to smuggle two of them off Linnisfarne to where, an adoptive family I suppose?"

Paragupta hesitated, clearly trying to decide how much he could say. "Jossi and Lanelle will make a total of fourteen I've managed to relocate, although they're the first on this ship, obviously. I hand them over to contacts at our first port of call, and I never see them again after that. It's for their own protection in case I'm ever found out. The Lectum on Linnisfarne does not believe in out of sight, out of mind. They've made efforts to track down fugitives, and they suspect there's an offworld connection."

Marym emerged at that point, her face expressionless but her eyes asking many questions. Dyle provided a condensed version of Paragupta's story, which hardened her eyes but left her otherwise visibly unchanged.

"So what are we going to do about this?" she asked at last.

"The children seem to be well as they are. Let's restore their privacy and move this discussion to some place more comfortable."

Paragupta seemed resigned rather than relaxed, but he nodded.

* * * * *

After dismissing the security guards and thanking them for their assistance, Dyle joined the others in a silent walk back through crew territory. They used the lounge that had been set aside for them, but sat away from the table, facing each other. Paragupta showed no inclination to initiate further conversation and Marym was initially content to study him silently. Dyle finally could stand it no longer, cleared his throat.

"I can't speak for Marym, but I'm inclined to ignore what we've discovered today, as long as I'm convinced it has no relevance to the death of Magnus Mercator."

Marym seemed less certain. "We're outside Linnisfarne's jurisdiction now. Why not tell the captain and move them to more comfortable quarters?"

"Pradesh is a major trading partner with Linnisfarne. They have an extradition treaty. I don't know about Scrimshaw, but I wouldn't want to take the risk. And even if I felt confident that they wouldn't be sent back, it would show our hand. The Lectum would know how the children were escaping and would plug that hole immediately. They'd be the last two children we'd be able to help, at least until we figured out some other method."

"And Captain Nicodemus already knows unofficially in any case, doesn't she?"

Paragupta looked distinctly uncomfortable and remained silent.

"The captain is far too thorough an officer not to know what's been going on. Mercator knew or at least suspected that you were involved in something illegal, didn't he?"

There was a single nod. "Eco and Memnon both had standing instructions to report to me if anyone expressed unusual interest in either the Stores area or my activities."

"My guess would be that he suspected something before he even came aboard, probably because of the sudden change in personnel in the Stores area. He probably checked on the captain as well as yourself, but she never came down here so there was nothing for him to find. And since her authority exceeds yours, she could have countermanded your watchdog instructions. I imagine she has also been keeping an eye on you, and I'd venture to guess she's spoken to you as well."

Paragupta let out a long, slow breath. "Captain Nicodemus has never been involved, and we have never discussed the subject even in passing. She has, however, suggested certain improvements in security arrangements and has requested that I increase the frequency of my inspections of the Stores area as a precaution against pilferage." He paused and wet dry lips with his tongue. "The captain has spent considerable time on Linnisfarne and has privately expressed her dismay at some of the local customs."

Marym visibly relaxed. "All right. I'm satisfied that we'd do more harm than good by interfering, at least given what we know so far. But this situation raises some troubling new questions."

"As, for example, would I have been willing to kill Magnus Mercator to prevent him from revealing the truth? I'm not sure myself, frankly, but I think yes, under the right circumstances, I would kill to save those children, and the others who will follow. But the situation didn't arise. I never saw him between the moment when I learned that he was tracking my activity until I was called to the scene of his death."

"Where were you at the time?" asked Dyle.

"I was off duty, but I had just received Memnon's message that Mercator had been examining my duty records. I didn't know what to do. I was too anxious to sit still so I walked around the ship, trying to think. Some of the time I was in crew territory but much of it was on the Promenade." He laughed uncomfortably. "I tend to think better in a crowd."

"Were you in the gardens at all?"

"No, but I can't prove it. There was plenty of time for me to have gone out there, tracked him down, and beaten him to death."

"Did anyone recognize you during your rambling?"

"I'm sure that many did. The uniform's quite distinctive. But it was always in passing, and even if I could point to a particular individual and say yes, I passed this passenger at this precise time, I couldn't possibly identify and confirm enough data points to provide a credible alibi. Yes, I had motive and opportunity. No, I didn't do it,

I don't have any idea who really was responsible, and frankly, I don't mourn the man's loss."

"You didn't care for him?" asked Marym.

"I know his reputation. He's no loss to civilization."

"You seemed to be on good terms with him at First Jump."

The first officer's expression turned sour. "Mercator and the captain didn't get along. She was going to be relieved when we reached Pradesh. I had heard that candidates for her job were waiting there to be interviewed by Mercator, and I also believed that he had not yet made a decision. My credentials are good and I thought I might have a chance. As captain, I would be in an even better position to help."

"Did Mercator give you any reason to believe that he might have chosen you?"

"No, quite the contrary. He implied that I didn't have the kind of leadership style that he preferred, and let drop that he'd already chosen Lydia's successor. I must have overplayed my hand and given him the impression that I was a little too interested in currying favor. I'm sure that's why he checked up on me."

"Does anyone else aboard the *Helen* know about the children?"

"No. One of the crew members suspected something when we were on Linnisfarne, but the organization I'm with arranged for a very attractive job offer at the last moment and he left the ship. Our last cargo master was lured away for the same reason."

"Did you have any other contact with Mercator or the members of his party?"

"Only casually, until his death, of course. I was alerted when his daughter disappeared but I wasn't involved with the search. That's all."

They tried to pin down his movements more precisely, but without success. Paragupta freely admitted that he'd had more than ample opportunity to stalk and kill Mercator, and return to be officially alerted when the body was discovered. "The only other thing I can offer in my defense is that I had no idea that Mercator was in the gardens at all, and alone at that. I assumed that the young lady would be somewhere in the Promenade, hiding among the other passengers."

Which didn't mean he hadn't spotted him in the Promenade and followed him afterward.

They thanked him for his time and he somewhat emotionally thanked them in turn for not revealing his secret. "I would not like to think that even in death Mercator had the power to reach out and ruin the lives of others." And then he was gone.

Dyle remained silent until Marym gave voice to what they were both thinking. "He's a good man, I think, but he's devoted to his cause. He would not have hesitated to kill to protect his secret."

"No, he wouldn't have. He would regret the necessity, but he'd do it. We can't cross him off the list of suspects, but I very much hope that he and his little hobby will escape further scrutiny."

"Tell me something. If you knew that Paragupta was guilty, that he'd murdered Mercator to prevent him from exposing the child smuggling operation, would you pretend otherwise?"

"No, I'd inform the captain of the facts."

"I'm curious. Why not weigh the welfare of countless children against the premature death of a single, reportedly ruthless, possibly monstrous man?"

"Because I believe that laws should not be broken lightly. The first officer looked at the laws of Linnisfarne and felt a moral obligation to circumvent them. In his place, I think I would have done the same. Laws are not evil, but evil people sometimes make the law. The deliberate taking of another human life is justified only in self-defense, in some instances for crimes against society, and in the case of war, in defense of the state. None of those apply here, at least not directly."

"What would you have done in his place then?"

"I'd have gone directly to the captain, told her officially what she already knew clandestinely, and requested asylum for the children. There's even a reasonable chance that Mercator could have been persuaded to forget the matter rather than risk having it known that one of his ship's officers made off with two underaged citizens of an independent planet. But for all his surface control, Paragupta is very emotionally involved in this matter, and he may not have been thinking clearly."

"Do you think he's our killer then?"

"I don't know."

* * * * *

The next person on their list was Tanith Mercator, but neither of them felt up to what was likely to be a difficult if not impossible interview, so they decided to refresh their minds and bodies instead. The fitness centers were all in use, but the free-fall gymnasium was available and they bounced around its interior, swatting at a padded ball designed to rebound at unexpected angles, making up the rules as they went along. There were old-style wet showers which they used separately, not quite ready to adopt the easy informality common among friends in most of the mainstream worlds of the Concourse. A light meal followed, during which conversation came in fits and starts. Both were preoccupied with their thoughts, and both were emotionally and physically fatigued, although not unpleasantly so.

They were on their way back along the Promenade when Marym spotted a familiar face in one of the small dining rooms. She nudged Dyle and nodded her head. Sondra Wong was sitting at a small table in the far corner, talking animatedly to her companion. Dyle expected the other figure to be Idrian Caserta, but it wasn't.

It was Morpheus Mercator.

"That confirms what I was going to suggest anyway," said Marym. "I think we should add Ser Wong to our list."

"Indeed, I think we should."

* * * * *

The following day did not start well. Feykirk returned from her quest to inform them that Tanith was confined to her quarters by the captain's orders and the family's request, and that she was not in any case feeling well enough to be interviewed. Dyle was inclined to insist and suggested that they interview her where she was, but Marym dissuaded him.

"Let's leave it for the moment. It might be more productive to talk to Wong first."

Feykirk was promptly dispatched to locate and retrieve this fresh quarry, which she soon accomplished with her usual efficiency.

Wong wasn't good at hiding her feelings; her face cycled through hostility, anxiety, and curiosity. She greeted them both by name, and took the proffered seat after only the slightest hesitation. As usual, Marym would conduct the formal interview while Dyle observed.

"I am at your service, of course, but I should not leave Idrian alone unnecessarily. His health is failing and he needs constant assistance."

"You left him long enough to meet with Morpheus Mercator yesterday," Marym responded promptly.

"I was there on his behalf. You already know that we came on this trip only in order to establish a significant commercial alliance with the Mercator family. In the light of recent events, it seemed wise to ensure that an amicable and mutually understood relationship still exists between the two parties. Neither of us is legally bound until the articles of incorporation are formally ratified. Idrian was not feeling well enough to meet with the younger Mercator, so I went in his place."

"You seem quite devoted to your employer."

Wong's face softened, became almost human for a moment. "I have the greatest respect for Idrian. He's led a very lonely life and he's been treated badly by a number of people, some whom he trusted. Despite that, and despite the nature of his business which requires a degree of callousness, he remains loyal to his employees and has never to my knowledge failed to keep his word or honor an obligation. His present financial difficulties are at least in part because of his pledge to provide continued livelihood for his crews even when they are limited to marginal or even unprofitable voyages. So yes, I am devoted to him, and will serve him as best I can for whatever remains of his life. Or mine." The little speech seemed to restore Wong's composure. Her back straightened and her voice lost even a hint of a quaver.

"Did you know any of the Mercators before coming aboard the *Helen*?"

"I knew Magnus by reputation, and I believe Idrian had mentioned his children by name on at least one occasion."

"But you yourself had never met any of them?"

"No, never."

"What was your impression of Ser Mercator? Was he what you expected?"

"I was disappointed. He did not live up to his reputation at all. I had expected a more formidable man."

"But you were satisfied with the terms of his offer?"

"My opinions in the matter are of no consequence. Idrian makes his own decisions and I have never had reason to doubt his judgment."

"But you did have an opinion."

"Yes. I thought that Ser Mercator's offer should have been somewhat higher with regard to subsidies, and some of the long-term provisions might be called exorbitant. On the other hand, it includes surprisingly generous provisions for our employees and is particularly considerate of Idrian's feelings. We would still face some difficulties but we would be out of any immediate danger. In the long run, the Mercators will receive a substantial return on their investment at the expense of Idrian's estate, but there are no children or other dependents, so that hardly matters. Given the state of his health, Idrian would theoretically be reasonably well off for what remains of his life, and would be an active member of the board of the Mercator family trust for as long as he wished."

"So your opinion of Magnus Mercator was favorable? You liked him?"

Wong shook her head. "I know his personal history, Ser Dunnis. I tend to be less judgmental than most people. I was a mercenary for several years." She lifted her artificial arm to underline the point. "I fought for and against people with the same conviction that their cause was right, that their decisions were above reproach, that the lives of others were somehow less important. No one likes these people; they do not even like themselves. Sometimes they make good leaders, but they are as likely to take the wrong road as the right one, and their supporters have no choice except to follow. I have even admired one or two, but I have never liked them. Mercator was the center of his own particular universe, and even his moments of charity were designed to please himself, not others. No, I didn't like him. But in this case, he was a near-ideal solution to a problem."

Marym was silent, but Dyle moved around the table and broke in. "Were you ever on Cathanor?"

Wong shook her head. "There were no mercenaries involved in the intervention, Ser Dyle. I was serving as a tech sergeant with Rossiter's Raiders on Falwell at the time. It was my last assignment. My unit was overrun and I spent six months as a prisoner, during which time I lost my arm. By the time I had access to advanced surgical techniques, the window for transplantation had closed and I had to be content with a prosthesis. I used up all my savings getting that done. The only merc units that would take me after that were out on the fringes so I went into personal protection instead. Worked as a bodyguard, improved my professional skills, eventually got picked up by Idrian on a temporary assignment that became long term."

"I thought merc units paid full medical for combat injuries."

Her face twisted as unpleasant memories surfaced. "That's right, for combat injuries. I lost the arm while I was in prison, so technically it wasn't a combat injury. That's how they argued it anyway, and I didn't have enough time, or credit, to fight them about it."

"So you had no reason to hate Magnus Mercator?"

She shook her head. "As I said, personally I was indifferent to him. If someone had attacked him in my presence, I'd have interfered for Idrian's sake. Otherwise I'd have left him to fend for himself the way his kind did to me."

"But the family has agreed to honor the terms he and Caserta settled upon, haven't they? Killing him after the final details had been settled would not have derailed things."

"Yes, but I had no way of knowing that until after the fact. You're dancing around the question you want to ask me, Ser Dyle. Please save us both some time and get it over with."

"All right. Did you or did you not kill Magnus Mercator?"

Her eyes never wavered. "I did not, and I don't have any information about Mercator's death that would help you in any way that I haven't already told you."

Marym asked a few more questions, thanked her and let her return to her duties. As soon as she was safely out of earshot, she turned to Dyle. "Do you believe her?"

"She was holding something back, possibly about the business arrangements, but I think she was telling the truth when she said she didn't kill Mercator."

"I can't imagine what her motive would be in any case." She suddenly sounded weary.

"Well, I did say very early on that I didn't think motive would help us determine the killer. Too many people had motives, and even in her case I can think of at least one very good reason why she might have wanted Mercator dead."

Marym raised an eyebrow.

"Suppose Mercator had second thoughts about his deal with Caserta. Their agreement was still informal and he could have reneged. If Wong knew or suspected that was the case, she might well have killed him. There was a chance the family would disavow their father's plans, but it would be better than no chance at all. I have no doubt she would cross the line without hesitation to protect Caserta. She's clearly devoted to him."

"So motive still doesn't help us. How about opportunity?"

"Same problem. I think this was a crime of impulse. The killer could not have anticipated the opportunity and either ran into Mercator in the gardens or followed him there from the Promenade. And none of our primary suspects have an alibi for the time in question."

"But are they all physically capable of the crime? Mercator was pretty well battered."

"The only person I'd rule out on that account would be Caserta and he's never even been on our list. The medicator's report indicates that Mercator was probably unconscious within the first few blows, possibly after only one. The substantial damage we saw was inflicted later and the effects were cumulative. The murder weapon was probably quite solid and heavy, but it could have been yielded by someone as small as Dorne or as large as Clout."

"So what's next?"

"I think it's time we spoke to Tanith Mercator. If she can't, or won't, come to us, then we'll just have to make a house call."

Chapter Thirteen

The guard posted at the airlock leading to the Mercators' private module was new, but he apparently recognized one or both of them immediately because he greeted them by name. The outer door was open as usual, but the inner one was secured.

"Who's presently inside?" asked Dyle.

"All of the residents except Ser Mercator, the younger one, I mean." The guard stumbled over his words and then looked apologetic. "They've left instructions that they are not to be disturbed."

"Tell them we're here to see Tanith Mercator, and that we won't bother her any more than is necessary."

The guard looked dubious, but he used the communicator to talk to someone inside. The conversation was brief. "Ser Clout will be out in a moment."

The inner lock opened almost within the same breath and Augustus Clout strode into view, wearing a casual robe apparently made from genuine animal skins. He wasted no time on formalities.

"Tanith is resting now and heavily medicated. We don't want her upset unnecessarily, particularly until the medications have had time to work. She's disoriented, subject to sudden mood swings, and delusional. You wouldn't be able to trust anything she said, if she even made an effort to respond to questioning."

"We appreciate your concern and the fragile stability of her mind, but we still need to speak to her. We'll be as brief as possible and we'll try not to cause her any additional distress."

"I'm sorry. I can't allow it. This module belongs to the Mercator family trust and is therefore private property."

"The right to absolute privacy was superseded when you docked. By Concourse law, it became a part of the entity known as the *Helen of Troy,* and it is therefore subject to the authority of its captain, and will remain so until the connection is physically severed. I wouldn't recommend disengaging at the moment, since you don't have your own jump drive, but that's the only way that you can legally prevent us from entering."

Clout's face clouded and his body tensed, but after visibly regaining control of himself, he nodded curtly. "If that's the way it must be, then you'll have to come inside. I won't leave her alone with you, however, and if I feel that you're putting too great a strain on her, I will physically eject you, and deal with the captain afterwards."

Tanith Mercator was indeed in her cabin, in her bed in fact. Dyle didn't notice her immediately upon entering because he was disoriented by the furnishings. For one thing, her quarters were better described as a suite than as a cabin, much larger than those of Callista Dorne, for example. There were at least four rooms, sitting area, bedroom, luxurious private sanitary facilities, and a fourth which Dyle would have called a den, with its own console and self-contained data unit, a holoprojector, and other electronic gear. The bedroom proper was that of a pampered child. The bed was a four-poster with what appeared to be gauzy curtains but which were actually insubstantial projected images. Toy animals, stuffed, carved, cast, woven, thatched, sculpted, painted, and sketched, were arranged in ranks along shelves affixed to the hull walls and internal partitions. There were at least several hundred, no two alike, and all of the soft and cuddly persuasion, although Dyle recognized at least one that was actually a deceptively gentle-looking but formidable predator.

Tanith was propped up on a nest of pillows, obviously awake, but she didn't react when they entered the room, and she continued to stare into some private universe of her own. "Let me speak to her first," said Clout.

"Does she know about her father?" asked Dyle softly.

"She's been told, but that doesn't mean she knows it at any given time."

While Clout spoke softly to the young woman, Marym swept the walls with her eyes, her expression one of vague disapproval. "How do they ever expect her to grow up if they keep treating her like a child?" She asked the question softly enough that only Dyle could hear her, and he had no answer.

Clout turned toward them. "All right, ask your questions. I think she'll respond, but you're likely to get little more than gibberish."

Dyle waited for Marym to step forward, but she stayed where she was, so he walked around the corner of the bed to where Clout had been standing only a moment before. The big man had retreated into the near corner, arms folded over his chest, face set in an expression of mild reproach.

"Tanith, my name is Sandor Dyle. I would like to ask you a few questions if that's all right."

She didn't say anything, but her eyes moved to his face and stayed there, and he took that as assent.

"I need to ask you about the day you went off all by yourself. Do you know what I'm talking about?"

"My self like to be with me," she said brightly, suddenly smiling. "Do you like your self?"

He nodded. "I like myself just fine, and I like your self as well. But do you remember being out in the ship alone?"

"Father doesn't like it when I go away by myself. He was very angry with me," her face turned dour, then brightened. "But he's not mad at me now."

"No, I'm sure he isn't. Tell me, Tanith, when you were out walking in the ship, did you see your father at all?"

Tanith shook her head. "There were lots of new people to see. I liked seeing new people, for a little while, but then there were too many of them and they started to crowd into my head so I thought I'd just go away and rest and then I didn't know where I was and. . . ."

Her voice had started to rise toward panic and Dyle instinctively took her hand in his and squeezed it. "It's all right, Tanith. There aren't too many people now, are there?"

Her eyes moved around the room, as though she were counting heads. "No," she pouted.

"So there's no reason to be frightened or upset. No one's going to hurt you. Now tell me, can you remember seeing your father while you were watching the new people?"

"The green man hurt me."

"Who is the green man, Tanith?"

"That's an old memory," said Clout quietly, without changing position. "A policeman on Gardia tried to arrest her during one of her first escapes. Their uniforms are green. He bruised her arm pretty badly. She broke his wrist and his nose and left him curled in a ball moaning."

"She doesn't look capable of it," Marym commented.

"All of the children have had excellent training in self-defense. Magnus thought it best that they not be completely reliant on the help of others."

Dyle tried to sound as reassuring as possible. "The green man isn't on the ship, Tanith. You don't have to worry about him." He decided to try a different approach. "When was the last time you saw your father?"

"I see him all the time." Her eyes had started to wander. "I was just talking to him."

"Her time sense is affected by the medication," explained Clout. "Events get all jumbled up in her memory. Sometimes people too. She confuses Callista with Absinthe, me with her father or sometimes Morpheus."

Dyle was ready to admit that this was a waste of time. He glanced at Marym for inspiration. She said, "Ask her if she saw her father in the gardens."

Dyle repeated the question. There was a prolonged silence during which Tanith apparently became fascinated by the way she could interlace the fingers of her two hands, and Dyle was about to try once more when she finally answered. "Father said he would take me to the gardens but that I have to get better first because sometimes when I'm sick I do things that make other people unhappy and I wouldn't want to do something like that except that I do really want to see the gardens because Callista says they're so beautiful and I would like it if you would tell Father that he must take me there soon because I need to see them." Her voice rose steadily and grew almost shrill toward the end of the outburst. Clout came forward and she saw the movement and rolled over, burying her head in a pillow, her shoulders trembling as she began to sob.

"I think it's time for you to go." Clout's voice was hot with anger.

"Yes, I think you're right," admitted Dyle. "I apologize for the necessity of intruding."

* * * * *

Feykirk was waiting outside the capsule. "Captain Nicodemus sends her compliments and wondered if it would be possible to meet with her for lunch today in the wardroom at the end of first watch."

Dyle was surprised it had taken as long as it had for Nicodemus to grow impatient. "Please tell the captain that it would be our pleasure."

As soon as Feykirk was out of sight, Marym nudged his arm. "You know she's going to want a progress report, don't you?"

"Of course. And energetic and thorough as we may be, we don't have anything to tell her that she's going to want to hear."

"Should we mention Paragupta's extracurricular activities?"

"No, I don't think so. Not at this point anyway. She already knows about it, at least in general terms, and if we made an issue of the matter, she might feel that she was obligated to act officially. There's a strong sense of duty among most starship captains and there's a limit to how much they can rationalize away. We can supply enough detail to reassure her that we actually have been looking into the murder, but I don't think we can offer her much hope of catching the saboteur."

"Eco! I'd almost forgotten about that. Are we considering them separate investigations or parts of a whole?"

"They're interconnected, although we don't know how closely. If Eco hadn't been destroyed, the murder would probably not have taken place. The surveillance system would have reported the attack as soon as it happened, which might have saved Mercator's life, and in either case the killer would have been easily identified."

"With Eco out of the picture, the killer would still have to find an opportunity to catch his victim alone."

"Unless there was a second part of the plan which was scheduled to take place later, and Mercator's solitary visit to the gardens precipitated a spur-of-the-moment improvisation."

Marym shook her head wearily. "Or a second party might have found a target of opportunity and taken advantage of the situation. Mercator certainly wasn't short of enemies on the *Helen*."

"No, he wasn't. And our original speculation might be correct. The saboteur might have had some other crime in mind and the killing is just a distraction."

"So what do we tell Nicodemus?"

"The truth, that we have learned a lot but know very little. We wanted to talk to her in any case, and now is as good a time as any."

They had some time before they needed to start for the wardroom, so they returned to the lounge where each reviewed the notes they had accumulated during the past two days. Dyle had entered his into an elaborate logic array which Memnon was manipulating for him. There were patterns in the data, of course. Accumulate enough related information and trends will appear. But the interrelationships which emerged in this instance were inconclusive or irrelevant. Magnus Mercator was the center of it all, of course, but was there a single enemy, two working together, or perhaps separately toward the same or similar purposes?

"You know, there's one aspect of this case that we've neglected."

Dyle looked away from the console. "You mean the murder weapon?"

"There was nothing at the murder scene. The killer must have taken it away and disposed of it."

"It's not that easy to dispose of a bulky object aboard ship. Passengers don't have access to the airlocks or recycling, although I suppose if it was a crew member who's responsible, that doesn't apply. Or someone might have bribed one of the stewards, although that seems unlikely. I don't think our killer would take the chance."

"Is there an exterior airlock on Mercator's module? Other than the docking port, I mean."

"Damn! I never thought of that. There's almost certainly a jettison chamber somewhere aboard."

"So we may never be able to identify the murder weapon."

"Other than by implication, no. It had to be something portable, something that could be carried about without exciting too much comment. Pylandris caught my attention because of the odd-shaped parcel he was carrying, after all."

* * * * *

The meeting with Captain Nicodemus went better than expected, but since their expectations had been low to start with, that wasn't much of a consolation. The wardroom was in crew territory, not far from the bridge, a handsomely laid out room in which slightly more than a score people could dine comfortably. It was used almost exclusively by the bridge crew currently on duty, although theoretically all of the ship's officers were entitled to eat there. An elaborate buffet had been laid at one end, and it was being replenished when they arrived.

Captain Nicodemus was sitting in one corner, talking to a female officer wearing a technician's bars and an administrative tassel. The wardroom was almost always empty around the time of watch changes. The outgoing crew were going off duty and the incoming would be preoccupied with bringing their stations up to date and would not be eating for some time yet.

The young woman left, offering them a polite smile as she passed, and then they were taking seats opposite the captain of the *Helen*. She looked tired but not unhappy. Although she was undoubtedly impatient to hear what they had to tell her, little though it was, she made polite conversation while they assembled plates of food. There were several beverages as well, but no intoxicants.

"Any change in the ship's status, Captain?" asked Dyle.

"Nothing of great interest. We should reach Scrimshaw right on schedule. The exterior hull damage has been repaired. My chief engineer believes that the problem with the malfunctioning drive is not as significant as we originally thought, so our layover there may well be considerably shorter than expected. We've had less luck augmenting Memnon, I'm afraid. Too many of the feeds are incompatible; we can adapt some but the technology is so sophisticated that it would be quicker to tear out the new circuits and replace them entirely, and we obviously don't have the resources to do that. We've reestablished surveillance at key points, but that only provides coverage of about ten percent of the common areas, and virtually none in crew territory. Other services are being restored where possible. Communication with Stores is completely operational and Medical and Security have just about all of their resources back."

"It sounds as though your crew has been busy," said Dyle. "So have we, as you probably know. Unfortunately, I can't pretend that we've been equally productive."

"I know you're doing your best under difficult circumstances," she replied. Dyle imagined that her voice carried a hint of chill, but it might have been his imagination. "I've made a realistic assessment of your situation and I don't expect miracles."

She might not expect a miracle, but she clearly hoped to hear that they'd come up with one. Dyle regretted the necessity of disappointing her. "Since it was obviously impractical to attempt to question everyone aboard, we confined our efforts to people with whom Mercator had more than casual personal contact since joining the *Helen*. That includes all of the members of his private party, at least two crew members, and some of the other passengers with whom he had had business relationships."

"My name should have been on that list."

Dyle nodded. "It is, Captain. We were hoping that information might flow both ways during this meeting."

She didn't seem at all offended. "I'm at your service, but I'd prefer that you summarize what you've found out first."

Dyle did exactly that, using his eidetic memory to provide exact quotes when necessary. He left out many of the details, as well as all mention of the children concealed in the Stores area, and most of their speculation about possible motives. "The physical evidence is limited, we don't have any useful surveillance records, the murder weapon is missing and possibly has been destroyed or removed from the ship. Almost everyone we've talked to had the opportunity to kill Mercator. Most have obvious reasons for wishing him harm, and those that don't may have hidden ones."

"Do you think further investigation will improve your chances of reaching a solution?"

"The more information we have, the more likely we are to perceive its underlying structure." He hesitated. "But frankly I'm not confident that we'll cross the threshold of discovery. If our killer acts again, it would improve our chances immensely, but if he or she simply waits patiently and inactively until we reach our destination, then there's a good chance we'll never find out who was responsible."

"Well, I don't know what information I can possibly provide, but ask your questions." If Nicodemus was disappointed by his pessimistic forecast, she gave no indication.

Marym had insisted that Dyle would be better suited for this part of the interview. "She's spent most of her life working in a formal hierarchy of authority. You'll have the advantage with her because she recognizes your reputation. All she knows about me is what you've told her."

"Had you ever met Magnus Mercator prior to his boarding the *Helen*?"

"No. We had communicated extensively, but it was never in person or visual. I learned of his role as chief investor some time ago, but hadn't realized how active a part he would play until quite recently. We only received word that he'd be coming along two days before departure." She sounded mildly annoyed. "We had to completely reconfigure the drive patterns. Mass didn't affect them as much as the change in exterior surface area, and Mercator insisted on adding his private module even though we'd passed the theoretical deadline for such modifications."

"Did he ever explain why his plans changed so suddenly?"

"I don't think they had. During subsequent conversations, he implied that he had planned this well in advance, but that he'd delayed notifying me for security reasons."

"Then you had reason to believe he was in some danger?"

"Given his past, Mercator was always in danger. I was irritated by the inconvenience his precautions caused my crew, but they were probably wise. Not wise enough, as it turned out."

"How often did you meet with Mercator?"

She paused thoughtfully. "I was too busy to meet him when he first came aboard, but I paid a courtesy visit just before departure. It only lasted a short while and nothing of significance occurred. We took a brief tour through crew territory. That was the first time we'd met in the flesh. You were present at our second encounter, the First Jump supper. I spoke to him briefly in person shortly after Eco was destroyed, and again a short while later to let him know I was employing your services to investigate the incident. I believe those are the only direct interactions I've had with him since Linnisfarne."

"It's fair to say you weren't on good terms, is it not?"

"Mercator was unhappy with the projected profitability of the *Helen*. I could sympathize with his situation and supported most of his cost-cutting proposals. Some of them affected the safety of the ship. I protested these and offered alternatives in some cases, but once he'd made a decision, it was almost impossible to change his mind. Eventually I told him that I would have to make my reservations and protests a part of the ship's official record. He was displeased with my decision. When the time came to confirm my long-term contract, I was informed that my services would not be required after we reached Pradesh."

"Did you ever receive an explanation?"

"No. Nor did I ask for one. The reasons seemed to me to be quite obvious."

"I apologize for the way this must sound, Captain, but you must have resented the situation."

"I felt some degree of contempt for Magnus Mercator, but I wasn't particularly angry. At worst I'd be mildly inconvenienced. With my record, I'll have another ship very quickly. It won't be as impressive and prestigious as the *Helen,* but I can wait for a good posting. And the severance package was quite generous. My original contract was negotiated before Mercator bought a controlling interest. I had good reason to dislike the man, but not nearly enough to kill him."

Dyle felt the urge to apologize but suppressed it. If he was going to fail, then he would fail, but not because he wasn't thorough. "We have to consider the probability that the murder was committed by the same person who disrupted the surveillance system and made it possible. If Eco was destroyed specifically to facilitate this more-serious crime, then the individual responsible had access to sensitive areas of the ship, or was working with someone who had it. On the face of it, there appears to be no way in which you or any of the other authorized individuals could be directly responsible unless you had passed the information on to someone else."

"Unless Mercator himself was the source of the leak, through someone in his family perhaps." The captain had obviously been giving the matter some thought herself.

"Which is why we have concentrated on the members of his party."

"But you have no proof of a link?"

He shook his head. "Mercator's death could just as easily be a crime of opportunity, in which case we still don't know the motive for the sabotage."

"We just don't have the resources to conduct an investigation properly," added Marym. "With the proper facilities, we could have interviewed a much larger number of people, potentially everyone aboard. No one person would likely be of much help, but the cumulative effect of their observations, particularly if we had caught them fresh, should have allowed us to eliminate at least some of the high-priority suspects, even if it didn't point directly to the killer."

"And if Memnon's inputs were compatible, we could have patched him into the surveillance circuitry," Nicodemus answered with a hint of impatience. "We're all working with inadequate tools and I can't expect you to perform miracles any more than I can expect it of my crew. So I'll ask the question again. Do you feel there is any point in continuing as you have been, or should we just hope that the authorities on Scrimshaw will be willing and able to help?"

"I'm not ready to abandon all hope," said Dyle. "So long as you understand that the odds are not in our favor."

"Understood. You have my authorization to continue for as long as it seems worthwhile."

* * * * *

Dyle felt mildly depressed afterward. He was not a storybook detective who always solved the crime in the final chapter. His successes outnumbered his failures, and there were a few of them of which he was particularly proud, but also some for which he felt considerable regret. He'd been unable to solve the brutal murder of Leslie Yulager on Demosthenes, failed to locate the missing artifacts on Widdershins, and his identification of the kidnappers of Crown Prince Dooly of Lustermount had come too late to save the child's life. Realistically he knew that he had human limitations, and that in this particular case he was effectively deprived of his most useful tool, data. Nor did he feel that the death of Magnus Mercator was a tragic loss to the civilized galaxy that cried out for vengeance. Given the man's background, it was surprising that it had taken this long for his past to catch up to him. With so many suspects, none of whom had alibis, and virtually no physical evidence, there was a good chance the killer might escape even if more sophisticated investigative tools were available. Crimes of opportunity were either very easy to solve, because the criminal lacked time to consider the circumstances of the act, or very difficult, because there was no preparation, no planning, nothing that might be detected after the fact through careful analysis.

Dyle had been dubious about their chances of catching the killer from the outset, but he had been more optimistic with regard to the sabotage. The circle of suspects was much smaller, and by necessity the act must have been planned in detail beforehand. It was the kind of puzzle he should be able to solve and the fact that he couldn't, that he didn't even have a useful line of inquiry, bothered him immensely. It was still early when he asked Marym if she'd excuse him.

"I'm feeling tired and wrung out. I think I'll just try to put everything out of my mind for a while and get some actual rest."

Marym expressed polite sympathy. "My nerves are on edge too. I think I'll walk a bit and possibly even indulge in an intoxicant."

Dyle doubted that she had an edgy nerve in her body, but on the other hand, he wasn't really planning to set the case aside. He just needed to play with it in his own way for a while.

He lay on his bed in the dark, fully clothed, hands clasped behind his head as he stared up at the ceiling he could not see. He imagined himself in a holographic theater with the *Helen* as the set, and very slowly began to play everything back, from the moment he first came aboard to the moment he left Marym walking along the Promenade. Whenever an event seemed significant, or even curious, he paused the replay and re-examined the scene from different viewpoints, concentrating on the inconsequential details which so often turned out to be consequential after all.

He reconstructed as much as he could of the conversations that had taken place at the First Jump dinner party, and the additional observations Marym had made afterward, this time against a background of the more detailed experience he'd had with the participants since then. Then came the sabotage, and there was a hint of something there, but nothing he could identify. He made a mental note to talk to the civilian consultant, Tharmody, then moved on to the first encounter with Idrian Caserta and Sondra Wong, the casual meeting with Abraham Baxter, and the events surrounding Mercator's death, including the discovery of the blood stain in Memnon's chamber and the discovery that Mercator had been spying on Cosmo Paragupta. He tried to imagine himself in the place of each of the participants, recreating what they might have seen, or even done.

It was late by then and he should have been genuinely fatigued now, but something had begun to stir at the back of his mind. He knew better than to concentrate on it, try to force inspiration. Best to continue as he had been and let whatever it was percolate until it was ready to spill over. So he painstakingly reviewed each of the interviews, relying on his memory rather than his notes. He had learned in the past that what he recorded was only a part of what happened, and that if he concentrated on his notes, they would shape and contain his thought processes and prevent him from seeing what might have escaped his attention previously.

When he had exhausted his memory, he sat up, tapped the manual light control, and briefly studied the hard copy of the ship's layout that he had requested. He toggled it back and forth from flat to holographic, then shook his head and set it aside. Whatever germ of an idea might have planted itself in his brain was not responding. Disappointed but not discouraged, he killed the lights and returned to bed, this time intending to finally seek the solace of unconsciousness, but his head had barely touched the pillow when he sat up in the darkness, tense with excitement.

"Of course," he whispered aloud, nodding with satisfaction. He didn't have the solution, not yet, but he'd experienced an epiphany. It was not surprising at all that they'd made so little headway. They were investigating the wrong crime!

He lay back down, dropping off to sleep almost instantly this time, smiling slightly at the reaction he expected to see when he told Marym what he'd realized.

Chapter Fourteen

Sandor Dyle had experienced a number of disappointments in his life, some big, some small. He resented a few and regretted them all, but few as acutely as when he met Marym Dunnis for breakfast, prepared to stun her with his acumen, only to discover that she'd come to almost exactly the same conclusion during the night. They had both examined the same evidence and had been similarly misled, and it was only when they had realized they were getting nowhere that they were able to relinquish their preconceptions, stand back and take a fresh look at what they knew, and what they thought they knew.

"It seems obvious now, of course," said Dyle.

"Hindsight always casts things in a simpler light. But now that we've unraveled the first layer, where does that leave us?"

"Well, for one thing, I have to retract my earlier assertion that motive is irrelevant."

"But that doesn't help us unless we can figure out what the real motive is."

"At least we have a whole set of new questions to ask."

Feykirk was waiting as usual when they reached their lounge, so Dyle dispatched her to track down Dona Tharmody and schedule an interview for later in the day. They started planning their next move as soon as she was gone, but only a few moments passed before they had an unexpected visitor. It was Gavin Pritchard.

He was obviously uncomfortable and ready to bolt at the least excuse, but Marym handled him delicately, got him to come inside and take a seat. She sat next to him rather than across the table and asked how the work on the ship's systems was progressing. Pritchard was soothed by talk of neutral, familiar topics and slowly relaxed, glancing nervously at Dyle, who remained silent and did his best to appear as innocuous as possible. He was in fact growing impatient with the pointless banter and was considering asking a direct question when Pritchard changed the topic without prompting.

"I need to know whether or not what I say here will be kept in confidence."

"That depends. We're not interested in petty scandals or minor infractions of ship's policy." Marym smiled warmly though no doubt insincerely. "If you have something to tell us that's pertinent to either the murder or the earlier damage to the ship's facilities, we need to know but we can't promise complete confidentiality. If there's no compelling reason to pass that information on, it will remain our secret."

"I don't think it's important, but I thought if you heard it from another party, you might misinterpret what happened." Marym nodded to show she understood, but didn't reply. Pritchard gave Dyle another nervous glance, then plunged into it, speaking so quickly and quietly that it was difficult to follow him. "I used my access to give Absinthe Mercator a tour of some restricted portions of the ship, including Eco's chamber. It was a few hours before the explosion. We were only there for a little while and I was watching her all the time. There's no possible way that she could have been responsible for what happened afterward and I promised her that I wouldn't tell anyone, but I was afraid that if you found out somehow, you might think I was hiding something more than just a foolish impulse."

"You never left her alone?" Marym decided it was best not to let on that she had already heard some of the more intimate details of his breach of discipline.

"No, absolutely not."

"Is there any way that she could have used your access code herself?"

Pritchard shook his head energetically. "Not possible. The codes are specific to individuals, except for the master access and only the captain and the owners know that."

"Did any part of your tour involve the maintenance area?"

Now that he'd said the worst, Pritchard seemed almost to relax. "Only peripherally. I mean, we went through part of maintenance to reach Eco, but that was the extent of it."

"Did she ask you anything about the maintenance robots, or did you volunteer anything about them?"

"No. It wasn't the kind of thing she seemed to find interesting."

"But she was interested in Eco?"

Pritchard shifted in his chair and Dyle knew that he was about to become evasive. "Not exactly. I think she only wanted to be there because her father had told her she couldn't. A lot of what she did was designed to make him angry. She, uh, she mentioned a few other incidents. Apparently his man, Clout, was supposed to be keeping an eye on her, among his other duties. Prevent her from embarrassing the Mercator name, though it's hard to imagine she could have done anything more controversial than her father's career."

"It sounds like he wasn't too good at his job."

Pritchard had the grace to blush. "She implied that he wasn't entirely unsympathetic to her cause. I gather there was some sort of arrangement between the two of them."

"I think we can guess their nature. Do you think she had turned Clout against his master?"

"We were not well enough acquainted to exchange confidences at that level." His expression soured slightly. "On the other hand, I have some doubts that she was entirely honest with me. We parted company amicably but she left me with the distinct impression that she had no interest in pursuing our acquaintance."

"So you were never alone with her again?"

"I've never even spoken to her since that day."

"Well, thank you for coming forward with this. I imagine it might be a good idea if you were less casual about obeying regulations in the future, even if you are trying to entertain the daughter of the majority owner, but I don't presently see any reason why this conversation would need to be repeated outside this room."

Pritchard hastily got to his feet, welcoming the dismissal. "It was a very uncharacteristic lapse," he replied quickly. "An impulse soon regretted. Thank you both for your understanding." And then he hastened away without a backward glance.

Dyle waited until he was out of sight before speaking. "Well, if we needed further evidence in support of our theory, that provided at least some of it."

"If Clout was involved with the daughter behind Mercator's back, it could certainly have caused trouble between the two of them, if they were caught at it."

"I imagine it would be quite difficult to keep a secret in that household. Even if Absinthe was capable of remaining silent, which I very much doubt, Mercator would have some clandestine method of finding out what his children were doing when they weren't within sight. He may even have played them off against one another."

"Do we gain anything by revealing what we surmise?"

"Let's not force the issue just yet, at least not publicly. We can only play that card once and I'd hate to waste it. If we're right, it won't make matters worse if we hold our peace for the time being, and a premature revelation might lead to yet another tragedy."

"Does this mean that our two crimes are not connected?"

"Not necessarily. Magnus almost certainly knew, or at least could have known, all of the necessary access codes."

"Would he damage his own property that way?"

"If the desired end was important enough to him, of course he would. He sacrificed the lives of many of his loyal followers on Cathanor in pursuit of what he considered worthy goals."

Feykirk returned then, with news that she'd taken the liberty of arranging for them to meet with Tharmody over a light lunch. "I can have it delivered here, or if you prefer, arrangements for a private meeting could be made elsewhere."

Dyle was in such a good mood that Feykirk's perpetual perkiness didn't grate on his nerves as it had in the past. "Here is just fine, Feykirk. And please order for yourself as well. Our conversation with Dona Tharmody will not be confidential and you deserve some small reward for running around for us."

"It's been a pleasure, Ser Dyle. I'd be standing watch at some quiet corridor junction or snaking new circuitry tape through the hull otherwise."

"Then we'll certainly require your services for a bit longer."

Feykirk returned to her post outside the lounge while Dyle played with his data array, examining the results when he changed a few minor and then one of the major assumptions upon which it was based. When he asked Memnon to calculate the probability of guilt of each of the major suspects, the results were in exactly the order of likelihood that he had expected, but the gap between the first choice and the rest of the names was even larger than anticipated.

He was about to describe the results to Marym, who was intent upon the notes in her datapad, when Feykirk stepped through the privacy screen in the doorway. "Excuse the interruption, but one of the other stewards just brought some news that I thought you might want to know right away. One of the passengers has been found dead. His name is Idrian Caserta."

* * * * *

Caserta was indeed dead, though not by foul play. Sondra Wong had raised the alarm when he didn't show up for breakfast and didn't respond to her efforts to rouse him. He had died in his sleep, and the chief medicator's initial diagnosis was heart failure. "He'd been patched and restored and augmented so many times that there probably wasn't any single cause, just an overall lessening of vigor that eventually dropped below the minimum required for life." He would not venture an opinion as to whether or not Caserta could have been saved if the life-signs monitor in his cabin had still been working. "It's possible that the immediate crisis could have been averted, but the end was inevitable, and near."

Sondra Wong was sitting in an anteroom in the medical section, somehow looking smaller than she had in the past. She sat motionless, head down, expression neutral, her artificial hand lying in her lap, the real one tangled in her hair. Marym and Dyle both offered their sympathies for her loss.

"It came a little quicker than we expected, but Idrian knew it wouldn't be much longer. We had hoped for at least a few months." Her voice was a monotone, devoid of emotion.

Dyle wondered what effect this might have on the merger, but it was clearly not a good time to ask. "What will you do now?"

"Take him home. He has no surviving family, but his friends will want to see him off." She dropped her hand and shook her head as though to rouse herself. "At least he got what he wanted before he died. Maybe the need to do that was the only thing holding him together."

Since she had raised the subject, Dyle thought he might probe gently. "Will this affect the arrangement with the Mercators?"

"Well, he won't be sitting on the board. Mercator would have had that in a year or so anyway."

"What will you do?" asked Marym. "Personally, I mean."

Wong stood up before answering, possibly to give herself time to construct an answer. "I haven't thought that far ahead. There have only been two things in my life that I've ever cared about strongly, and my obligations to both have ended during the past few days. Or will end once I've seen to the last of Idrian's wishes." She glanced up suddenly, as though seeing them for the first time, then rose to her feet. "If it's not rude of me, I think I'd like to be alone with him for a while."

They watched her go inside, then turned away.

* * * * *

Dona Tharmody arrived promptly, obviously curious about why she'd been summoned. Marym had asked Dyle what he expected to learn from her, since they had no reason to consider the consultant a suspect, and he had been forced to admit that he didn't have a firm idea himself. "Sometimes there's just enough of a pattern that one element seems out of place or significant in some way. She did have access to Eco, after all, and she's an outsider, hired through the influence of the consortium. Pritchard hadn't met her before she came aboard, nor had anyone else in the crew."

"And even if she's not the mind behind everything else, she might be an accomplice?"

He nodded. "She understands artificial personalities better than anyone else on board. Given the right access code, she would have had no difficulty redirecting the maintenance robot, and she already had intimate knowledge of the layout and safeguards in Eco's chamber."

"So someone might have paid her to disable Eco, with or without explaining that it was designed to mask a second, more deadly crime."

"It's possible."

She seemed an unlikely criminal now, however, as she draped herself casually in one chair, lifting her legs onto a second and crossing them at the ankles, nibbling at the meat-filled pastries that Feykirk had provided along with beverages, a large vegetable platter, and a variety of desserts. "Sorry, but I've been on my feet all morning and they ache. I've been pressed into duty tracing circuitry wires since there's not a lot I can do with Memnon."

"He's less sophisticated than Eco, I take it." Dyle was seated opposite her while Marym reversed her usual role and moved restlessly around the room.

"Well, yes, but that's not the issue. Memnon is set in his ways, quite literally. His personality was adjusted during his first few flights and then locked down once the staff was satisfied that he was at close to optimal."

"I thought the whole point of installing Eco was to improve the interface."

"Pretty much. Eco could discriminate in finer increments. In gross terms, Memnon's responses are limited to yes, no, and maybe. Eco added probably yes and probably no."

"You've done this sort of thing before?"

"Not on a starship, but yes, I've done quite a few planetary installations. You would think that the solution in one case would apply to others that are similar, but that's only true to a limited extent. You might have three identical AP's and install them in a government complex, one to oversee family development and welfare, one to administer the criminal-justice system, and one to administer offworld trade relations. The core personalities might be identical, but the data in their memory would be different, specialized to serve their designated purpose, and the divergence would grow greater with the passage of time. The first example might eventually become either more sympathetic or more callous, depending upon the sensitivity settings of the core program, the second more autocratic, and the last more sophisticated and prone to a wider variety of responses."

"You make them sound like people."

She nodded. "They react that way, but they're not people. They aren't self-aware, no matter how realistic they seem. The core programs are set to react as a human would, and most of the time they do. But we can't anticipate every possible situation, and once in a while they'll respond in a way that is totally inappropriate, because they've followed a train of flawed logic to an absurd conclusion."

"I've known people to do that as well."

She laughed. "Good point. But people expect a higher standard of efficiency from machines than they do from one another. It's rather sad, isn't it?"

"Tell me, had you ever met any of the Mercators before you joined the *Helen*?"

"No, definitely not. They're a memorable lot."

"Had you ever worked for them?"

She shrugged. "Not that I know of, but that doesn't mean anything. I've worked for at least a couple of dozen private firms. Mercator could have owned any or all of them without my knowledge."

"Is there anyone else aboard whom you'd met previously?"

"I'd met Gavin Pritchard once or twice, but only casually. And I once worked for Senator Baxter."

"You worked for Abraham?"

"Sure. His office AP is named Cecilia, and she's a nice old girl. Uses his grandmother's voice and speech patterns. I don't think he remembered me though. We hardly exchanged a word at First Jump and I haven't seen him since."

"Was Eco really as advanced as Pritchard implied?"

She pushed one cheek out with her tongue in an exaggerated expression of deep thought. "Yes and no. The technology isn't new or radical, just more complex."

"But she was expensive to install."

"Yes, although it was the initial development that really ate into the credits. Fortunately, she's backed up on Linnisfarne, and I think elsewhere. We've lost all of my tinkering, which is a great tragedy, but my salary isn't so high that the accounting programs will cry foul."

"How about the physical installation? That's obviously a complete loss."

"Eco's core is gone, all right. But the big installation expense was running new circuitry wire through the hull and installing all of the microcameras and vodal nexi so that she could see, hear, and speak. None of that was damaged by the explosion. A few of the interfaces were fused or shorted, but a new version of Eco could be up and running very quickly. We're lucky that no one decided to rip out Memnon's existing connections. The *Helen* was only dysfunctional for a microsecond before he automatically began assuming control. There were some minor delays restoring certain of his functions because of the way they'd be reconfigured, but he was fully operational very quickly."

"Is there any way, in your opinion, that Eco's security could have been compromised?"

"Without the access codes? No, impossible. I mean, sure, if you used a boomer to blow up the airlock, you could have entered the chamber and done whatever you wanted. But she would not have opened the door for an unauthorized person unless that individual was accompanied by someone who did have authority. And before you ask, she would have scanned for any visible sign of duress even in that situation."

"There were only seven people on the access list?"

"That's correct. And each of them had an individual code that was linked to their personal image. There's also a master code, but none of us have that, except Gavin and maybe the captain. I've never asked."

"So no one could have used another person's code?"

She squirmed in her seat. "Not exactly. Anyone with a code could have instructed Eco that another party was entitled to use their code on a limited basis. They would have access physically but that's about it. The only time we use it is when we have physical maintenance done, so that we don't have to keep an authorized person with the work crews."

"And all of these codes were known back on Linnisfarne. Suppose, for the sake of argument, that someone acquired that information and subsequently came aboard. How would Eco respond if that individual demanded access?"

"Well, first of all, there are levels of access assigned to each code so it would depend on which one was invoked. The lowest would require confirmation from one of the seven already known to her, and that would be the preferable choice to what we call loaning out our own codes. The highest would, well, would let this theoretical newcomer do anything, even change or remove access from everyone except Captain Nicodemus."

"And how would I be identified if I had stolen the information? How would Eco know who I was? Could I give a false name?"

"There's a retinal scanner in the chamber. You'd have to use that if you wanted to alter the access list. If you just wanted personal access for yourself, you'd be matched visually against the passenger list or crew lists. Eco has very sophisticated optical recognition techniques. Her microcameras can pick up your fingerprints and retinal patterns and match them."

"So she wouldn't just take my word if I told her my name?"

"No, neither would Memnon for that matter. It would be an enormous security gap." She shrugged. "But if you had previously corrupted the information in her recognition system so that she thought you were genuine, you'd be accepted. No system is completely foolproof."

"You mentioned that the captain is exempt?"

"Deference to the ship's captain is hard coded. Technically, she doesn't even need to be on the access list, but if she wasn't it would introduce additional strains into Eco's judgment circuits."

"All right, say I came aboard, used the highest-level access code, spent some time in Eco's chamber, then told her to forget I'd been there. Would it work?"

"It would depend to some extent on how you phrased the instruction, but yes, you'd have the authority to permanently erase your visit from her memory."

"Records of access to Eco were immediately replicated to Memnon as a security precaution, were they not?"

Her eyes widened. "Yes, they are."

"Would an instruction to Eco to erase her memories have been passed on to Memnon?"

"No! Not unless Memnon were given the same instructions. He and Eco are, or were, two distinct personalities."

Dyle nodded to himself. "Thank you very much for coming by, Ser Tharmody. You have been quite helpful."

She stood up, nodded to Marym, and started for the door. Dyle pursed his lips. "Wait!"

She turned to look back at him.

"You were about to go to Memnon and ask him about Eco's visitors, weren't you?"

Tharmody smiled at him. "The thought had occurred to me."

"Well, you might as well stay and we'll ask him together. You might notice something we'd overlook." He glanced toward the console even though it was unnecessary. "Memnon, which individuals whose names are not on the formal access list entered Eco's chamber after we left Linnisfarne but before the explosion?"

"Passenger Magnus Mercator. Passenger Absinthe Mercator. Passenger Augustus Clout."

"We already knew that," said Marym. "Magnus and Clout went with the captain, and Absinthe was there with Pritchard." Tharmody twitched and gave her an amused look.

Dyle nodded to himself. "Memnon, did any of those three individuals ever enter Eco's chamber alone?"

"Yes. Augustus Clout accessed Eco at her source on two occasions."

"When?"

Both visits were within the first few hours of their departure. "What was the nature of the interaction between Eco and Augustus Clout on these two occasions?"

"That information is unavailable. The data resided in Eco's memory and was not replicated within my system."

"Memnon had enough capacity to replicate more information," explained Tharmody, "but we were being very cautious about their interface. This is the first time, to our knowledge anyway, that two AP's were functioning simultaneously on the same ship."

"Don't other starships have backup systems?" asked Marym.

"Yes, it's called the crew. Not entirely, of course. There are passive automatic safeguards, particularly in life support, propulsion, and navigation. If Memnon failed right now, we'd still have a good chance of reaching Scrimshaw safely. It would be prohibitively expensive to install two parallel systems, but Memnon was already here, and there was ample room for Eco's more compact circuitry."

Dyle turned immediately to Tharmody. "I trust that you will not repeat anything you have heard here, at least until an appropriate time."

She nodded assent. "You have my word on it. But I hope that eventually someone will tell me what's been going on."

"We hope the same," he admitted.

As soon as she was gone, Dyle called in Feykirk and told her what he wanted. For the first time, she sketched a frown.

"I'll have to clear that with Captain Nicodemus, Ser Dyle."

He nodded understandingly. "Tell her that I think it's necessary."

The steward still looked uncomfortable. "She will want to know if there is any danger to the ship."

"No, but it's possible that we're finally getting close to the truth, and someone doesn't want us to know what has really happened aboard the *Helen*."

"I'll speak to her immediately." Feykirk took the communicator from her belt and spoke into it, frowning. "She's outside inspecting the hull repairs. I'll have to use an external communicator to contact her." Dyle nodded his understanding and watched her disappear, then waited patiently for her to return.

Feykirk's mission was apparently successful because she was back before they had finished sampling the desserts, carrying two small objects, one for each of them. Dyle made his vanish into the inner pocket of his vest, while Marym concealed hers somewhere within the baggy folds of her pantaloons.

"Now what?" asked Marym.

"I can't see any reason to delay. If we're right, it is unlikely but not impossible that there is any further serious danger, but there's still the possibility, however remote, that we've been fooled by yet another layer of deception. I think it's time to confront the source of our problem directly and see where that leads us."

"Very well then." She turned to Feykirk. "Would you please ask Augustus Clout if he could join us here."

Feykirk still looked vaguely troubled, but she nodded and turned away with most of her usual enthusiasm.

Feykirk returned alone, looking apologetic and somewhat cowed. She'd had some difficulty locating Ser Clout, she explained, because no one in his party knew where he had gone, or at least admitted to such knowledge. Security had no reason to keep track of him, but she'd tried there anyway and finally had a bit of luck, because someone mentioned that Clout was spending a good deal of his time in the fitness center. Sure enough, he'd been exercising and was not happy about the interruption. He had grudgingly agreed to answer the summons, but not until he had finished his routine. Dyle expressed his sympathy to Feykirk, who looked only slightly cheered. He suspected that the response to her intrusion had been considerably more unpleasant than she'd reported.

They waited in relative silence, lost in their individual thoughts. Dyle was convinced that he had pierced the outer layer of the puzzle, but there was a second, tougher skin lying inside. He was concerned that they might be playing their most powerful card prematurely, but on the other hand, if they held it too long, it might prove less effective.

Clout appeared eventually, swathed in a voluminous robe, his face betraying obvious irritation. He marched around the table and dropped into the chair, leaning forward in what was an obvious effort to make the room his territory rather than theirs.

"Now what's this all about?"

"We're still pursuing our inquiry into the unfortunate incident in the ship's gardens. Now that the immediate stress has passed and you've had time to reflect, we thought you might have remembered something else. You did, after all, discover the body."

"I answered all of your questions, and my recollections are not affected by stress."

"Then you still insist that you saw no one else in the vicinity of the body."

"I can't tell you anything more concerning the death of Magnus Mercator."

"No, I don't imagine you can. Would you tell us then the purpose of your two solitary visits to Eco before she was destroyed?"

For the first time, Clout seemed shaken. It was only a momentary thing, an uncertainty in the eyes, a tightening of the jaw, but Dyle saw it clearly.

"What makes you think I did any such thing? I'm not on the access list. I was there with the captain and with Magnus once, if that's what you mean."

"As a security precaution, all direct access to Eco's core was replicated in Memnon's memory."

Clout digested that, and the faint traces of alarm slowly faded. "All right, yes I had access to Eco. Magnus gave it to me so that I could conduct some confidential work for him."

"What kind of work?"

"As I said, it was confidential."

"Isn't your obligation negated by his death?"

"I work for the family, the trust. My duties have not changed, even under these circumstances."

"I see. What if we asked Absinthe Mercator to release you from your oath of confidentiality? Would that soothe your conscience?" It was a bluff, but if he was called on it, he'd carry through on the off chance that she'd cooperate.

Clout must have been considering the same possibility. "You're obligated to report your findings to the captain, aren't you?"

Dyle relaxed invisibly, knowing that he'd won the point. Marym answered Clout's question. "In general terms, yes, but only information which proves relevant to our investigation. There have been other confidences which we've respected, as we will respect yours if that's possible."

"I was implementing a procedure designed to alter a single element of hardwired programming. The technique is complicated and would have required at least two more sessions to complete. It would not have affected the safety of the ship in any way."

He fell silent, but Marym pushed. "We have to know what it was, I'm afraid."

"I was removing the component which made it impossible to delete Captain Nicodemus from the access list."

That caught them both by surprise, but Dyle recovered first. "Why would that be necessary? Was there reason to believe that the captain had or might act in a manner that would justify her removal?"

"She was rigid and uncooperative and had already been told that her services would no longer be required once we reached Pradesh. It was just a precaution. Magnus only lived as long as he did because he believed in precautions, even those you might consider unnecessary."

"Yes, we're quite ready to believe in his survival instinct."

"Well, it failed him at the last."

Dyle shook his head. "That's not true, actually. You see, all three of us in this room know that Magnus Mercator is very much alive."

Chapter Fifteen

"I very much doubt that the chief medicator would agree with your diagnosis," said their companion drily.

"Oh, the man you found in the gardens was dead all right, but he wasn't Magnus Mercator. You are. I imagine his real name was Augustus Clout, unless that was just another clever blind."

There was a prolonged silence during which they could almost hear the other man think, at the end of which he sat back, looking almost relaxed for the first time since they'd met him. "All right, you've found me out. What gave me away? I thought we had the act worked out pretty well."

"You had us fooled," said Dyle, hoping to play up to the man's ego. "If it hadn't been for the murder, we would never have looked at the two of you so closely. That's when the anomalies started to crop up. You always seemed slightly more assertive and knowledgeable than Clout, even at the First Jump dinner, not at all like a subordinate. We wondered at the time if the legendary Magnus Mercator hadn't lost his edge at last."

"Gus was usually much more in control. He'd been drinking Cyranos earlier. I spoke to him about it afterwards."

"He also displayed visible interest in one of your daughters. I confess that we interpreted that as a worse sin than it was."

"Absinthe, no doubt. She makes a point of seducing all of my key employees. She even attempted to entice Callista into her bed. I know she'd been involved with him in the past, but I wasn't expecting a return engagement. She grows bored so easily."

"There were other things that suggested a substitution sooner. There was that cut on his arm, for example. He let it go without treatment for several hours. Your profile suggested that you would not have delayed any longer than is necessary."

"A failing, I admit. I take disproportionate pride in my body, I suppose, but of all my possessions, it's the only one that I can neither replace nor do without."

"The strongest clue was the depilatory, although I confess it didn't occur to me until long after I'd noticed it. It made sense for Magnus Mercator to have lost his body hair; it's a common side effect of regeneration therapy. But it made less sense for you to be removing your legendary shock of hair voluntarily, less sense than for your bodyguard to be using it to emphasize the resemblance between the two of you, or to further a masquerade."

Mercator ran one hand over his bald crown. "I do miss it, but it was a necessary sacrifice. I stay out of public view as much as possible, but enough people knew about my baldness to make it necessary for Gus to follow suit, at least temporarily."

"There were other clues. The accounts of the initial search for Tanith were contradictory about your movements. The members of your party all know the truth, obviously, but they're not as well disciplined about it as Clout was, and under stress they occasionally forgot who was supposed to be who. When we asked Absinthe how long Clout had worked for you, she hesitated, then provided information that contradicted what we'd heard elsewhere. That should have clinched matters, but Absinthe apparently lies even when it's unnecessary, so there was still a degree of uncertainty. Then Tanith mentioned seeing her father after his supposed death, and while it was entirely possible that she was delusional, your insistence on that point was suspect. It was also rather surprising how quickly the terms of your arrangement with Idrian Caserta were confirmed following the supposed death of the principal negotiator and owner, although that didn't strike us as significant until we'd had time to sit back and sift through what we knew and realize the truth."

"Poor Idrian. I did actually feel considerable sympathy for the man, you know. He handicapped himself with all manner of restrictions on the way he pursued his business, but still built himself an efficient and profitable enterprise. He would have continued to flourish if it hadn't been for circumstances beyond his control. What I knew and he didn't was that the Tenebrian War will be over soon. There are secret treaty talks underway already. Trade routes there will be particularly lucrative during the reconstruction."

"So Caserta would have been able to survive even without the influx of credit from your merger offer?"

"Probably, but he was a dying man and the effort might have been beyond him. I offered him a fair deal, Ser Dyle. I took advantage but I didn't cheat him." For just a moment, Mercator appeared uneasy. "Can I rely on the two of you to keep my identity to yourselves, at least until we reach Scrimshaw? I'd prefer not to have a repeat performance, with the right target this time."

Dyle hesitated. "I'm not sure if that's going to be possible. There are, you realize, very good reasons why we must suspect your involvement in the death of Clout. And I do think you would be wise to take Captain Nicodemus into your confidence regardless of the circumstances."

He shook his head. "I can't confide in her yet. Oh, I don't think she's a threat and she's certainly discreet, but she has enough difficulties to deal with at the moment without yet another distraction. And I didn't kill Clout. I give you my word that he was dead when I found him, just as I described. Nor did I arrange to have him killed by a third party."

Dyle ignored the latter comment. "Nicodemus seems both capable and discreet."

"I've never doubted her capabilities, and I hope to hire her services through another of my holdings. But she's too conventional to be patient with cloak-and-dagger antics and she's not particularly good at concealing her feelings. Her profile also suggests that she would not be sympathetic to certain events scheduled to occur after we reach Pradesh, if we ever do."

Marym broke her silence. "Will your plans for the merger be disrupted now that Caserta has passed on?"

Mercator shifted his weight restlessly. "No, I don't think so. There's no reason for his successor not to honor the terms of the agreement and I expect it to be ratified without difficulty. It is, as I said, a fair arrangement for all parties concerned."

"Although you'll get the lion's share." Dyle wondered if her pun had been intentional.

"The trust will be the prime beneficiary, but profit is, after all, the purpose of conducting business."

"Why is it so necessary to conceal your identity?" asked Marym.

"Would you like a summary of the various attempts that have been made on my life, Ser Dunnis? They have been numerous, inventive, and in one case almost successful. I have not traveled on a commercial vessel in more than three standard years and I am forced to relocate my home from world to world so frequently that I rarely have time to fully adjust to the local gravities and atmospheres."

"Then why are you on the *Helen*?"

"We joined the ship at the last moment to prevent anyone from anticipating us, but we made the news public enough to attract attention. Captain Nicodemus is leaving the ship once we reach Pradesh and although officially we're still interviewing candidates, her replacement will be one of my closest associates." He paused, looking back and forth between Dyle and Marym, then apparently made an internal decision to trust them. Or perhaps accepted candor as unavoidable. "An accident would have been staged while we were orbiting Pradesh, during which Magnus Mercator would lamentably perish. His family would carry on the trust, of course, hiring one Forbes Bowie to watch out for the family interests as general administrator. Bowie is, of course, fictitious, but I've expended considerable time and effort in order to construct him retroactively so that I could step into the role."

"And Clout? The real one, I mean."

"I wasn't going to kill him, if that's what you're suggesting. The stand-in body is already at Pradesh. He died through natural causes, I assure you. Clout wished to retire to a life of wealthy indolence, which I promised him in return for his act as decoy during the first leg of the voyage. It was an extra layer of insurance."

Marym's face had grown unfriendly. "When did you decide to simplify things by destroying Eco and killing Clout prematurely?"

Mercator laughed, genuinely amused. "I thought that would be your interpretation of events. I regret the necessity of disappointing you, Ser Dunnis, but I did neither. Eco was far too expensive an asset to destroy impulsively and unnecessarily."

"But less expensive than supporting Clout in the style he aspired to for the rest of his life."

"The thought had occurred to me, but no, I didn't kill Clout. He was loyal and I value loyalty above all else."

"You don't appear heartbroken about his death."

"I didn't say that I liked him. He was lazy, occasionally cruel, and he went behind my back with Absinthe."

Marym shook her head, her expression sour, and Dyle decided to take up the questioning.

"Obviously his death disrupted your plans."

"Only superficially. Particularly in a crisis, decisions must be made quickly. Failing to make an overt choice is a decision in itself.

I regret Clout's death, but as a practical matter, it furthered my own purposes. My children and Callista were used to calling me Clout, and it only took a few seconds to bring them up to date, except for poor Tanith, of course. But no one really listens to her anymore."

"How long had Clout been with you? Truthfully, this time."

"Several years, as I said. I had employed him briefly shortly after the exile, and when my former bodyguard died during one of the assassination attempts, I sought him out to fill the vacancy. He was quite a formidable man when I first hired him, though he's softened a bit over the years. I needed someone with military and security expertise who could also help with administrative duties. Gus had been a mercenary of sorts for four years and made quite a name for himself, although he was never enlisted with one of the licensed units. He became an officer very quickly, then edged away from field duties. Later, he operated a supply depot, a communications center, spent a year or so as warden of a prison camp, went into procurement and negotiated a shrewd contract with the Falloway Commercial Union. That's where I met him. I own a chunk of Falloway."

"What happened when you found his body?"

"I give you my word that he was already dead when I arrived. Death has been a common companion during my life, Ser Dyle. I recognized his presence even before I was close enough to see the physical evidence. I was surprised by what I found, but not particularly shocked."

"And you didn't see anyone else in the vicinity?"

"Gus had been dead for some time when I arrived."

Dyle noted without comment that Mercator had evaded answering the question, and he could tell by her subtle change of breathing that Marym had made the same observation. "So you would have us believe that someone aboard the *Helen* sabotaged Eco in order to kill you without being recorded, then happened to find your stand-in alone long enough to subject him to a prolonged and deadly assault?"

"You'll believe whatever you wish regardless of my intentions, won't you? Personally I am convinced that the opportunity arose by chance. The killer probably spotted Gus at some point while he was searching for Tanith, then followed him or possibly even offered to help and accompanied him openly. I'm surprised that even under those circumstances Gus could be assaulted without inflicting damage on his attacker, but we all let our guards down occasionally."

"And Eco?"

"I'm genuinely puzzled. I do have the access codes, as you no doubt suspect. So did Gus, and it pains me to admit that he might have shared that information with Absinthe. As far as I know, both were in their cabins during the critical period, or at least both were in one or the other, but I admit that it's possible for them individually or in consort to have acted without my knowledge and against my wishes. I did wonder about them, as a matter of fact, but by the time it occurred to me, it was too late to determine their movements."

"So who do you think was responsible for the sabotage?"

He shrugged. "A disgruntled crew member working through an accomplice? That seems the likeliest scenario, although I readily admit I don't believe it. You have my word that I don't know anything more about it than you do, and probably less."

"I'm sure you know which members of the crew have access and I'm sure you had them investigated. Would any of them have good reason to wish you harm?"

"To my knowledge, only Captain Nicodemus has a personal reason to dislike me, admittedly with good reason. But despite my differences with Lydia, she's honest and aboveboard. Even if I'd given her sufficient provocation, which I have not, she would never resort to subterfuge, nor would she have attacked me without warning."

Marym responded immediately. "How do you know Clout didn't have warning?"

"Because his was the only blood found at the scene. If he'd remained conscious after the initial blow, he would have found a way to fight back. Gus had grown lazy but he hadn't lost his gift for self-preservation."

"We might be able to clear up that matter as well if you tell us the whole truth. You've asked us to conceal the secret of your real identity, but you're holding something back."

Mercator's expression didn't change. "It's an imperfect universe."

"Why continue to pretend that you're Clout?"

He gave Marym a strange look. "Surely that's obvious. Someone aboard the Helen has gone to great lengths to kill me, Ser Dunnis. At the moment, they believe they've accomplished their goal. But even if that were not the case, I have now by purest chance an alternative to my own more elaborate and expensive plans to permanently remove Magnus Mercator's name from the universe. I would not have sacrificed Gus for this purpose, but now that he's already dead, I'm willing to let him perform this one final service for me."

He met her eyes and held them, unashamed of what he'd just told her. Dyle felt mildly revolted, but he had to admit that on some level, it made cold, rational sense.

They made no further progress. If Mercator knew anything more, he wasn't about to admit it. Marym was openly hostile but Dyle had preemptively agreed to honor Mercator's wish to continue the pretense that he was Clout. But he wouldn't promise not to tell the captain the truth. "We'll decide that when we next report to her."

Once Mercator was gone, Marym was even more visibly angry. "I'm halfway convinced that he killed Clout himself. He admitted that he knows the access codes and could have sabotaged Eco, and it was simpler and cheaper for him to murder his stand-in than to stage an elaborate and expensive accident at Pradesh. I don't say that he planned it that way from the outset, but he could have taken advantage of the situation and acted on impulse. And maybe he resented Clout's relationship with his daughter more than he's letting on."

Dyle shook his head. "If it was on impulse, then he wouldn't have sabotaged Eco, and I doubt that Mercator has ever acted impulsively. He might be responsible in both instances, but I think not."

"But he knows more than he's telling. You can see it in his body language."

Dyle nodded agreement. "I don't think he murdered Clout, but I think he knows who did."

"Then why not tell us?"

"That, Marym, is a very good question, to which I presently have no good answer."

Much to their surprise, Feykirk was waiting to deliver a message. Melanctha Korisov, chief of maintenance, had asked to see them at their earliest convenience.

"Do you suppose she's discovered something new about the maintenance robot?" asked Marym.

"There's only one way to find out." They dispatched Feykirk with word that they could see her immediately if she was available.

Feykirk returned after only a short delay, followed by Korisov, whom they knew only slightly, an older woman with a shock of thick white hair and a slender frame that nevertheless looked quite solid. She was accompanied by a younger version of herself, slightly taller, with long, straight hair the color of starless space. Korisov seemed calm but determined, while the younger woman—possibly her daughter—appeared uncertain and possibly just slightly frightened.

"Thank you for seeing us on such short notice. This is my niece, Dani Kinsarah. Dani is a greeter at one of the holotheaters on the Promenade. She has something to tell you."

Dani still seemed uncertain, but Marym dropped her professional coolness and warmly invited her to make herself comfortable. Dyle decided to stay out of the way, since the younger woman was still giving him wary sidelong glances, taking a seat where she could see him and he could watch her out of the corner of his eye without being too intimidating. Her aunt, Korisov, apparently preferred to stand.

The story came out haltingly at first but once she had started, Dani seemed to find continuing easier than stopping. Her job was to help customers choose a particular holo to experience, so she had been trained to recognize behavioral cues from potential customers. "We get first timers who are uncertain, or browsers who might change their mind at any time, or the ones from more conservative backgrounds who want something a little bit daring but aren't comfortable talking about what they're looking for. And, of course, there are others who really don't want to be shocked." On the second night aboard ship, she'd had an unusual customer. "He was hoping to get plugged in directly. I know that's legal on some worlds but ship's policy prohibits it. He wasn't very happy to hear that.

"We offer two levels of immersion. The viewer can simply assume a static position and watch the story take place, or we can provide a sensory helmet with various degrees of interaction. The viewer becomes one of the characters to a limited extent. The helmet adds tactile and olfactory input to the audio and visual, and the viewpoint shifts to follow the character. At its highest level, you could actually participate directly by reading the dialogue off a tiny screen inside the helmet. This customer wanted more than that. He wanted to jack in directly." Dani sounded indignant and a trifle shocked.

"I don't understand the implication," prompted Marym.

"On some worlds, you can link the helmet directly into the brain. It's not quite the same as reality, but it comes very close." She glanced nervously at her aunt. "I've never experienced it myself, of course, but we were told about it. Your own identity becomes partially submerged by the input and you actually believe that you're the character whose part you're following."

"I see. Is it addictive?"

Dani shook her head. "In most cases, no. But addicts often use it as a temporary fix, and most worlds decided that it was better to be safe than sorry, so the procedure is usually contrary to local laws."

Marym was beginning to see what this was leading to. "Your client was a stim addict."

Dani nodded. "I didn't know for sure until later, when he sort of told me. But I suspected it right off. He was irritable but kind of sad."

"His name was Morpheus, wasn't it?"

"Yes. I'd heard of his father, of course, and I was kind of curious. And he was obviously unhappy and needed someone to talk to, so I told him I was going off shift and asked him if he'd like to have a drink with me."

"Fraternizing between crew and passengers is never a good idea," said Korisov dourly.

There was a hint of a flare in Dani's eyes, but she didn't turn her head so her aunt couldn't see it. "There was nothing improper about it and I'm in services, not crew. We had a couple of drinks in a public place and we talked."

"What did you talk about?" asked Marym gently.

"Oh, lots of things, but most of it was just casual, you know?" Marym didn't know, although she suspected there'd been some mild flirtation going on, at least on Dani's part. Morpheus was not unattractive, and his lack of focus might even be interpreted as a kind of lofty sophistication. "There was one thing he said that kind of stuck with me, and with what happened later, I started to worry about it. He was complaining about how hard it was to get to know anybody when he couldn't stay in one place for very long before his father would move them again. I could tell he was unhappy and I asked if he'd ever just told his father he wanted to settle someplace. I mean, he was old enough to make his own life a long time ago."

She glanced around the room, apparently looking for confirmation of her opinion. Marym dutifully nodded, waiting for Dani to get to the point.

"Well, I asked him if his sisters felt the same way about it because if they did maybe it would carry more weight if they went to their father together. He just sort of looked at me as though he couldn't believe what I said and then told me that one of his sisters usually didn't even know which planet she was on and that the other liked things just the way they were because whenever they moved they'd meet a whole new group of people she could take into her bed. He said she was currently involved with her father's bodyguard but that she was getting bored like she always does."

Marym and Dyle exchanged looks. If this was supposed to be a revelation to them, it was well off the mark. But just as Marym was about to say something, Dani took a fresh breath and blurted out the rest. "Then he sort of laughed and said his sister would be furious if she knew that her lover was arranging to see someone else aboard behind her back. I asked who it was, but it was kind of a nervous reaction, you know, because it really wasn't my business, but he wouldn't tell me. That's all. Is it important?"

"It might be." Marym's voice was noncommittal. "Thank you for telling us, Dani. We'll get in touch if we need you for anything else."

Dani looked around uncertainly, but her aunt tapped her on the shoulder. "Come on now. We've wasted enough of their time with your prattle."

Marym and Dyle had little to say while they waited for Feykirk to fetch Morpheus Mercator. The possibility that Clout had arranged a secret meeting with someone since coming aboard the

Helen might or might not be important, if it was even true. And was he meeting her as Augustus Clout or as Magnus Mercator?

The young man appeared fairly promptly this time, settled down into his seat with considerably less truculence than before. He seemed calm but depressed, and Dyle wondered if he'd been recently medicated. Although he had originally planned to skirt the issue initially to put Morpheus off guard, he changed tactics at the last minute. "We would like you to tell us about Augustus Clout. And before you say anything, we know that he and your father switched identities before joining the ship."

Morpheus' eyes had become wary and he seemed slightly more focused, but he nodded. "This isn't the first time they've played that game, but it was supposed to be the last. My father usually doesn't like it when things don't work out the way he planned them, but this time he was pretty pleased."

"Are you saying Magnus was happy about Clout's death?"

Morpheus shrugged. "My father is rarely happy about anything. I'd describe him as satisfied. Clout's death provided him with another opportunity. It's important to watch for opportunities and exploit them when they present themselves, that's what he always says."

"Were there bad feelings between your father and Clout?" asked Marym.

"Bad feelings?" Morpheus laughed humorlessly. "Magnus Mercator doesn't lower himself to experience bad feelings. Or good ones either, for that matter."

"Are you telling us that he didn't resent the fact that Clout was involved with Absinthe?"

Morpheus turned to look at Marym directly. "Why should he? She was using him, not the other way around. Sinthy changes partners whenever she gets bored, and she gets bored very easily. She's even tried to get me to play games with her, and she knows I can't stand her."

"Clout's been with you for years," said Dyle. "I'm sure he knew what to expect."

"Of course he did. This isn't the first time they've been together. Neither of them takes . . . took it very seriously. Ask her; she likes talking about it almost as much as doing it."

"We have reason to believe your sister might not be the only woman aboard with whom Clout was involved."

The wary look was back. "I wouldn't know about that." It was an obvious lie.

"Yes, you do. You were overheard talking about it in fact." Which was also a lie. "You said that he was seeing someone in addition to your sister."

Morpheus was obviously uncomfortable and his voice had acquired a whining note. "I don't want to talk about it."

"Then perhaps we ought to ask your father to clear this up."

"No, wait!" For the first time, Morpheus' eyes lit up, with panic rather than interest. "We don't need to tell him about this, do we?"

Dyle didn't let the feeling of triumph show on his face. "If you tell us what we need to know, we'll do our best to keep your name out of it. But you have to tell us everything. We can only help you if you help us."

The issue remained in doubt for a while longer. The internal battle within the young man's mind played across his face as well, his expression switching from sullen to sly, from frightened to defiant, before finally settling back into resignation. "I had a deal with Clout. I wasn't supposed to leave the module without father's permission, but he'd look the other way if I promised to be careful."

"You were friendly with him then?"

"I paid him. Clout didn't have any friends, just people he knew. He and my father were more alike than either of them realized, except that Clout was corruptible and my father isn't. Anyway, I couldn't stand being cooped up anymore and I told him I wanted to go for a walk. He made me wait until Father's sleep inducers had had time to kick in, and we sat around and talked a little, just to pass the time. He knew that I didn't like him being with Sinthy and he teased me about it, and I guess he decided he might have pushed too far because he almost apologized and told me that it wasn't going to last much longer, that she was getting tired of the game. But then he said something like how lucky it was that he'd found another woman aboard who was interested in him."

"Did he say who it was, or anything about her?"

"No, just that she was his kind of woman, whatever that meant."

"Was this woman interested in him as Augustus Clout, or as Magnus Mercator?"

"How would I know?" His voice had turned petulant. "I think he said more than he had intended because he shut up after that and reminded me that I would be in big trouble if my father found out I'd gone off on my own. It was probably a bluff, because he couldn't give anything away without admitting that he'd helped, but I didn't argue with him."

"And the subject never came up again?"

"I never spoke to him after that. We just nodded to each other when I got back afterwards, and then Tanith went off and we were all sent to look for her."

"And you have no idea who this woman was?"

He shook his head. "None at all. I didn't care who she was. If Clout wanted to sleep with the captain herself, it was no business of mine." His face changed, eyes widening. "Maybe it was the captain. He did say that Father would be furious if he knew."

Dyle walked Morpheus through the conversation a second time, but without uncovering anything else. Morpheus grew increasingly sullen and withdrawn, and when he was told that they were done, he got up and left without another word. Feykirk poked her head in but Dyle waved her off.

"Clout and Nicodemus. Now there's an implausible couple for you." Marym was shaking her head wearily. "So we have another mystery, possibly relevant, probably not."

"Why do you say that?"

"Because there's no evidence that they ever actually met. We don't even know if this woman, who might just be the product of some imaginary bragging on Clout's part, was interested in him personally or was just trying to get close to the Mercator fortune."

"Do you still think Mercator himself was the killer?"

She made a disgusted sound. "I'd like it to be that way. It would tie up all the loose ends. I don't like the man personally, and I think he's perfectly capable of a cold-blooded murder. From his point of view it simplifies the process of faking his own death and it eliminates a possibly troublesome involvement between his daughter and an employee. He was the first to discover the body, and it would have been comparatively easy for him to dispose of the weapon before sounding the alarm."

"But you don't believe it."

"No," she said with considerable regret. "I don't. He strikes me as too methodical to have acted impulsively. I suppose he could have set things up so that Tanith escaped, planning to stalk and kill Clout in the aftermath, but too many things could have gone wrong. A carefully orchestrated shuttle accident at Pradesh is much more his style. Assuming that Morpheus was telling the truth, this isn't the first time Absinthe had invited Clout into her bed, and there's no particular reason for Mercator to have taken umbrage on this particular occasion, especially if the affair was nearly over." She stood up and began pacing. "I'm used to not knowing who the murderer is, but this time we can't positively identify the victim either. Was the killer after Mercator or Clout? Almost everyone aboard had a potential motive to kill Mercator, but I can't think of anyone who had sufficient reason to kill Clout. So don't ask me to explain this, but a little voice in the back of my mind tells me that Clout was the intended victim right from the start. Am I out of my mind?"

"No," he smiled broadly. "Because you're absolutely right."

Chapter Sixteen

"Well, great. I'm glad to hear it. Would you mind telling me how you know?"

He answered her question with one of his own. "Are you familiar with the concept of pre-imposition?"

"It's a term used in pattern analysis. That's when the analyst allows preconceived opinions to affect the interpretation of data."

"Correct, at least partly. The most obvious application is as you describe it. I am employed to deduce the reason why traffic has been disrupted in the capital city of Provencia. I assume that there has been some alteration to either traffic patterns or to the overall volume, so I search the data for evidence of either. I discover that certain routes have experienced a significant and unexpected increase in volume and make recommendations to augment the existing traffic lanes or divert traffic elsewhere. What I have failed to notice is that certain alternate routes have deteriorated in surface quality due to difficulties scheduling routine maintenance, a problem which will resolve itself in due course rendering my recommended expenditures unnecessary."

"That was my understanding of the term. I don't see how it applies here. We haven't been working toward any preconceived goal. We've been at a complete loss from the outset."

"Not entirely true. We were predisposed to believe that each development was part of an organic whole. But there's a more subtle form of pre-imposition in which the analyst attempts to fit all aberrant data into an evolving pattern. Sometimes there are multiple patterns, which might interact but which are nevertheless separate. The problem that faces the analyst is in determining which elements belong to which pattern, so that they can be segregated and evaluated independently."

"All right, I see that. So you're saying that we have two different problems mixed up together and that the reason we can't solve either of them is because of extraneous data from the other."

"Exactly, except that I think I know the truth now, or at least enough of it to let us sort out the rest in due course. Do you still have the stunner security provided?"

She nodded. "It's in my cabin."

"I have mine with me." He patted his side pocket. "Might I suggest that you retrieve yours while I send Feykirk to see Captain Nicodemus."

"To what end?"

"Why, to solve the mystery, of course. Don't you think it's time?"

Dyle's message was a long one and Feykirk repeated it back to him to make sure she'd gotten it correctly. He assured her that her recitation was impeccable and she hastened off. Dyle spoke to Memnon extensively until Marym returned, but a theoretical observer would have been puzzled by the lack of substance in his remarks, which had nothing at all to do with the murder of Augustus Clout. Feykirk's first mission was obviously successful, because a lone figure appeared at the door. Dyle stepped outside, engaged in a brief but pointed conversation, then watched as his visitor left to comply with his request, albeit reluctantly. He was sitting at the console again when Feykirk and Marym arrived almost simultaneously, the former with assurances that his requests would all be met and at the appropriate time, the latter now armed but not with knowledge.

"Are you going to tell me what's going on?" she asked, somewhat testily.

So he did, explaining his reasoning in detail. She listened attentively, saved her questions until he was finished, nodding occasionally as she recognized the logical steps he'd taken to solve the problem. "But that still leaves one question unanswered," she said at last.

"True. I believe I can lay that to rest also, but would you be very insulted if I left that until later? I enjoy a touch of theater and I also have a very good reason which I can't explain just now."

She glanced at her chrono. "I've waited this long, I can hold on a while longer."

* * * * *

Dyle made sure they were the last to arrive at the wardroom. He didn't want to have to fend off questions before everyone was present and he had the general outline of what he wanted to say all worked out in his head. Experience did not favor his being able to strictly adhere to his prepared agenda, but he hated walking into situations such as this without having a plan of attack. Chief Korisov was sitting in the vestibule just outside the privacy-shielded entrance, looking impatient and slightly puzzled, and two bored-looking security operatives were flanking the door. He could see the others inside, although the privacy shield dampened all sounds, and he paused, taking attendance.

Magnus Mercator sat directly across from the door, arms folded, his face calm but probably a mask concealing simmering anger. He would not like being kept waiting. Callista Dorne was on his left, looking smaller than he remembered, her pose casual but her face betraying barely controlled tension. To her left sat Morpheus, glowering slightly and with his head hunched forward. Next was Absinthe, who leaned across the corner of the conference table to flirt with Abraham Baxter, who looked alternately amused and distressed by her attentions. Next to him sat Sondra Wong, her back straight, eyes moving slowly around the room. It was impossible to read her mood. Around the next corner were two empty seats, then one occupied by Dona Tharmody, who seemed relaxed, although they could not see her face. To her left, at the head of the table, Captain Nicodemus sat impassively, but she had positioned her left arm in front of her so that her chrono was visible.

"I guess it's time." There wasn't much of a rise in the sound level when they passed through the privacy shield. Absinthe's chatter died away immediately and it appeared that no one else had been speaking at all. Dyle made a point of sweeping his eyes slowly around the table, during which Mercator abruptly broke the silence.

"Tanith is under heavy medication and is unable to attend your little soiree. And some of the rest of us have business to attend to. Would you care to explain why you've asked the captain to inconvenience us all?"

Dyle wasn't at all ruffled by Mercator's tone. He simply nodded and waited until Marym had taken one of the empty places. "I'm sorry if we've disrupted anyone's plans, but it was necessary and if you'll bear with me, I think you'll agree that this shouldn't wait. Everyone in this room is familiar at least in part with the unfortunate events that have taken place aboard since we left Linnisfarne, but I'd like to start with a brief summary so that everyone understands where they have led us."

Although Dyle professed to dislike presenting lectures, he'd been asked to speak at convocations of pattern analysts from time to time, his business interests had required a certain amount of public speaking, and his not entirely voluntary avocation as an investigator often led to formal presentations. Truthfully, he rather enjoyed having an audience, although he wouldn't admit it, even to himself. He rested both hands on the back of the remaining empty chair, but remained standing.

"Shortly after First Jump, a maintenance robot was reprogrammed with instructions to convey a capsule of liquid oxygen into Eco's inner chamber and detonate it. The resulting explosion completely destroyed Eco and inflicted incidental damage to the drive system which has necessitated our detour to Scrimshaw. Other consequences included a dramatic decline in personal services and the loss of the extensive surveillance system aboard the *Helen,* although we were fortunate enough to have a backup AP, Memnon, which maintains the ship's essential services and to whom direct access is slowly being expanded." He gestured toward the console at the far end of the wardroom, which currently betrayed the mnemonic glyph that was Memnon's ready sign. "Memnon has also been invited to attend, as you can see.

"Several possible motives have been suggested for the sabotage but we have not been able to identify anyone among the passengers or crew whose movements were not accounted for at critical times and who had or reasonably might have had knowledge of the access codes required both to redirect the robot and to bypass Eco's own security system. The most reasonable explanation is that the party responsible was in fact one of that group, but that he or she had an accomplice to which critical information was passed. Given that possibility, it becomes very difficult to definitely eliminate anyone aboard, particularly since surveillance records covering the critical time period were stored in Eco's memory, which is no longer available."

"Is this going somewhere?" asked Mercator impatiently.

"I beg your indulgence for the moment." Dyle clasped his hands behind his back and began to stroll slowly around the table, clockwise, passing behind Captain Nicodemus, whose face remained expressionless, although her shoulders had suddenly tightened with tension. "There was considerable speculation about the motive of the saboteur, everything from an elaborate attempt to commit suicide to an attempt to damage the Mercator family's fortunes to a simple desire to eliminate surveillance in order to facilitate another crime. None of these seemed probable to me but I was forced to entertain them for lack of a better alternative.

"Now we come to the more serious matter. Tanith Mercator is a troubled young woman prone to periods of irrational behavior." He paused to let Mercator protest, but the silence was unbroken. "She eluded the system designed to monitor her activities and escaped into the ship, after which members of her party and others were enlisted into an informal search. At some point, the man we all knew as Magnus Mercator entered the gardens, whether alone or accompanied we do not know, and some time later he was assaulted and killed. His assailant left no direct physical evidence behind and the attack, though impressive in its cumulative effect, would not necessarily have required much physical strength. Anyone in this room, almost anyone aboard the *Helen,* could have accomplished it, if provided with a suitable weapon."

He let his eyes trail around the room. Dorne looked even more upset than before, but no one else showed any change of expression. "Once again, we had too many suspects. Magnus Mercator's controversial past might well have caught up with him. There were many people aboard ship who had known reasons to wish him harm, and almost anyone else might have had a hidden motive. In the absence of any other evidence, and hampered by our lack of resources to mount an effective investigation, we knew from the outset that it was unlikely that we would be able to identify the mastermind behind the two crimes. As it happens, we made two errors in that assumption." He was passing behind Absinthe and he paused, waiting until he was certain he had their attention.

"Our first error was in believing that the two crimes were connected. They were not. The killer had nothing to do with the destruction of Eco. Our second, and more serious error, was in believing that we were investigating the death of Magnus Mercator." He waited as Magnus turned toward him, his eyes threatening reprisals. "I know that we promised discretion, but what I'm about to say is known to everyone in this room with two exceptions, and I think Captain Nicodemus has already guessed the truth. The man murdered in the gardens was not Magnus Mercator. It was Augustus Clout. The two men swapped identities for purposes of their own which are presently irrelevant."

Only Dona Tharmody reacted physically, her eyes widening and lips thinning. There was a hint of a smile, but she wiped it away almost immediately. Captain Nicodemus just nodded, as though Dyle had just confirmed something she had already known, and she spoke for the first time since he'd arrived. "You don't get the true sense of a man through messaging so I couldn't be certain, but it just felt wrong as early as First Jump." She turned to Mercator. "I've questioned your judgment on several occasions in the past, but I've never known you to be hesitant or uncertain of yourself."

Magnus nodded to her. "I regret the necessity for the masquerade, Captain, but I assure you I had what I believed to be good reasons for it." He glanced around the table. "I know your reputation, Ser Tharmody, and I hope I can rely on your discretion."

Tharmody nodded back, and the hint of a smile came and went once again.

Mercator's eyes strayed to Sondra Wong. "But I think you've miscounted."

Dyle shook his head. "Ser Wong has known the truth for some time as well." Wong's face remained impassive. She didn't so much as nod to confirm Dyle's assertion, but her lack of denial was answer enough. "Among other things, she had approached Clout about meeting clandestinely for what he thought would be a romantic encounter. She would never have dared suggest such a thing to Magnus Mercator." Wong's eyes flickered this time, but her face remained immobile otherwise.

Baxter spoke up suddenly, his voice hoarse. "What led you to believe that I knew the truth, Sandor?" He made no effort to deny it.

"When you were talking about your service on Cathanor, you mentioned the shock of seeing Mercator again, without his hair. I didn't think anything of it at the time because you also said that you never actually met him."

"I was a low-ranking officer at the time, but I was part of his escort after the surrender." He looked directly at Mercator. "You have aged remarkably well. I recognized you immediately."

Captain Nicodemus stirred. "So with the exception of Tanith Mercator, everyone who knows the truth about the switch of identities is gathered in this room?"

"I believe so. The solution to our mystery is entangled within that masquerade."

"Then may I ask why Ser Tharmody has been included in our number?"

Dyle began walking again, passing Wong and reaching the next corner before he responded. "Dona provided unconscious but invaluable aid in solving part of our mystery, and she may well have been instrumental in preventing an even more tragic sequel." There were puzzled looks all around the table, including Marym, but Tharmody's face stayed neutral.

"I know most of the story, I believe, but there are some minor points which I need confirmed or filled in. Could we have Chief Korisov's assistance for a moment?"

Nicodemus nodded and signaled the security operative at the door. Melanctha Korisov passed through the privacy shield and looked around uncertainly.

"I'm sorry to have interrupted your duties, Chief, but I wonder if you could answer a few questions for us? Would you like to sit down?"

"I'm fine standing, if you don't mind, Ser Dyle. But I don't know how I could help you."

"I understand that the maintenance robots, including the one destroyed in the explosion, are semi-autonomous?"

She nodded. "That's right. Unless they receive overriding orders, they perform a preset round of duties. The one we lost was used primarily for heavy work that didn't require much discrimination. It moved waste materials from holding areas to the disposal dock, cleaned corridors and aisles in the cargo bay, and delivered heavy items from Stores to designated locations."

"But it was capable of more sophisticated tasks."

"Oh, very much so. We used it to load cargo back at Linnisfarne. It had a nice, soft touch. It can do external hull work in a pinch and a limited amount of microelectronics repair."

"I understand that it was equipped with a welding unit."

"An arc sealer, actually. It could have handled a small hull breach on its own. That particular unit was originally equipped to work in a vacuum and weld heavy plates to the hull's exterior, but we adapted it later rather than buy another unit."

"What is the procedure for overriding its orders?"

"Well, first of all, there's only six of us aboard who could do it directly. There's a nine-character access code that has to be inputted to put it in a waiting state. The task menu comes up on a little screen after it acknowledges. It's a list of every task that has been programmed into it, with the scheduled ones highlighted. If you want to add one of the others to the schedule, you just toggle it and then toggle the time slot or priority level you want. We keep these units pretty busy so there probably wouldn't be a time slot in most cases unless you demoted one of the scheduled tasks to make room for the new one."

"What if you wanted the robot to do something that wasn't on its task list? Would you be out of luck?"

"Well, it would be more difficult, certainly. The easiest way would be to find a similar task and modify it. If I wanted to have it move some repair parts to a corridor junction, for example, I'd replicate the existing stores replenishment task and modify the start and end points."

"What if you wanted to order the unit to go to security, access the brig, and repair the weld on a cell block?"

"I'd order it to follow me there and supervise it directly. That's a pretty complex job. There are too many ways it could go wrong. The robot might select the wrong unit to work on, or ignore the danger to humans in the vicinity. You can't weld without proper ventilation."

"Theoretically, then. Assume that for some reason it was essential to complete the task without human supervision."

"Well first of all, we don't have the old-style cell blocks, so there'd be nothing to weld."

Dyle rolled his eyes. "Theoretically, if you did have something that needed welding there. How would you instruct the robot?"

"I'd probably initiate a blank task, establish beginning and end points, access the specialized repair submenu to pick the welding icon. I'd have to input the security area access code with an order to wipe its memory immediately afterward, and provide disposal instructions for any waste products, including ventilation and fire prevention. That would be the easy part. Then I'd have to go to vocal mode and describe the work I wanted done in as much detail as possible. There's a rudimentary intelligence unit, about that of a bright toddler. I'd make it repeat the instructions back to me and then send it on its way and hope for the best."

"Or let it wait until the time slot you had preselected?"

"That's correct."

"Would it balk at orders which would result in its own destruction?"

She shook her head. "The self-preservation protocol is rudimentary. We can trust these units to take care of themselves on their own, but they'll follow a foolish or unintended instruction blindly."

"Is there any other way that the robot's task list could be altered?"

"Well, if there was a ship's emergency, Eco could override directly. The robots are technically part of the *Helen*'s infrastructure, so ordinarily instructions would still come from Memnon, but Eco had the ability to supersede the older system under certain sets of circumstances."

"Would there be any record if that had happened?"

"Sure. It would reside in the robot's local memory until upload, and Eco would have a permanent entry in her emergency intervention log."

Captain Nicodemus stirred. "Dona, isn't the emergency log backed up to Memnon on a real-time basis?"

She nodded, but it was Dyle who answered aloud. "We've reviewed Memnon's copy of the emergency files. Eco's most recent override occurred while the *Helen* was still orbiting Linnisfarne, a minor hull breach."

There was some stirring around the table. Absinthe Mercator was either bored or pretending to be. Baxter had settled back in his chair and was staring down into his lap with a bemused expression. Sondra Wong and Magnus Mercator exchanged a cryptic look, and Morpheus was moving his lips, very slowly and very slightly, as though engaged in a secret conversation with an invisible companion.

"Thank you, Chief. I think that's all we need for now."

Korisov glanced at Captain Nicodemus, who nodded dismissal, then turned and left, clearly puzzled by the interview.

"Is this going anywhere?" asked Mercator.

Dyle was behind his own seat now, but he remained standing. "Just a few more questions, if you don't mind." He turned his head.

"Ser Wong, could you tell us about the status of the agreement between Idrian Caserta and the Mercator family trust?"

She blinked and paused, either replaying the question in her head or considering how she should answer. "Since, as you have pointed out, Magnus Mercator is still alive, the tentative agreement is still in force, subject to the formal acknowledgment and registration which will be consummated on Pradesh. Assuming we ever reach our destination."

"But Caserta himself has died, unfortunately, without completing the formalities."

"The terms of the negotiations are binding upon his successors."

"And who would the successors be?"

"The Windrider Cooperative. Most of Idrian's employees became vested shareholders some time ago, although they had no voting power while he was alive."

"Then how can they authorize the completion of his negotiated merger?"

"They can't. Idrian also designated a temporary successor whose term expires once the formal contracts are complete. The successor then becomes an ordinary shareholder and all authority shifts to the board of the new entity."

"Which essentially means the Mercator trust, I take it?"

"That's a fair characterization," she admitted.

"And just who is this temporary successor?"

She didn't hesitate for a heartbeat. "I have that honor."

"Then you had something to gain from the death of Idrian Caserta, did you not?"

For the first time, there was evident emotion in her face, anger boiling to the surface. "My stipend as successor is identical to what I was being paid as his secretary, to the very last credit." Her fury was almost a physical force and Dyle had to resist the temptation to retreat before it, but the flare-up passed almost immediately. "I felt nothing but respect and affection for Idrian, and I deeply regret his passing."

Dyle felt a moment of great compassion for the woman, but consciously set it aside for the moment. Individual tragedies could be dealt with later.

"Having realized that Magnus Mercator was still alive, we found ourselves with an even more complex problem. There were too many questions whose answers were interrelated. Why did the saboteur destroy Eco? Was the sabotage designed to facilitate the murder? If not, then was the same individual also the killer or was it someone else taking advantage of the unexpected opportunity? Was the intended target Magnus Mercator or Augustus Clout? Why was a member of the crew summoned to help administer medication forcibly to a passenger identified as Tanith Mercator but who was actually her sister Absinthe?" For the first time, Mercator lost some measure of control. His face shifted from surprise to fury to resignation within the space of a single breath. Absinthe lowered her head with a low cry and refused to look up. "We lacked sufficient information to resolve these questions all at once, so we began to consider them independently. We also accepted the fact that our resources were severely limited. Virtually everyone aboard ship was potentially a credible enemy of the probably intended victim"—he glanced significantly at Mercator—"but what if Clout was the target right from the outset?"

Mercator sat up in his chair. "Are you implying that it was someone from my party who killed Gus?"

"I'm not implying anything at the moment. I'm describing the process we followed to reach our present conclusions. Practically speaking, we had no way to eliminate the possibility that you were the intended victim. The possibility that your bodyguard had an enemy of his own was a much more manageable question. Even if the result was only to eliminate that alternative, it would at least reduce the level of distraction."

"But no one else aboard the *Helen* knew Gus. We couldn't have carried off the impersonation otherwise."

Dyle smiled, but it wasn't warm. "I think it's time to drop the pretense, don't you? There was in fact someone else aboard the *Helen* who knew Clout, knew him from a long time ago, before he worked for you, although you couldn't have known that when you planned your little deception. I don't pretend to know the details of their relationship, but I could hazard a guess. I'm confident that this was a chance encounter, that the killer had no foreknowledge that Clout would be on the *Helen,* and I'm also reasonably sure that the recognition was one-sided. Clout had no idea that he was in any specific danger, and might well have enlisted his killer's aid in the search for your daughter, effectively collaborating on his own death. The murderer was patient, waited until they were in a location in which they could not be observed, then struck him down, repeatedly, and continued the assault long after he was dead. This was a crime of passion and impulse, emotionally premeditated but committed on the spur of the moment."

Captain Nicodemus stirred restlessly. "Personally I don't care whether the victim was Magnus Mercator, Augustus Clout, or the exiled King of New Etruria. If the connection was so vague that even the dead man didn't recognize his assailant, I don't see that this revelation or speculation or whatever it is advances matters. We still don't have a witness or any other means by which to identify the guilty party."

Dyle scratched the side of his nose with his forefinger, staring down at the floor. "Well, that's not exactly true either. There was a witness to the crime. Ser Mercator, what restrictions have you placed on the movement of members of your party?"

"I don't understand. What has that got to do with anything?"

"Humor me. Other than your daughter Tanith, have you placed any constraints on your children? Can they come and go as they wish?"

Absinthe laughed quietly, possibly amused by the idea that anyone could prevent her from doing anything she wanted. Morpheus looked uncomfortable. "Morpheus is recovering from a prolonged illness so I keep a close watch on him but Absinthe and Callista are free to come and go as they please."

"Do you think that's wise given that someone apparently just attempted to murder you in a quite brutal fashion?"

There was a very brief hesitation, but Mercator's voice was as firm as ever. "My enemies are after me personally, not my children."

"Is that why you keep them with you all the time? Is that why they have always been covered by your security umbrella even when they weren't living in your current home? Is that why you had Absinthe under covert surveillance during the brief period in which she tried to strike out on her own?" This last was a guess, but it clearly hit home.

When Mercator didn't deny it, Absinthe slowly turned her head toward him, and her expression was cold and speculative. He sighed. "Tanith's difficulties result from an infection that lodged itself in her brain before she was born. It's a mutant version of a virus native to Cathanor that adapted itself to live in a human host. Absinthe was diagnosed as having the same infection but in her case it was latent, at least most of the time. I was watching her just in case the virus became more active, which it has recently. That's why we were forced to medicate her." He drew a deep breath. "I consider this to be an intrusion into my private affairs, Ser Dyle, and I fail to see how it is relevant."

Dyle nodded as another suspicion was confirmed. "I regret the need to speak of these things but I won't apologize. Your secretiveness forced us into this situation. I submit that you made no effort to improve your personal security because you knew that your family was in no immediate danger. Almost everyone on the ship accepted you as Clout except for the killer, who knew the truth, and who had already exacted vengeance."

"How could I possibly know that?"

"You knew it because you witnessed, if not the crime itself, its immediate aftermath. When you found him lying in the gardens, his killer was still there, possibly still methodically battering him. You know the murderer's identity but for reasons of your own, you have refrained from revealing the truth."

Chapter Seventeen

"Now why in the universe would I conceal that fact if it were true?" Mercator's voice and posture indicated that he was genuinely curious, though probably not as much in the answer as in Dyle's method of reaching that conclusion. There was a suppressed stirring around the table as most realized the significance of Mercator's refusal to deny the charge.

"Because it would be more profitable for you if the solution did not come to light, at least not in the short run. Tell me, what happened to your professed loyalty to your employees? Clout had been in your service for a long time."

Their eyes met. Mercator folded his hands on the table in front of him, let out a long breath. "He was already dead. There was nothing more I could do for him. I would have intervened if I'd arrived earlier, but what's in the past is forever beyond our reach. If a cherished possession is irredeemably broken, you look for a replacement, or alter your habits to fit the new situation, don't you? I was presented with an unexpected scenario; I evaluated the possibilities and chose the course I thought best."

The captain's normally emotionless face was distorted with anger. "Are you saying that you know who has been endangering my ship, and have suppressed the information for reasons of your own?"

Dyle intervened. "It's not quite that bad, Captain. He also knows that the person who murdered Clout was not responsible for the sabotage. The two incidents are linked only in the sense that the first made the second possible without detection."

"Then who did kill the man?"

A steady voice from the far end of the table answered. "I did. Ser Dyle is correct. I had no idea that Angus Boden—that's the name I knew him by—was aboard until I saw him in the receiving bay." It was Sondra Wong speaking, her face perfectly calm, but her eyes were looking into a distant place or time invisible to the rest of them.

"My first impulse was to kill him immediately, to fulfill the oath I took years ago, but I had another obligation, to Idrian. I couldn't abandon him while he was dying; I had to see that his wishes were carried out. Boden didn't recognize me. I've changed a lot since we first met, and I don't think he ever recognized any of us individual human beings even back then."

"The prison camp?" prompted Dyle.

She nodded, not surprised that he knew. "On Paramour. It was a fringe world, probably still is. I was with a merc unit working for the separatists when we were sold out by one of the local militias and captured. Boden was an ex-merc, so he knew the rules, written and otherwise, but he ran his prison camp by his own set of laws. The Uniform Codex prohibits mercs from trying to escape after they've been moved to permanent detention so he knew we were no threat, but he liked exercising power and he liked making examples." She raised her artificial limb and put it on the table. "Someone stole extra rations so he took one arm from every cell block. I drew the unlucky number."

"You followed him into the gardens?"

"No. I was with him. Ran into him in the Promenade. He told me what had happened and I offered to help. I didn't have anything specific in mind at the time, but when he told me that the girl liked finding secluded spots when she escaped, I knew this was likely to be my best chance. I hesitated the first time we were obviously alone. In some part of my mind, I'd been anticipating that moment for years and when it finally came, I had doubts. Not about killing him. Boden was an animal and I don't regret his death for a moment. I doubted myself. Could I kill in cold blood, striking from behind? I actually felt a twinge of sympathy for the bastard, standing there not knowing that his death was so close. And I was also afraid that I'd fail. He was still in prime shape, and I'm not. He had weight and reach on me, and probably retained better skills. So I hit him when he wasn't looking. I told myself it was a mercy, that I was putting him out of his misery for good and sufficient reasons but that I wasn't being cruel. The truth is, if I'd given him a chance to defend himself, he would probably be alive and I'd be either dead or in the brig. In either case, I wouldn't be able to help Idrian. And once I started hitting him,"—her voice didn't quite break, but it was a close thing—"it was even harder to stop."

"You used your prosthesis."

She nodded. "It's coated with duroplast so it didn't leave any traces. But I did a job on the internal alignment."

"Caserta mentioned that you were having it repaired."

"I told them it got caught in a flittercab door on Linnisfarne."

"You were still there when Mercator showed up."

She shrugged. "I'm not sure when that happened. When I ran out of breath, or hate, I staggered back, not really taking in what I had just done. And I saw him standing there. He didn't look happy and I thought I'd failed after all, that Idrian would have to go on without me."

"Why didn't you kill him as well?"

She looked suddenly offended. "Angus Boden deserved to die, but I had no right to take another life. And it was essential that Mercator complete the arrangements with Idrian."

Dyle nodded as she fell silent. "And Mercator was equally determined that the merger should occur. So much so that he was willing to conceal your identity."

"He assured me that we could hide the truth. He even helped me clean myself in the fountain. I believed him when he said the deal was more important to him than punishing his bodyguard's killer."

"Understandably, since it was essential that you be capable of serving in Caserta's place if his obviously failing health made that necessary. What happens now? If the captain surrenders you to the authorities on Scrimshaw or Pradesh, will the merger still be consummated?"

"Almost certainly, although the process will take longer. I have no designated successor, so the members of the cooperative will have to be polled individually. There might be a few holdouts, but the vast majority understand the situation and the merger would certainly be ratified."

"How long would this process take? A standard year perhaps?"

She shook her head. "Not that long, no. Perhaps half as much or a little longer. It depends on where the ships are at the time and how quickly they can be reached."

"I see." Dyle resumed his perambulations, noting that Magnus Mercator's face remained impassive but that he was shifting his weight restlessly. "I don't suppose that he told you that the Tenebrian War is about to end?"

Wong's face clouded. "I don't understand."

"There are secret negotiations underway to bring the conflict to a close. What impact would peace have on Caserta's commercial interests?"

"We're the only trade ships still working that part of space. We'd be able to negotiate exclusive terms with the lesser worlds and very favorable ones with the others." There was a hint of anger in her voice and her eyes had moved toward Mercator.

"I see. Did the two of you leave together?"

It took her a second to understand his question. "No, I left first. I walked for a while; I'm not sure exactly where. I think I was suffering from mild shock. When I collected myself, I was outside the casino, and after that I went back to my cabin, washed and changed, and then looked in on Idrian, who was napping."

"Did either of you ever discuss the matter again?"

"Never."

"Thank you for your candor." Dyle turned to Captain Nicodemus, who could barely contain herself.

"And you're quite certain that Ser Wong had nothing to do with the earlier sabotage?"

"Quite sure."

"How about Ser Mercator?"

Dyle allowed himself a moment to reflect on the possibility of seeing Magnus Mercator thrown into the brig, but he shook his head. "Only in the most indirect manner and certainly not with his knowledge or consent."

She looked disappointed as she gestured for the security people to enter the wardroom. "Ser Wong, I'm ordering your detention in my capacity as captain of the *Helen of Troy.* You will be confined to the brig pending my further disposition."

Both security people drew stunners, but Wong stood up slowly and spread her hands. "I'm unarmed except for this"—she moved the prosthesis. "I planned to surrender myself once my other obligations were satisfied. I won't cause any trouble. It would serve no purpose."

Absinthe Mercator stood up the moment the threesome passed through the privacy shield, obviously believing that the convocation was over. She glared at her father for a second, but remained silent and didn't even glance toward Dyle. Magnus also shifted his seat backward, preparatory to rising, but Dyle broke the awkward silence. "I don't want to hold you against your wishes, but we're not through yet."

Only Tharmody and Marym seemed to have expected this. Absinthe remained standing but was uncharacteristically quiet, and Magnus leaned forward again. "I had good and sufficient reasons not to divulge what I knew, and I judged that Wong was not a danger to anyone else aboard."

"The authority to make that decision was not yours," said Nicodemus icily. "Even a ship's owner is subject to a captain during transit, particularly in emergency situations. I could have you locked in a cell next to Ser Wong." Her face changed subtly and her eyes fairly twinkled. "The worst you could do is to fire me, and you've already expended that option."

Mercator took it in surprisingly good spirits. "That was probably the first of several bad decisions I've made recently." He settled back in his seat. "Ser Dyle, I assume you have more revelations for us? Do they include the identity of our mysterious saboteur?"

"In a manner of speaking." Absinthe hastily resumed her seat, and even Marym looked at him curiously. Senator Baxter had become more animated during Wong's confession and even Morpheus seemed to be following the conversation avidly. Only Dona Tharmody remained silent and apparently disinterested. "We suspected from the outset that Eco was attacked in order to render the surveillance system inoperative, thereby facilitating another crime. The subsequent murder seemed logically to fill that role and we wasted a good deal of time trying to find the common factors between the two events. The truth is that Wong acted entirely independently, although obviously she took advantage of the situation as she found it."

"Then there is still another crime to be discovered, or not yet committed?" Captain Nicodemus sounded angry rather than alarmed.

Dyle shook his head. "No, the attack on Eco was an end in itself."

"And you can identify the person responsible?"

Dyle glanced at Tharmody, who shook her head almost imperceptibly. "No, Captain, I cannot name the party responsible. At least not yet. I have to ask you to be patient for a while longer."

Nicodemus made an exasperated sound. "I don't see that we can accomplish anything further here if you don't know who is responsible."

Dyle looked momentarily flustered. "I didn't say that I don't know. I said that I can't tell you quite yet." He glanced at his chrono and frowned. "Indulge me for just a short while longer. As you are already aware, Eco was possibly the most advanced system of its type ever built."

Mercator sighed. "If you're going to say this was an attempt to embarrass me financially, then it was a wasted effort. The physical damage is covered by insurance and the basic programming has been replicated elsewhere. My only out-of-pocket loss is Ser Tharmody's extravagant but admittedly deserved consulting fee."

Dyle shook his head. "The fact that you had a financial interest in Eco had no effect on the motive. Your efforts at economizing are more relevant."

Mercator's eyes narrowed. "I never stinted in the security arrangements for Eco. They should have been more than sufficient."

"And under ordinary circumstances they would have been." Dyle spotted movement out of the corner of his eye. Tharmody had jumped as though she'd been jabbed by a needle. She turned toward him and nodded, ever so slightly. "You won't need another cell, Captain Nicodemus, because no one aboard the *Helen* was responsible for the destruction of Eco."

"But how is that possible?" Marym spoke out for the first time. "We know that the instructions were delivered to the robot shortly before the explosion, because otherwise it would have uploaded the revised work schedule into the maintenance system."

"Absolutely correct, but nevertheless, no one aboard this ship issued those orders." He was enjoying himself immensely now.

"Are you trying to say it was some kind of malfunction?" asked Mercator.

"Yes, in a manner of speaking. The robot received the orders that resulted in Eco's destruction from the ship's AP operating system."

There was silence all around the table. Marym was nodding, as though a flood of new ideas were passing before her eyes. It was Nicodemus who finally broke the silence. "Are you saying that Eco killed herself? That the system self-destructed?"

Dyle shook his head. "No, Eco was too stable for that. Using the term very loosely, Eco was the victim of a jealous rage. She was murdered by Memnon."

Several voices spoke at once, but it was Captain Nicodemus who pushed back from the table and stood up. "Ser Dyle, under the circumstances, perhaps we should adjourn for the moment." Her eyes moved toward the console which provided two-way communication with Memnon.

"It's all right, Captain; we're not in any danger. I was just waiting for Dona's signal. Gavin Pritchard has just performed a precautionary lobotomy on Memnon. He's going to be dull company from now on because the artificial personality has been disconnected, but he'll keep the ship running and follow your orders. Unfortunately, he won't have any initiative left so services to the passengers are going to be reduced again, but he no longer poses any danger. I doubt that he would have harmed a human being in any case, although I admit I feel much more comfortable knowing that he can no longer act on his own initiative."

"Memnon's imperatives would almost certainly have prevented him from harming anyone even now," explained Tharmody. "But given the aberrant behavior we knew of, it seemed prudent to avoid any unnecessary risk."

The other voices had died down when it became obvious that Dyle was ignoring them, but it was also clear that they were waiting for further explanation. Dyle deliberately stepped back from the table. "Dona, why don't you describe the basic situation?"

Tharmody drew a deep breath. "Okay, here's the short version. Artificial personalities are designed to mimic human personalities. That makes it more comfortable for the average person to interact with them and gives us a structure around which to arrange subsidiary programs. Even the people who create the base code fall into the habit of thinking of them as intelligent and self-aware, even though we know they are not. We give them names and voices, and we identify different modules as ambition, pride, self-preservation, sociability, and so forth, and that nomenclature reinforces the misconception. A given system has an array of responses from which it chooses in response to a stimulus—a request, order, or less overt act. For example, a moderately sociable system might draw a level-three response to a greeting from a passenger and respond with a cheery reply and a request to be of service. If the overall system design increased the emphasis on sociability, the response might be drawn from a much deeper level, resulting in wildly exaggerated compliments. The different modules interact with one another and mutually affect decision making. The real art in developing a first-class AP is to fine-tune those interactions, because that's where we have difficulty predicting the response. What made Eco so effective was that she'd been given four times as many possible responses as Memnon, and even more importantly, she had a much more sophisticated conflict-resolution and discretionary profile. She did a vastly better job of matching an appropriate response to a stimulus."

Captain Nicodemus nodded. "It was a pleasure working with her. At his best, Memnon comes across as a touchy old man. There were times when I thought of Eco as another crew member."

Tharmody nodded. "That's exactly the effect the designers wanted. But there was one thing in her environment that they hadn't anticipated."

She paused and it was Dyle who took up the narrative. "Originally, Eco was supposed to replace Memnon entirely, but late in the game it was decided to keep Memnon where he was."

"It made sense financially," said Mercator grumpily. "There was no need to remove the old, incompatible circuitry, and the space we would have gained by removing his central units was negligible. It cost virtually nothing to keep him in place and as it turned out, he serves as an acceptable backup to the main system following its loss."

"A loss that wouldn't have occurred if Memnon had been decommissioned," corrected Dyle. "You deprived Memnon of his purpose, so he acted to restore the status quo."

"You talk about it as if it was a person."

"Because that's how it's designed to function!" Tharmody almost shouted the words. "He's designed to mimic humans and that's what he did. Every AP has a primary module, the one designed to shape its performance. The model used for Memnon was self-esteem. Humans take pride in their accomplishments and usually measure that pride by the responses of other humans. Memnon's creators made him immensely proud of his work, and his work was defined as preserving human life and providing satisfaction to passengers and crew. Positive responses from humans were even more important to him than his own continued existence. It was a simple concept in AP terms but it worked."

"Until you added Eco to the mix," added Dyle.

"But Eco was accomplishing the same thing, with even greater success," protested Mercator. "Memnon should have welcomed her, not murdered her."

Dyle shook his head. "You know better than that. Even among humans, jealousy would have been a powerful motivator."

"But Memnon's not human."

"No," Tharmody resumed. "But his programming mimics us, remember? And his judgment is heavily influenced by how well he satisfies his prime motivations."

"Which were being satisfied better than ever before!"

"Ah," said Dyle. "But not by him. What do you suppose an AP is supposed to do when a situation arises which interferes with its job performance?"

Something moved behind Mercator's eyes as he began to realize the implications. "Eliminate the source of the interference."

"Correct," said Tharmody. "Unless eliminating it causes a serious threat to human life. Eco wasn't human. She was interfering with Memnon's job performance by superseding him and completing those tasks herself. His self-esteem level began to drop until it reached a point where the balance between the blow to his pride slipped below that of the negative effects of damaging ship's property." She settled back, letting Dyle tie up the loose ends.

"Memnon still had primary control of life support and routine maintenance. He changed the robot's programming—the procedure is much too complex to have been done by someone not familiar with the technique—and since even Memnon lacked the access code to Eco, he told Eco to let the robot in. She had no reason to suspect what was about to happen and complied. We immediately became dependent upon Memnon for all services and support, and his self-esteem quickly returned to normal levels."

There was a brief silence before Captain Nicodemus spoke up. "Very fine work, Ser Dyle. How in the world did you ever guess the truth?"

"I didn't guess, I only considered the possibility. So I asked Memnon and he told me. He's not human, after all, and made no attempt to be evasive. We had asked previously if he knew who was responsible and he responded that he was unable to identify any human agent. That, of course, was absolutely true. Eco was an impediment to Memnon's function which he removed in accordance with his interpretation of his directives. Although I don't believe there was ever any real danger to anyone aboard, I didn't dare take the chance that he would interpret imminent discovery as another problem to be solved. I spoke to Dona where Memnon couldn't overhear us, and she contacted Pritchard, who signaled her by personal buzzer when he had finished bypassing Memnon's discretionary modules."

"So where does that leave us?" asked Mercator.

"It leaves us two days from Scrimshaw," replied the captain, who stood up abruptly. "If that's all you have to tell us, Ser Dyle, I have a ship to run."

Chapter Eighteen

Captain Nicodemus invited Dyle and Marym to dine privately with her that evening. She thanked them again for their services, but didn't mention their investigation otherwise, and swapped stories of exotic planets with Dyle for a while until they both realized that Marym's isolated background on Tashista had left her with little to contribute. Their talk drifted after that to Concourse politics, speculation about the length of their stay at Scrimshaw, and other matters of even lesser import.

It was only once it was obvious that it was nearly time to leave that Dyle decided to broach a potentially touchy subject. "What will you do about Sondra Wong, Captain?"

"I don't think she's a danger to anyone except possibly herself, but she'll remain in confinement for as long as she's on my ship."

"Will you turn her over to the authorities on Scrimshaw then?"

Her face darkened. "Are you familiar with Concourse guidelines in cases like this?"

Dyle shook his head. "Only vaguely, I'm afraid. Doesn't jurisdiction reside with the planet to which the vessel is registered?"

"Unless it's under charter, yes, according to the strict letter of the law. Unfortunately, the *Helen* isn't registered to any planetary body."

"I assumed it was Linnisfarne," said Dyle thoughtfully.

Nicodemus shook her head. "The consortium has yet to declare an affiliation. Mercator was probably hoping to avoid registration fees and home port taxes for as long as possible. Linnisfarne was paid an orbital lease fee but that's as far as it went. In any case, planetary jurisdiction can be superseded at any time by a vessel's captain, though it's rarely done. I can pretty much deal with her any way I want, anything from setting her free or ejecting her through the disposal bay without a lifesuit."

"So what will you do?"

"Linnisfarne won't want her back there. I could probably talk Scrimshaw into taking her, but if so, they'd almost certainly require that the primary witnesses remain to provide testimony. Mercator and the two of you would be detained, and they might delay our departure as well. As much as I would enjoy inconveniencing Mercator, I don't want to prolong my acquaintance with the man any longer than is necessary."

"It's a difficult situation."

"Yes, it is, and the fact that I am not entirely unsympathetic to Ser Wong doesn't help. My brother is a mercenary colonel and I'm familiar with their code. I have reached a decision in her case, but I'm not prepared to reveal it unless I have your word that neither of you will repeat it outside this room."

They both gave their assurances.

"Wong will leave the ship at Scrimshaw. She will then find other passage as required to allow her to finish the job that she undertook for Caserta. I haven't asked, but I imagine she will use her authority, and your recent revelation about the future prospects of her friends, to withdraw from the agreement Caserta made with Mercator. I freely admit that I enjoy the chance to hit Mercator in his credit balance, but my decision would, I think, have been the same even if I thought she would confirm the merger as it stands. She has given me her word that once she has accomplished this, she will turn herself in to the authorities on Paramour, confess her crime, and accept whatever punishment they impose."

"Why Paramour?" asked Marym.

"Because Wong told me how she regained her freedom. The separatists eventually won the war. Clout, or Boden I suppose, was forced to flee the planet and could never have returned." She smiled. "I don't imagine they will impose too harsh a penalty for the unofficial execution of a fugitive war criminal."

* * * * *

They arrived at Scrimshaw without further incident, taking up orbit as instructed. A shuttle came up from the surface carrying an official greeting party and the first of the technicians who had arrived to begin the repairs. The system was too underdeveloped to have a permanent orbiting facility and was still essentially a company fiefdom, with a population well under a million. From space it looked to be an attractive and varied world, with tiny icecaps at both poles and large oceans. The land masses were varicolored, suggesting desert and forest, jungle and grassland. There were no other ships in orbit except for a small freighter that barely looked spaceworthy.

Word spread through the *Helen* that passengers were welcome to visit the planet, so long as they paid shuttle fees, but they were also warned that facilities were limited and comparatively primitive. Dyle asked Marym if she wanted to explore, but she seemed diffident and he himself was lukewarm to the idea. Although it was true that no two worlds were alike, most of the company-operated colonial worlds were distressingly similar.

A second shuttle arrived as the first was departing, and Dyle watched its approach from the observation dome. He had no reason to think it significant, but he was surprised when Marym appeared a short while later. "There you are," she said quietly. "I thought you might still be here. We have a visitor."

Dyle raised his eyebrows. "A visitor? I don't believe I know anyone on Scrimshaw. In fact, I'd never heard of the place until the captain mentioned it."

"No, but they've heard of you. And our visitor is the secretary to the planetary governor."

Dyle was not prescient. In fact, despite repeated claims and rumors, he doubted that prescience was a scientific reality. But if it existed at all, he experienced it during that moment, because he could almost have spoken Marym's next few words before she opened her mouth.

"They need your help. They have a mystery that needs to be solved."